the love of my life

Louise Douglas is a journalist and lives
near Bristol with her three children.
The Love of My Life is her first novel.

'A passionate and enduring love story which
has unexpectedly captured my heart . . .
An outstanding debut, written with assured
confidence . . . lingering and haunting . . .
likely to set tongues wagging on the
book club circuit'
Bookseller choice from Kate Bradley, BCA

louise douglas

the love of my life

PAN BOOKS

First published 2008 by Macmillan

This edition published 2009 by Pan Books
an imprint of Pan Macmillan, a division of Macmillan Publishers Limited
Pan Macmillan, 20 New Wharf Road, London N1 9RR
Basingstoke and Oxford
Associated companies throughout the world
www.panmacmillan.com

ISBN 978-1-447-20027-7

9 8 7 6 5 4 3 2 1

A CIP catalogue record for this book is available from
the British Library.

Typeset by Intype Libra Ltd
Printed in the UK by CPI Mackays, Chatham ME5 8TD

Visit **www.panmacmillan.com** to read more about all our books
and to buy them. You will also find features, author interviews and
news of any author events, and you can sign up for e-newsletters
so that you're always first to hear about our new releases.

for my family and friends, with love

acknowledgements

I will always be grateful to Marianne, who
read the manuscript and liked it enough
to become my agent, to Vicki, and to
Pat, who has held my hand throughout.
You've been wonderful, thank you.
Also heartfelt thanks to Josephine and
Kate for their kindness and wisdom along
the way. Finally, thank you to the team at
Pan Macmillan: Trisha, Fiona, who designed
the cover, and especially Imogen, my editor,
who thought of the title and suggested many
improvements. Working with you has been
a privilege and a complete pleasure.

prologue

I shall never go back to Watersford.

It is where my husband Luca lies buried, but I won't go there again.

Luca's family has won. Angela and Nathalie have found a way to keep us apart. It is what they have wanted for years and I don't think I'll ever be able to forgive them for that.

There is no way to atone for what I've done, either. There is no way back to how we were before, no way to make things better. We shall all just have to learn to live with ourselves and the consequences of our actions.

After the truth about the Felicone family came out on that stormy summer evening, I never wanted to see any of them again. So I left the restaurant and got into my car which was parked outside and drove through the night to my sister Lynnette's house in London. Lynnette loves me. She didn't ask why I had arrived on her doorstep at three o'clock in the morning with mascara all over my face. She didn't ask why I had turned up without a suitcase or even a toothbrush. She gave me a mug of milky hot chocolate to drink while she made up the bed in the spare room, found a pair of pyjamas for me to wear, tucked me between the clean sheets like a child, and left me to sleep.

If I had been born five hundred years ago, I would have been sent to see out my days in a convent. Today, the convent isn't an option but Lynnette still believes in the principle of redemption. Now I am feeling stronger, she has brought Sean's old laptop up to the bedroom and told me to write down everything that happened. She believes that once I've done that, I will be able to put the whole affair behind me. I don't know if she's right, but I have nothing else to do.

I am sitting cross-legged on the yellow bedspread. Beside me is a photograph of Luca, taken outside a restaurant in Sorrento last summer. He is squinting at the camera. The sun is in his eyes, and he has a cigarette between his lips and a bottle of Peroni in his hand. I miss him with every breath and heartbeat. He should have been my happy ending. Instead, he is the sad beginning to this story.

This is what happened after Luca died.

one

It started on the day of Luca's funeral. It was the third week in January and it was one of those cold, bright days when the sun makes the winter appear beautiful and when your heart wants to soar like a seagull above the city.

Instead, we were grounded like cannonballs in Luca's parents' house in Waterstord by the obligatory rituals. The family and their guests hovered in the living room, fussing over one another. Under the direction of my mother-in-law, Angela, my sisters-in-law were making themselves useful, pressing cups of coffee and bite-sized sugared pastries on people who didn't really want them.

Everyone was gentle with me, except Nathalie, who simply avoided me. I was aware of her watching me across the room and wondered if she was still angry with me and if she still hated me. I thought, perhaps, that she was glad things had turned out the way they did, and that I was the one who was suffering most. Maybe she thought I deserved to be a widow. Maybe she thought it was my fault that Luca was dead.

Gracefully, if grudgingly, the family treated me as guest

3

of honour at my husband's funeral. I had never been welcomed into his family, and nobody pretended that I had been, but they were generous enough to show me a modicum of respect and kindness. They asked me simple questions about my journey and my hotel, which I answered, but I found elaboration difficult. It was the first time in more than fifteen years that I had been with the Felicone family *en masse*, without Luca acting as my defence counsel, public-relations consultant and sponsor.

In truth, I was terrified of what lay ahead – not just the funeral, but the rest of my life. I felt as if I were moving in exaggerated slow motion, shackled by fear. My senses weren't working properly. Sometimes I heard things too clearly – a voice would be like a bell clanging – sometimes every word and noise dissolved into an aural soup. My mouth was dry. My fingertips tingled. I had to remember to breathe.

Two of the four surviving brothers, Stefano and Luca's twin Marc, were brotherly to me. They hugged me and kissed my cheeks and were solicitous. I was aware of them but only vaguely. They were like breaths of wind around me. The other two behaved true to form. Carlo was his usual distant, disapproving self. Fabio, the youngest brother, was upstairs, playing computer games. I had tried to talk to him earlier, but either he was too engrossed in the game to speak, or else he chose to ignore me.

Downstairs, the older brothers went outside to smoke, and through the low-voiced, churchy buzzing of conversation in the living room I heard anxious laughter coming from the garden. It must have been Marc. It sounded like Luca. I picked up a couple of empty cups and saucers and took them into the kitchen. Angela was packing the uneaten food back into plastic containers. With her was an elderly, frail-looking woman wearing an old-fashioned, long-sleeved cleaning overall with buttons down the front over a faded brown skirt. Her narrow face was framed by salt-and-pepper hair curled painfully tightly. She was wearing yellow rubber gloves.

'You don't need to do that, Olivia,' said Angela without looking at me. 'Mrs McGuire's going to clean up later. She knows where everything goes.'

I smiled tentatively at the woman as I passed her the soiled crockery. Her expression was stern but she looked up at me and gave me the briefest nod of thanks. I could see in her eyes that she was trying to work out who I was. Of course, it never occurred to Angela to introduce us.

'Can't I do anything to help?' I asked.

'No thank you. We can cope,' said Angela.

I wandered back into the living room. Luca's father Maurizio was staring out of the front window, fingering his newly shaved chin and gazing into the street where people were going about their business as if this were just another ordinary day. I went to stand beside him with my back to the room. Maurizio and I had always been comfortable together, and this way I didn't have to talk to anyone.

Luca's nieces and nephews, who were all beautifully turned out, had been given the job of standing in the front porch on the look-out for the funeral cars. Eventually one of them came running inside, pulled on Maurizio's hand and said, 'Nonno, they're coming.'

There was a communal intake of breath and a flurry of activity.

People put down their sherry glasses, their coffee cups and sandwich plates, and wiped their fingers on Angela's starched linen napkins. Maurizio went upstairs to fetch Fabio. With elaborate consideration, people helped one another into their coats, and then they headed down the polished wooden hallway to the front door, pausing at the tall mirror in the curlicued gilt frame to smooth a wisp of hair or dust their shoulders. Mrs McGuire emerged from the kitchen to tidy the living room.

I turned the other way, into the cloakroom, and sat on the lavatory with my head in my hands, trying to compose myself. My heart was racing, my hands trembling. I thought I might faint. The cloakroom was dark and cool and smelled of lilac air freshener. I held the hand towel to my face. It was damp.

There was a rap on the door.

'Liv, are you all right?' It was Marc. 'Is it OK if I come in?'

'Yes.'

The door opened. The anxiety on Marc's face mirrored my own.

He touched my cheek with his fingertips. 'Oh, Liv.'

'I can't go to the cemetery,' I whispered, hunching down into myself. 'I won't be able to bear it.'

'You have to.'

'I can't. I'm really scared.'

'I know. So am I.'

I was wringing my hands. I looked up at Marc. He was pale and gaunt.

'Drink?' he asked.

I nodded.

Marc took a hip flask from his pocket, unscrewed the lid and passed it to me.

'Drink as much as you can then use the mouthwash in the cupboard under the basin.'

I did as I was told. It was whisky. It was good. Marc drank after me, then we both rinsed our mouths and spat out together, like children preparing for bed.

'Did you hide the mouthwash there on purpose?' I asked.

'I thought it best to be prepared. Don't breathe a word.'

I smiled.

Marc topped up the hip flask from a whisky bottle concealed with the mouthwash amongst Angela's clean towels, spare toilet rolls and air freshener.

'We'll get through this, you know,' he said, helping me to my feet. 'Today and afterwards. I'll help you and you can help me, OK?'

I wiped my mouth and nodded.

two

When I stepped out of the house into the cold morning light, I could not look towards the hearse. Instead I watched my feet, unsteady in their high-heeled black boots, as they followed one another down the stone steps, on to the pavement and into the back seat of the first limousine, where Luca's immediate family was waiting. I sat down beside Angela. She moved aside to make space, and turned her body away from mine. She was an icy presence beside me, exuding a miasma of deep, black grief, yet completely composed. I put my gloved hands between my knees, and held them together tight.

I couldn't look at the coffin.

I stared at my knees throughout the journey to the cemetery, which seemed to last for ever, and the next thing I remember was the terrible sound of stifled male sobbing in the chapel, icy despite the electric bar heaters. Music chimed from the coloured glass dome high above us; there was a smell of cough sweets, must and decaying flowers. Although I could not look at it, I knew the coffin was lying on the catafalque in the middle of the aisle, covered in white lilies, carnations and roses, and I knew, although it was difficult to believe, that Luca was inside the coffin, on his own, shut away from the rest of us. I wondered if it was completely dark inside the coffin, or if there were slivers of light at the rim of the lid. I hoped his head was rested on a silk cushion, I hoped he was arranged comfortably.

The prayers, the testimonials and affectionate anecdotes were delivered in halting voices while I, afraid to listen, drifted off instead to the memory of last summer's holiday and Luca sleeping on a sunbed by the pool, his face turned towards mine, and how I put down my paperback for the pleasure of simply watching him breathe.

It was a conventional service. I don't remember the prayers or the hymns – I wasn't concentrating – but they would have been beautiful. Angela, perfectly coiffed, hatted, veiled and turned out in a suit which looked like Chanel, would have seen to that. I sat next to Luca's eldest brother, Stefano. His thigh was warm against mine throughout the service. He shared his hymnbook although I couldn't read the words and didn't make any attempt to sing.

When it was over, Stefano squeezed past my knees to join the other brothers to lift the coffin and carry it up the hill to the grave. I walked on my own, behind the coffin, up the hill. My breath shrouded my face but I kept my eyes on the ground.

I can't recall any of the words the minister said at the graveside, but when the coffin came to be lowered, he gave me the gentlest word of encouragement to throw the rose I was holding into the hole. I had to look at it then, and that's when the grief came over me like a wave. I don't think I made a sound as I stood there in my high heels and my new coat and my silver earrings but inside, every hope and wish and dream I'd ever nurtured tore itself up by the roots and miscarried into bloody little disasters inside me. Stefano's wife Bridget was holding their youngest daughter, Emilia, in her arms but she must have seen the crisis in my face because she nudged Stefano, who came to me and put his arms around me and I closed my eyes as he pulled me to him, holding my head as if it were something precious and fragile against his shoulder. I could feel the shudder of his sobs through the rough masculine fabric of his coat.

When it was over, the lesser mourners drifted away from the grave, back down the hillside towards the area outside the chapel where the cars were parked. The sisters-in-law, the nephews and nieces and uncles and aunts, the long-standing family friends and employees of the business peeled off one by one, leaving the immediate family, the four brothers, the parents and me, to pay our last respects. And for a while we stood there around the grave, casting long shadows in the late-morning winter sunlight. Nobody said anything, but eventually Carlo wandered away on his own, and Stefano put his arm round Fabio's shoulders and turned him away from the grave, and Marc whispered in my ear: 'They deserve a moment to themselves,' and I nodded and allowed him to guide me away from the grave, leaving just Angela and Maurizio standing together but slightly apart, like statues in the cemetery beside the grave of their prodigal son.

We were halfway down the hill when Marc started to cry, loudly and fiercely like a child, and that set me off, and it seemed natural to take our gulping sobs and blinded eyes and dissolving mascara and snot and hide them from the others, so we left the main footpath and followed a horizontal one which was smaller and wound in between the trees that framed the chapel below. And there on the path we cried together long and noisy and cathartic, holding hands; and then, without any words being spoken, we kissed. It was a sweet kiss, like a glass of water after a week in a sandstorm or a lungful of oxygen when you thought you had drowned or a kiss from the only person on earth who had loved Luca as I did. Marc's tongue, salty with tears, was like a gift in my mouth, his hands gentle on my wet cheeks, our teeth getting in each other's way. Marc kissed me sweetly but deeply, as if he were drinking Luca's essence out of me and I, feeling his weight against me, his thigh between my thighs, knew that I was the lucky one: I still had Marc to remind me of Luca, but Marc only had me.

three

My husband died in a car accident on the southbound carriageway of the M1 motorway on 7 January last year.

It was a particularly cold and icy New Year, although the coroner's report concluded that the weather had not contributed to what happened. The dull, late-afternoon light may, however, have been a factor. Luca, who was speaking to me on the telephone a few moments before the accident, had described the motorway as 'filthy northern grim'.

I don't like to think of the details. Occasionally I find my mind wandering down a dangerous, dark alleyway where fear rushes towards me like the shadow of a jack-knifing lorry and adrenalin surges and glass shards and bone fractures and caves. If I catch myself off guard, I'll sometimes wonder what Luca actually saw and heard, what he felt, whether he had time to be afraid. My story is that he died instantly, that he did not suffer and that he wouldn't have known anything about the accident. 'That's a blessing,' people say kindly. They think my story is true, but I don't know whether it is or not.

Luca had a premonition that he would die on the motorway, in an accident. Whenever we were stuck in traffic jams, no matter how long and tedious, he would always tell me not to complain.

'At least you're not the poor bastard at the front of this queue,' he would say, and I would think of the poor bastard and how he or she would have left home that morning just as they did every morning, with no idea of what lay in store. Now, at best, they would be in the back of the ambulance hurtling down the other side of the road with its sirens screaming and its lights blazing. And I would sigh and tuck my hair behind my ears and say, 'Yes, I know. There but for the grace of God.' Luca, who didn't believe in God but was certainly not lacking in self-esteem, would say, 'See, if I hadn't spent that extra ten minutes watching the football results . . .' So we were late for the wedding, so we missed the support band, so bloody what?

four

Luca had broad shoulders and slim hips and long, foot-baller's legs. His eyes were dark and his eyelashes were dark and if his eyes had been slightly larger he would have looked quite feminine. Because he was so dark, he always looked as if he needed a shave. His hair was black and fine with a wave in it, which meant that when it was long it almost had ringlets. When he was younger, he wore his hair down to his shoulders. More recently he had it cut, but it was still longer than was the fashion. It didn't matter in London. There you can be who you want to be.

Luca was always scruffy. He never perfected the habit of tidiness. I don't recall him ever tucking in a shirt. Often his socks didn't match. More often he didn't wear socks at all, even though this made his trainers smell. I didn't mind the smell of his trainers but other people would complain.

Luca was opinionated. He used to say this was a virtue because, according to him, all his opinions were right. Everything was black or white with him. He either loved or he didn't love. He either cared or he didn't. There was no middle ground.

Luca was a chef. He cared about his job. He loved his colleagues. He wouldn't tolerate sloppy presentation or poor ingredients, overcooked fish or undercooked pasta. He was a perfectionist in his work. He laughed a lot. He shouted a lot. He made a good deal of noise. He was emotional. In that respect, he was very like his father.

When he was watching football on TV, Luca would sit forward in his chair, with his elbows on his knees, urging the players on and shouting instructions to them. If they followed his instructions and scored a goal, he would say, 'Good boy! Well done!' If they didn't he would groan and sit back in the chair and slap his forehead with the heel of his hand and it would be like the end of the world for a few moments.

Luca loved football almost beyond the point of reason. He followed Team Napoli and said that Diego Armando Maradona was the best football player in the world, ever. Stefano said it was embarrassing these days to admit to supporting Napoli because they were so crap. In spite of this, sometimes Luca and I and Stefano and his family would all go to Italy so that Stefano and Luca could watch Napoli being beaten while Bridget and the children and I swam in the pool of our rented villa on the shanks of Vesuvius. On those magical Italian evenings, we would drink wine as the sun set and dip bread into olive oil before eating whatever feast it was that Luca had prepared for us. 'Here, Liv, taste, taste!' he would order, emerging from the plastic stripping which kept the flies out of the kitchen with a plate of something fresh and fragrant. He would press a titbit between my

15

lips whether I wanted it or not. The children would squeal with delight. Stefano, a bottle between his legs, tugging at the corkscrew with both hands, would say, 'Oh, leave the girl alone!' out of the corner of his mouth, without dropping the cigarette that was stuck to his lip.

Luca used to play football all the time, everywhere. If he didn't have a ball he would use a scrunched-up cigarette packet, or a conker, or an empty Coke tin, or anything else he could kick.

Luca smoked more than anybody else I have ever known – except perhaps Marc.

Luca could play bass guitar quite well. Sometimes he gigged with a band from Southend called The Piers.

Luca was completely physically unselfconscious. He wore an earring in each ear. That was his only affectation.

When he was in the bath, Luca liked to put a flannel over his face, hang one leg and one arm over the side, the dark hairs flat against his skin, and listen to the Red Hot Chilli Peppers.

Luca turned me on. At work, on the tube, in the supermarket, whenever I was bored, I would dream of our lovemaking. I adored him. I would never have been unfaithful. Why would I have looked at any other man when no other man came close?

Luca had my name tattooed on his left arm, close to his heart.

five

Luca was buried in a plot already reserved for the Felicone family in Arcadia Vale, a sprawling, overgrown Victorian cemetery close to his parents' home in the northern city of Watersford. The city lies about twelve miles east of the small seaside town where we both grew up and is known for its university, its cathedral and its glassworks. These used to produce highly prized goblets in pink and white marbled glass, before the seam of coal that fired their furnaces was exhausted a century ago and they all closed down. Angela and Maurizio live in a grand, bay-fronted semi in one of the more upmarket suburbs of the city. The road outside their house is wide and bordered by lime trees whose roots buckle the pavements at intervals. The original settlement of Watersford was built on a hill in the curve of the river, and a small part of the old city remains intact behind a section of stout, defensive wall. There is a tangle of impossibly steep and narrow streets connected by flights of dipping and sloping stone steps. Beyond this is a much greater, grander city built by the show-off Georgians and Victorians which

17

stretches down to the river and beyond. It contains Watersford's neo-classical civic buildings, tall and elegant with
sandstone façades, the university, the grammar schools and
the main shopping roads. There are fountains and churches
and little parks with wrought-iron fences and statues of the
great men of commerce. Parts of the city were destroyed in
the war and the gaps were filled with concrete and brick
constructions which haven't worn nearly as well as the older
buildings. There's an ugly shopping centre where the drug
addicts hang out and a bowling alley and a car park and the
former Romeo and Juliet's nightclub which is now a casino.
The residential areas radiate away from this hub, crescents
and avenues and streets of villas, houses and tenements. As
the glass industry brought wealth and opportunity to
Watersford, so its population grew. The small church grave-
yards were soon overcrowded and Arcadia Vale was created
to prevent an impending crisis. The elegantly landscaped
cemetery was situated on the far side of the river. It over-
looks the city and the city watches back and the river curls
like a ribbon in between.

Given the choice, Luca would probably have preferred
a quiet cremation followed by a noisy, drunken wake in
the Bow Belle, which was our local pub in London, but
in the face of his parents' grief I didn't have the heart to
insist upon this, or even to suggest it. They wanted their son
to be buried in traditional fashion in Arcadia Vale where the
family could visit him whenever they wished, and I concurred. It was the least I could do after everything I had put

them through and I didn't think it would matter to me where he was.

But it did.

By mid-February a black dog of depression and misery had come to sit on my shoulder. I'd heard of such creatures before, of course, but never encountered one. My dog was not an evil presence; more, as is the nature of dogs, a loyal and trustworthy companion, an embodiment of my unhappiness. It was always with me. It weighed heavy on my shoulder. I could feel its weight in my bones, causing me to stoop and walk with my head lowered, my eyes cast down. The dog was on the pillow beside me when I awoke, and curled up on my chest when I fell asleep. On the occasional instance when I forgot what had happened, the dog was there to remind me, its breath hot in my ear. At some point, I thought, I would have to chase the dog away, throw metaphorical stones at it or something. But for the time being I welcomed the dog into my life, and even went so far as to talk to it. Only the dog understood the depth of my loneliness and the enormity of my fear. The dog, I reasoned, had come to fill the gap, large as a universe, left by Luca.

In March I started scanning the recruitment sections of national newspapers for jobs in Watersford, but public-relations posts are hard to find. After a dozen letters, and God knows how many online applications, I secured an interview with a PR company that specialized in the leisure sector and flew up to Watersford, but I could see in the directors' eyes that I hadn't got the job even before they stood up to shake my cold and trembling hand. I probably smelled of the previous evening's gin.

I would have to come up with a different plan.

After the funeral, Angela called me occasionally. During these calls she made an effort to sound attentive and affectionate, as if she were speaking to somebody she cared about. She must have been calling out of loyalty to Luca. We both knew it wasn't out of love for me.

Before Luca died, we used to maintain a polite distance. We would be cordial to one another at family functions, and if Angela called and I answered the phone, our exchanges would be short but civil. She sent me birthday cards, but didn't write *With love* on them, and I dutifully sent her birthday cards but deliberately picked embossed, flowery cards with poems when I knew perfectly well she would have preferred a tasteful watercolour. It was my way of retaliating for the myriad minor snubs she dealt out to me over the years.

Luca never seemed to notice, but I was always aware of how she favoured the other daughters-in-law, particularly Nathalie, and always found something to criticize in me. Nathalie could do no wrong. As the years went by, she became more like Angela and the bond between them grew stronger. It became clear that, although the blood-link was tenuous, they had genes in common. They shared the same values, beliefs and prejudices. They enjoyed the same music and disliked the same television programmes and they concurred in the opinion that there was little I had to say that was of any interest. I understood, of course, why

Angela behaved like this, but after so many years of being cold-shouldered at family get-togethers I had tired of my black-sheep status.

It didn't help that, after all I had put the family through, I had failed to deliver the expected grandchildren. Bridget, Nathalie and Carlo's wife Sheila had all produced babies without any fuss or difficulty. Angela, who had also excelled at motherhood, regarded conception as a straightforward matter.

'No good news for us yet then, Olivia?' she would ask every time we visited. Luca said it was just her way of being interested in me. I regarded it as very bad manners. I'm sure she believed my failure to fall pregnant was proof that I was not committed to her son. In truth, Luca and I did want children. We had tried for years, but there were physiological issues that had stopped us conceiving. My physiological issues. He wanted to tell his mother about them, but I thought it was none of her business and was damned if I was going to humiliate myself by airing any aspect of my private life or the deficiencies of my private parts in her restaurant. So I pretended that I was just too busy to think about babies, having too much fun, enjoying my life too much. Angela would sniff and shake her head and use this 'selfishness' as another example of my bad character. I didn't care. It was better than her knowing the truth.

Before Luca died, Angela was my nemesis. She enjoyed humiliating me, in little ways and big ways, especially in front of Nathalie. Now we were both bereaved, things were a little different. We were a little more considerate towards one another. I appreciated her concern, which seemed to be almost genuine, and although we struggled to find new areas of conversation once we had enquired after each other's health and exhausted the topic of the weather in our respective parts of the country, she continued to call.

After Luca's death, when she saw the way I was, I think she finally believed that I had loved her son. For that, she would never forgive me.

When I told Angela I intended to move back to Watersford, she sounded surprised, and far from enthusiastic about the idea. I heard her take a deep breath when I broke the news, almost a gasp, and then there was an uncomfortable pause before she responded.

'Olivia, I'm sure Luca wouldn't want you packing up and moving.'

I twirled the phone cord around my fingers. 'It's something I have to do, Angela. I need to be close to him for a while.'

'You're not thinking of staying permanently then?'

'No, not at the moment.'

'Well, that's something.'

I made an effort to ignore this remark.

'So what are your plans?' she asked.

'I don't really have any plans.'

Angela tried a different tack. 'Is it really a good idea to leave your whole life behind you? Your house, your job, your friends . . .'

'Luca *was* my life. Nothing else matters. Being in Waters-ford, near him, is the only thing I care about right now.'

'But what about Lynnette? She needs you to be in London.'

'Lynnette's fine about it,' I lied. I hadn't even mentioned the move to my sister. 'She thinks it's a good idea.'

'Right. I see. And have you told your mother?'

'I'll let her know my new address.'

I could imagine Angela exhaling and tapping her pen against her accounts book as she acquiesced. She wasn't going to talk me out of this plan, no matter how much she disliked it, so, typically, she began to take control of it.

'Well, of course, Olivia, you must come and stay with Maurizio and me in Watersford. We'd be pleased to put you up for a few days.'

I was ready for this. 'No, Angela, thank you, I'll look for somewhere to rent.'

Angela sighed again. It was a habit she had picked up from her husband and modified over the years so that her sighs could convey a variety of emotions and messages. This one signified frustration tinged with disappointment.

'All right. But when you've found somewhere, you let me know where you are so that I can keep an eye on you.'

I promised, although in my heart I knew the last thing I wanted or needed was to have my mother-in-law watching my every move.

six

I don't remember the first time I met Angela, but she does. As you might expect, I come out of the encounter in an unflattering light. 'Not a pretty baby,' is how Angela describes me. I was about a year old, bald, fat and red-faced, buttoned up in a knitted jacket and screaming in my pram. This was a big, old-fashioned, second-hand affair which was being pushed by my long-suffering mother, a newcomer to Portiston, the seaside town to the east of Watersford. With us was my sister, a quiet, well-behaved four-year-old. A squall had blown up outside on the seafront, and my mother, anxious to keep her daughters out of the rain, had taken us into Marinella's Restaurant. Her immediate priority was to buy something sweet that she could put into my mouth to shut me up.

My mother and Angela were of a similar age. Both my mother's parents hailed from Lancashire. Angela had been born in Glasgow, the only daughter of second-generation Italian immigrants who owned and ran a chain of fish-and-chip shops. Both women had been encouraged to learn a useful skill and had left school at sixteen to take secretarial classes which equipped them for office work. At the age of twenty, both had started courting and at the age of twenty-two both were married. The difference was that Angela's marriage was successful.

When my mother arrived in Portiston with her two small daughters, she was on the run from a small-town scandal that was nipping at her heels. Up until then our little family had been living in an upmarket suburb of Wigan in what appeared to be complete propriety. This image was shattered when it transpired that my father, an electrician, was romantically involved with the teenage girl who kept the books at the shop he owned. My mother, with her secretarial certificates, could have kept the books herself, but she didn't believe it was 'done' to be a mother and to work.

This is obviously conjecture, but knowing my mother as I do, I imagine the neighbours would have been outwardly sympathetic, but inwardly just a little pleased at this turn of events. My mother was, and most likely still is, a snob, and there would have been those who thought she got what was coming to her.

Mum's overriding concern was to avoid being the subject of gossip. She craved respectability and the admiration of her friends and neighbours above everything else. She cared profoundly about what other people thought of her, and their pity would have been as wounding to her as their *Schadenfreude*. The situation was intolerable.

Fortunately, as well as her pride, Mum also had access to a small inheritance which she'd wisely squirrelled away from her husband. She had the keys to the house of a spinster aunt who had lived, and died, in Portiston. Nobody had bothered to sell the house; it was fully furnished, and available. So we upped sticks and decamped to Portiston, where nobody knew us and our history. Mum allowed people to believe that she had been widowed. Lynnette was somewhat confused but everyone else, including me when I was old enough to understand, accepted the lie. For the first seventeen years of my life, I really believed that my father was dead.

Angela, on the other hand, had married Maurizio, a gentle, hard-working Glaswegian whose family originally hailed from Naples. Maurizio's catering skills complemented Angela's administrative abilities: they made a good team. Angela's wealthy parents gave the young couple Marinella's as a wedding present. They worked hard to establish the restaurant, living in the large flat above it and expanding their family in line with their profits.

My mother looked down her nose at Angela, despite the fact that she had money in her pocket and a good-looking, cheerful husband who adored her. She thought it wasn't right for a pregnant woman to be working behind the counter of what she termed a 'jumped-up ice-cream shop'. She thought that only lower-class people worked in the catering industry and only bad mothers worked at all. She also thought it wasn't right for a pregnant woman to be wearing high heels and make-up and looking for all the world like somebody out of a fashion plate.

So in the early months of our time in Portiston it was my mother who enjoyed a relative life of leisure, while Angela worked every moment that she wasn't asleep. My poor, thick-ankled, lonely mother passed her days polishing the furniture and scrubbing the floors in the dark, draughty house in which we lived. She only had my sister and me for company. God knows she must have felt isolated, so it's little wonder she turned to religion. On nicer days, she would sometimes take us out for fresh air to play on the pebbled beach, waving the seagulls away from the fish-paste sandwiches she had prepared for our lunch. She would sit and knit and watch the ferry travelling to and from Seal Island while Lynnette and I made mermaids out of seaweed. Luca's mother, meanwhile, was managing a home, a pregnancy, four sons, a business, a loving but unpredictable husband and the two local girls who worked as waitresses in the restaurant.

The two women never became friends, but they soon became courteous acquaintances. As well as my mother's carefully rationed visits to Marinella's for coffee and cake, she and Angela met at school functions and, inevitably, given Portiston's size and lack of amenities, in the shops, the doctor's surgery, the post office, the bank and the church.

Angela's fifth child was another boy. Maurizio was '*fam al settimo cielo*' – over the moon – Angela less so. She told my mother that she'd ordered some pink fabric to make smocks, and knitted pink matinée jackets, so convinced was she that this baby would be a little girl. She sat down at our table and stroked Lynnette's dark hair and sighed for the plaits she would never have to twist and the ribbons she would never have to tie. The baby, Fabio, a bonny, happy, wide-eyed boy without an ounce of malice in him, sat in his pushchair opposite mine and blew bubbles at me from his little pink lips while I sneakily kicked him with my own fat little legs, hoping to make him cry.

seven

I moved into my flat on the top floor of a tall, terraced Georgian house at number 12 Fore Street, Watersford, on 17 March, St Patrick's Day. The pub windows were full of Guinness promotions, there was a shamrock on every street corner and the inhabitants of Watersford, still suffering the tail-end of a long winter, cold even by the standards of this north-easterly ridge of the country, were in the mood for drinking – especially as it was a Friday. It felt like a party the day I moved into my flat. I had equipped myself with wine and diazepam so that I could join in.

The flat was in good order and newly painted. The land-lords had had the place professionally cleaned so there was a strong smell of disinfectant, with an underlying odour of drying carpet, about it. I had paid a stupid price for a man with a van to transport three hundred miles the bed Luca and I used to share, the settee, the TV, several potted plants whose chances of survival had diminished exponentially over the last few weeks, boxes of books and CDs, and vari-ous other bits and pieces that either smelled of Luca or were stained with wine he had spilled or burned with cigarettes he had dropped, or that he had chosen, or repaired, or broken.

The flat was clean, but it was cold. I turned the central heating up as high as I could, and scorched my calves in front of the old-fashioned three-bar electric fire in the fireplace in the living room. Because the flat was in the eaves of the house, the ceilings sloped and once it was warm the double glazing kept the heat in. There was no need for curtains, because nothing overlooked the flat, but I tacked nets up over the front windows anyway, leaving the back-bedroom window clear. It had comforting views to the dark space on the hill beyond which was the cemetery.

I had broken my promise to tell Angela when I arrived in Watersford. I had no inclination to speak to her.

I made up the bed, and aired it with the electric blanket and a hot-water bottle. The bed had got used to our bodies over the years. Now I would have to get used to sleeping on Luca's side, my hips in the slight indentation where his hips used to be, my face turned towards the place where my face used to be. In this position I could see out of the window and fall asleep as close to my husband as circumstances permitted.

That weekend I explored my new neighbourhood. I found it difficult to go out by myself. It was like being in another country where I didn't speak the language or understand the culture. Several times I walked into a shop and then felt panicked because I didn't know where to find the item I needed. My accent didn't fit any more, I'd been too long in

London and had lost my northern lilt. Once I attempted to catch a bus into the city centre but as I stood at the bus stop I realized I didn't know which number bus I needed, or how much the ticket would cost. I abandoned the plan and ran back to the flat. Inside, I leaned on the door, shutting out the world. My hands were shaking. I wondered, not for the first time, if I was going mad.

Fortunately, there was a small supermarket tucked into the ground floor of a student house at the end of the road. It was stocked with enough basic provisions to keep me going for the foreseeable future, and the off-licence was the same distance in the opposite direction, so there was no practical need to wander far.

I didn't need a job – Luca had been earning good money and his life insurance had been up to date. I had also spoken to an agent about letting our London house out to tenants and he had assured me that this could be done quickly and easily. Sooner or later I would have to find work, for the sake of my own sanity, but I could deal with that later, when I felt stronger. For the time being, everything I needed was within walking distance of the flat.

By Monday it was all beginning to feel familiar. I was used to the way the doors opened and closed, I knew which ring on the gas cooker didn't work, I knew how to set the mixer tap on the bath so that the water was at the perfect temperature. I had stocked the tiny kitchen cupboards with tins of soup, crispbreads and cereal, food that didn't require thought or preparation. The television was tuned in and working. I had seen to all my practical requirements. It was time to visit Luca.

March was as cold as January had been. If anything the trees and shrubs of Arcadia Vale looked bleaker and blacker than they had at the funeral; the headstones hunched their shoulders against the wind and the inscrutable angels were sadder than ever, their poor bare ankles and shoulders exposed to the biting air.

I walked up the hill to Luca's grave. Despite the gloominess of the surroundings, I had an irrational sense of pleasurable anticipation at being physically close to him again.

The cemetery was full of primroses. Prettier and more subtle than all the shop-bought flowers and plastic ornaments on the graves, they grew wild and promiscuous in every available slope and crevice. God, they were sweet, their pale yellow flowers like glimmers of sunshine amongst the greyness. Primroses lined the path up to Luca's grave, and I felt almost like a bride treading the marital aisle as I climbed that path, a wrap of thin, unnaturally yellow forced daffodils in my hand.

At the grave I stopped.

'Oh,' I said. 'I'm sorry, I didn't know . . .'

Marc was there. He was squatting on his heels, his chin resting on his fists, staring at the head of the grave. His eyes were red and swollen. It might have been the cold but I doubted it.

'Hey.' He turned and smiled, jumped up, wiped his face with the back of his hand. 'Liv, what are you doing here?'

'I couldn't stay away any longer,' I said.

'Me neither.'

We stood for a moment, each of us not looking into the other's eyes.

'Is it the first time you've been back here? To the cemetery?' he asked.

'Yes.'

'I've come a few times. It doesn't seem to help much.'

I nodded. I didn't know what to say to him.

'How've you been?'

'Oh, good,' I said. 'Fine. Yourself?'

Marc shrugged. 'You know,' he said. 'OK.'

I jiggled my heels. 'It's so cold.'

We both glanced down to the grave. Poor Luca was down there with that cold weight of earth above him. Down there with the frost. A sorry little sigh slipped between my lips like an exhaled breath. The black dog on my shoulders grew heavier.

'Shall I fetch you some water for the flowers?' asked Marc. 'Give you some time . . .'

I nodded. 'Yes, thank you. That would be nice.'

Marc took the flowers and left me alone with the grave, which hadn't yet been colonized by primroses. The carcasses of other shop-bought, rootless flowers, blackened by repeated frosts, littered the grave. Somebody had planted something, but it was too small to know what it was yet. There was a sheet of paper on the grave, weighed down with a pebble, a letter or poem, too water-damaged to read, and a damp little blue teddy bear from one of Luca's nephews.

I knelt down at the head of the grave and tidied the soil, as if it were Luca's hair.

'Darling, I'm back,' I whispered. 'I'm just down the hill there.'

I closed my eyes and tried to summon up my husband, but I couldn't reach him.

I was calm, but there was a thought inside my head. I imagined scraping away at the soil with my hands, digging down to Luca, opening the coffin, climbing in beside him and just lying there, watching the sky change colour. Looking out into the universe like a tiny dot at the eyeglass end of a huge telescope.

Around me were thousands upon thousands of headstones, every one commissioned by somebody who had been left behind. The grief of all these abandoned husbands and wives, parents and children lapped at my ankles. It was a lake, a sea. And beyond Arcadia Vale was a whole ocean of death and loss and grief. It was unbearable. How could a world have evolved where such sadness was the inevitable result of love? There was a spasm in my heart, and I thought: Yes, I will bring tablets and gin, and I'll dig down to Luca, and I'll lie there and watch the sky and that's how they'll find me.

The thought was so comforting that it filled my cold eyes with hot tears. The black dog lay down beside me and put its chin on my lap. I stroked its head.

'Liv? Are you all right?'

Marc's nose and cheeks were red but his eyes less so. He was proffering an old pickled-onion jar half full of water and my poor forced daffodils with their unnaturally orange trumpets.

'I'm fine, thanks,' I said.

'No worries,' said Marc. He was wearing boots, jeans and an old leather jacket over a baggy old jumper, with a woollen hat pulled down over his ears. He had a stud in both ears and there were shadows of tiredness on his face. 'Look,' he said. 'I'm off now, I'll give you two some privacy.'

'Marc,' I said. 'Please don't go.'

When we were children it was always the three of us, Luca, Marc and I. None of us was ever excluded. We were a perfect triangle. I didn't see why it should be any different now.

Marc shrugged, patted his pockets, located his tobacco and started to make a roll-up.

'I don't like the thought of him being up here on his own.'

'I know,' I said. 'Actually that's why I've moved up here.'

'You've moved to Watersford?'

'To be close to Luca.'

'You're back in Watersford! I can't believe it.'

'I didn't realize how much I would miss him.'

'But you were so happy in London. All your friends . . .'

'Everything's changed. I need to be here now. I can see the cemetery from the back window of my flat and it's better than . . . than nothing.'

Marc nodded and offered me a drag of his cigarette. I shook my head.

'Do you want to see the flat?' I asked. 'It's not far. I could make coffee.'

'I'd rather have a proper drink.'

'OK,' I said.

Marc's car was parked at the side of the main ceremonial garden at the entrance to the cemetery. We left it there, turned right out of the gates, and walked along the main road for half a mile or so, before turning left into a road that lay parallel to Fore Street. There was a good, old-fashioned pub built into the bottom half of one of the buildings, the Horse and Plume. Marc pushed open the door for me, and I walked out of the cold into a pleasant cushion of warmth, the friendly pub micro-climate of woodsmoke, alcohol, exhaled breath and vinegary chips. The afternoon clientele was already ensconced, a mix of regulars who leaned on the bar with one elbow while they discussed the rugby, which was showing on the television in the corner, and tourists, gradually shedding layers of clothing as the warmth of the pub permeated.

'What do you want?' Marc asked.

'Red wine, please.'

'A large one?'

I nodded.

I found a table by the window and sat on the red plush bench by the frosted glass, picking apart a beermat while I waited. Marc returned with the wine and a pint. I'd noticed him knock back a chaser at the bar.

I took a big mouthful of the wine.

35

'You're looking tired,' said Marc.

'So are you.'

'I never thought anything like this ever happened in real life,' said Marc. 'Not to me. I just assumed – no, I didn't even assume, I just knew – Luca would always be here. With me. For me.' A big, fat tear rolled down his cheek and flattened itself in a starburst on the polished tabletop. 'Fucking hell,' he said. 'I've cried so many tears you'd think I'd be all cried out by now.'

I gave a little smile. 'I know.'

'Do people keep telling you it'll get easier?'

'I don't talk to people,' I said.

'That's a sensible approach. I've heard enough well-meaning but totally bloody inane condolences to fill a book.'

He was *so* like Luca.

He pulled a bitter face and said, 'Time's a great healer and life goes on and these things happen for a reason and one day we'll understand how Luca's dying fits into the great scheme of things. I just wish somebody would tell me how to fix the fucking great hole in my heart.'

Marc was not speaking quietly. A couple at the neighbouring table were giving us disapproving looks. I scowled back, almost willing them to make something of it.

'It doesn't help,' said Marc, 'being in Marinella's all the time. Every inch of that place is full of Luca. Every spoon I polish reflects a memory.'

'It's harder being away,' I said. 'That's why I've come back.'

'I'm glad you've come back.'

'I haven't told anyone I'm here yet. Angela doesn't know.'

'I'd worked that out for myself, considering she hasn't mentioned it.'

'She knew I was thinking of it. She wasn't very happy about it.'

'Well, she wouldn't be, would she?'

'She even said I could stay with her and Maurizio for a few days.'

'Blimey, she must be worried. And you declined?'

'I didn't want anyone interfering with how I feel.'

'What? The Felicone family interfere? Oh please, Liv, I think you're confusing us with somebody else.'

I almost laughed.

'How are Nathalie and the kids?'

'They were perfectly fine last time I looked. We don't talk much about Luca. Nathalie is of the "Least said, soonest mended" school of cliché.'

'You can't really blame her, Marc.'

'I know,' he said, tipping back his pint and swallowing the last few ounces of beer. 'But let's not go there. Come on, Liv, drink up. You're going way too slow.'

We had three or four more drinks each, I don't remember. We did some reminiscing. We laughed like monkeys at the memory of the eight-year-old Luca getting stuck up a lamppost on the seafront which he'd climbed for a dare. Eventually, panicked, I'd run to fetch Angela, who called the fire brigade. In the meantime Luca managed to climb down safely. So worried was Angela about the indignity and humiliation she would feel were she to be given a lecture about wasting the firemen's time that she made Luca climb the lamppost again in order to be properly rescued.

We talked about our friendship. Marc told me that, as children, he and Luca used to argue about which of them was going to marry me. They decided the matter, he told me, by tossing a coin.

'So how did you feel when Luca won?' I asked.

'Actually, Luca lost,' replied Marc, and I snorted.

Some time later, when it was dark outside, Marc stood up and pulled his hat down over his ears. 'Perhaps we should make a move,' he said. 'Before it gets too late.'

We went out into the bitter evening air. I was drunk, but not so drunk I wasn't aware of the crossroads at which we stood. Marc pulled up the collar on my coat and buttoned it round my chin, just as Luca used to do. I linked my arm through his.

'Would you mind walking me home?' I asked, choosing the path we were to take. Marc came with me.

Marc was almost the same size and shape as Luca, he smelled like Luca, he swore like Luca, he tipped his head back to laugh like Luca, he was the closest thing in the world to Luca, and I was longing for Luca like a moth longs for the moon.

A few hundred yards from the pub, in the deep cold black of the Watersford night, we collided as if by accident, and kissed. This time it was a different kind of kiss from the one at the funeral. Marc's hands cupped my head and pushed me back against the wall and this time I kissed back with a passion I didn't know I still felt. And then we were groping and kissing and stumbling all the way back to number 12 Fore Street, through the lobby and the front door, up the party stairs, into the flat, and as we kissed we undid the buttons on each other's coats. I hopped as I pulled off my boots while he tugged at the waist of my jeans, our mouths still together, our bodies sliding against one another. I wanted the comfort of being as close as it's possible to be with another human being. This was nothing to do with death and everything to do with life. It was the only thing we could do given our grief. It was the only possible way to exorcise the terrible loneliness. Marc pulled down my jeans and I helped with the buckle on his as we backed on to the sofa, and then it was just a tangle of breathless, rough sex and God when he came it was such a wave of emotion, such a catharsis, and I stroked his head as he cried and told him that we would be OK.

We fell asleep on the settee in each other's arms and for the first time in weeks the black dog left me.

I had forgotten how it felt not to be lonely.

It was his mobile phone that woke me, that and the weight of him on top of me. Marc was deeply asleep, his snores, like Luca's, trusting as a baby's. His head was still on my shoulder; my shirt, beneath it, was still damp. The phone meant trouble, I knew. Yet I didn't feel guilty, or worried, or anything really. All I knew was that I was reluctant for the moment to end. I smoothed the hair from his dear face, and whispered: 'Marc, wake up, your phone's ringing.'

Marc moved and grunted slightly.

'Marc . . .'

He opened his eyes, looked completely confused and then said, 'Oh *Christ*! Oh Jesus Christ. What time is it?'

I didn't have a clue. I had no need of a clock in my unstructured life. Marc found the phone in the pocket of his jeans and answered.

'Nat? I'm fine, I'm fine. I just had a bit too much to drink and fell asleep in the car . . . No, I'm OK to drive . . . I . . .'

I shook my head at him. The car was in the cemetery. The gates would be locked by now.

'I think I'm locked in the cemetery . . . I don't know . . .'

Nathalie, thank goodness, couldn't leave the children to come and fetch him.

'No, I'll be fine. I'll get a taxi. I'll be back soon. Don't worry.'

He put the phone down and put his head in his hands. 'God, oh God.'

'I'll make a cup of tea,' I said. 'Then I'll drive you home. It's OK, Marc, honestly it's OK.'

Marc looked like a different person from the mad-eyed man who had tumbled into the flat with me a few hours earlier. Now he just looked tired and worried and haggard. He sat on the settee, his boxers round his ankles, his head in his hands.

I wriggled out from behind him and went into the kitchenette to put the kettle on. I smelled of sex, a reminder of Luca. I felt exhausted. I felt alive.

Marc and I sat together on the settee and drank our tea. I leaned my head on his shoulder and he kissed my hair softly.

'Do we need to talk about this?' he whispered.

'I'd rather not.'

'Thank God it's you,' he said. I knew what he meant.

My old Clio had been abandoned at the side of the road for several days. The engine was cold and complaining, but it eventually obliged us by coughing into life. I drove Marc the twelve miles to Portiston and dropped him off at the end of the main street with a whispered goodbye and a squeeze of his warm hand. Then, for old times' sake, and because nobody was awake to see me, I drove slowly along the seafront. The lights of Seal Island across the channel reflected into the sea. I wound down the window and inhaled the familiar cold, damp air, heard the shushing sound of the tide rolling the pebbles up and down the beach. I passed a spot that reminded me of a winter's night when Luca and I had sat together in his father's van and watched snow falling over the sea and the memory cheered me. But I must have left the window open too long, for on the road back to Watersford I noticed the dog curled up in the passenger seat, drawing attention to the fact that nobody else was there.

I was alone again.

eight

The Felicone family are in all of my best early memories.

When I was little, my mother used to take Lynnette and me to Marinella's every Saturday afternoon. It was our treat and we looked forward to it all week. Before we went to the restaurant, Mum would put lipstick on her pale, dry lips and roll them into her mouth to make sure the colour was even. She would fluff up her hair, which was sparse and flat, put on her good shoes and check her appearance in shop windows *en route*. We sisters associated visits to Marinella's with Mum being almost cheerful.

Angela was always working in the restaurant or the office, Maurizio would divide himself between his customers and his kitchen, and the twins would be playing with their toy cars or their Action Men, either in the restaurant itself or on the steps outside. Fabio, the quiet, serious little boy, would sit and watch his brothers, but never joined in their games.

Maurizio, perhaps out of sympathy for us fatherless girls, always made a big fuss of us. He told us we were beautiful and exotic creatures. He gave us little gifts and treated us

like princesses. Lynnette and I lapped up his attention. He
was the same with Mum. He was the only man I ever saw
make her blush. He used to kiss her hand, and ask after her
health, and if there was any bad news he would clasp his
hands together in front of his chest and exclaim, '*Dio mio!*'
Then he would come up with some speciality of the house
which he assured Mum would remedy whatever it was that
ailed her. He would serve it to her himself. After she'd
eaten, Mum would pat her lips with her napkin, leaving a
dark pink imprint on the white linen, and assure Maurizio
that she was, indeed, healed. Maurizio would cross himself
theatrically and say a little prayer. Lynnette and the twins
would exchange glances. I watched Mum's face move through
various degrees of pleasure. Behind the counter, Angela
looked on. Her lips were smiling but the skin round her eyes
didn't move.

Music would be playing in the restaurant, usually a man
who sounded like Tom Jones but who was singing in Italian.
Marinella's was busy and bright and smelled delicious, and
there was laughter and conversation. People came and
went. The grown-ups talked to us and smoothed our cheeks
with their knuckles. It was the opposite of our quiet, cold
house with its dark corners and washing-up-water smells.
Even Mum was different at Marinella's. She had more
colour. She smiled. I used to imagine what it would be like
to be a Felicone. I imagined being tucked up in bed at night
by Maurizio, and the scenario made me squirm in my seat
with pleasure. I imagined meals with all those boys. It would
be so noisy, so much fun. I imagined shopping trips with

Angela. Almost all my clothes were Lynnette's hand-me-downs, but Angela, I was sure, would take me on the bus into Watersford and buy me new things all for me. I imagined what it would be like to be part of a real family, with grandparents and cousins and so many brothers that there would always be somebody on my side. I imagined the Felicone Christmas tree, covered in fairy lights and almost dwarfed by the pile of presents that would be necessary to service that great family. I imagined living above the restaurant. I thought the Felicone boys were the luckiest children on the planet.

On summer Saturdays at Marinella's, if we had been good girls, Lynnette and I ate strawberry- or cherry-flavour *gelati* served in quail's-egg-sized scoops in frosted-steel dishes, each one placed on its own paper doily on an elegant little china saucer, and served with a quarter-circle of the finest butter wafer and an ice-cold spoon. On winter days we drank hot chocolate from slim glasses slotted into metal holders. There were two inches of whipped cream floating on top of the chocolate and on top of the cream were slivers of real chocolate. It was the most delicious thing I have ever tasted to this day.

If we (or more usually I) had been naughty, we would be excluded from the weekly trip to Marinella's. It was dreadful to be locked in my bedroom knowing that I was missing all the fun. If we were particularly good, or if my mother had one of her migraines and wanted to bribe us into silence, extra visits would be dangled in front of us as treats.

Portiston is a small town with just one primary school, so

it was inevitable that Lynnette and I would grow up with the
Felicone boys. Stefano had already moved up to grammar
school by the time I started at the primary. Carlo was in the
same year as Lynnette. Luca and Marc were two years above
me. The year I started school, there were just twenty children aged between four and eleven attending Portiston
Primary and we shared the same classroom.

It was a friendly school, still housed in purpose-built Victorian premises with separate doors marked GIRLS and BOYS
for when even the infants used to be segregated. I can't
remember the name of our teacher, but she was young
and had dark frizzy hair and glasses and she smiled a lot and
used to put her hand on our heads if we were becoming
overexcited – it had the effect of calming us down.

Our classroom was bright and airy, with pictures tacked
up on the walls, and it was alive with the bird-cage chatter
of the infants. I remember sitting in between Luca and
Marc, colouring in a picture of a dragon with fat, wax
crayons. I was good at colouring, and so was Marc, but Luca
found it tedious and scribbled all over the black lines
that were supposed to contain the colour. He was quite a
naughty child. He used to spend more time out in the
corridor, excluded from class for misbehaviour, than any of
the rest of us. Even these minor separations made Marc
uncomfortable. While Luca was excluded, Marc would be
constantly wandering over to the door and standing on
tiptoe to peep through the glass window and make sure his
brother was in sight and all right.

Both boys had very skinny legs with bony knees. Their

shoes looked far too big for their feet. They wore black lace-up shoes whilst I had brown sandals. When I was little, I preferred Marc to Luca, because he was patient and obliging. If I told him to do something, he generally did it. Luca refused to co-operate with anything I suggested. Even at the age of six, he liked to be the one in control. Marc and I were usually happy to be his foot-soldiers.

The three of us built a den in the wooded area behind the school, which was officially out of bounds. We thought we were being very daring. There was a brick-lined hole in the ground already, which must originally have been part of some earlier building, or perhaps an old bomb shelter. We covered the roof of this hole with sticks, and then covered the sticks with grass and leaves. We had to leave a space to climb in, but when we were inside we filled in the gap so that we were completely hidden.

The hole was tiny. There was just room for the three of us to squeeze in with our chins on our knees and our arms folded round our legs. It smelled of wet leaves, mud and fungus and once we had hidden ourselves inside it was dark and green, like being underwater. I worried about spiders dropping into my hair. We used to pretend we were hiding from the enemy. I didn't know who the enemy was. This was the twins' game; I didn't have any say in its content or its outcome. Sometimes they made me be captured by the enemy, which meant I had to hide in the playground until they came and rescued me. They didn't always bother.

Sometimes Lynnette let me play with her, and I had a

46

girlfriend of my own age, Anneli Rose. I preferred playing with the twins though.

As we progressed through primary school, I spent more and more time with Luca and Marc. We were a gang of three.

Out of school, we had a pretty idyllic childhood. By the time I was about eight, Mum used to spend most afternoons lying on her bed with the heavy brown curtains drawn. She said it was migraine, and Lynnette and I were forbidden from disturbing her. The only way to avoid this was to go out. As a result, although Mum endeavoured to keep her daughters on a very short chain, when she was lying down with migraine we had limitless freedom. Lynnette was happy reading or drawing on the beach. I would seek out the Felicone twins. The three of us were forever up on the cliffs spying on people (a favourite pastime) or bobbing about in the harbour in Maurizio's boat. It was anchored and we were forbidden to touch the rope that held the anchor, but we pretended we were out at sea and we caught fish and, occasionally, swam, although the water was so cold it took my breath. When we were hungry, which was often, we went back to Marinella's. I would sit at a table on the terrace at the front, swinging my bare brown legs, peeling my sunburn and making ersatz grown-up conversation with the tourists while the twins begged whatever food they could off Maurizio. He would make a big show of bringing a tray of cakes and fizzy drinks out to us.

'For you, *signorita*, the chocolate fudge cake,' he would

say, squeezing my cheek, and I would be so pleased that my face ached with smiling.

Occasionally Fabio tagged along with us, but by then we all knew that he wasn't quite like other children. He was silent. He didn't join in with anything. He would come with us if Angela told him he must, but it was as if he didn't care if he was there or not. We liked him well enough, but he was never one of us.

It's difficult for me to tell different summers apart now. One runs into another in my mind. I recall one summer when Luca and I made a small fortune telling Japanese tourists on the literary trail that we were direct relatives of Portiston's very own famous writer, Marian Rutherford. For 50p we would pose for photographs beneath the blue plaque on the wall of the house where she used to live, now the Rutherford Museum. The tourists were too polite to question our authenticity, but word got back to Angela, who immediately put an end to our entrepreneurial enterprise and told us we must give all the money we had made to charity. My mother told me she was bitterly ashamed of me and due punishment was inflicted. Marc had refused to join in the scam. I can't remember his objections, whether they were moral or if he just didn't want to get into trouble.

Those summers seemed to last for ever, and when there was a sniff of autumn in the air it would be time to go back to school, me in one of Lynnette's hand-me-down pinafores, Luca and Marc in new trousers and shirts two sizes too big, so that they had to fold back the cuffs. We all thought our childhoods would never end.

Then, the September after my ninth birthday, I went to school as normal to find the twins weren't there. They'd both gone up to Watersford Boys' Grammar School in the city. By the time the summer holidays came round, the boys had no interest in me at all, having discovered more interesting pastimes like football and Army Cadets. We had nothing much to do with each other again until we were teenagers, and very soon after that I found out that my place in the triangle had been taken by somebody else. That somebody was Nathalie Santo.

nine

I decided to take the bull by the horns and call in to Marinella's. Angela would be wondering what had happened to me, and I wanted to see Marc again. I had a new ache and it was centred on him.

Early in April I coaxed the Clio, now covered in birdshit, back into life and followed the road back to Portiston. I parked the car in the seafront car park. In summer there's a warden because a good many literary tourists end up in this remote little seaside town. In April, however, the inclement weather keeps most of the tourists away.

Beyond the seafront is the town's main street with its single line of pastel-painted bars, restaurants and shops facing out to the sea. Marinella's is the biggest and grandest of these establishments. It was founded in 1890 as part of a chain belonging to a *gelato* entrepreneur, a chain that stretched throughout Scotland and the north of England. In summer they sold ice cream, in winter their speciality was hot peas and vinegar. They were remarkably successful. In 1901 there were twenty-one ice-cream shops in Watersford and two years later the number had risen to 115. I know this because the history of the UK ice-cream industry is written on the inside of the menu in Marinella's, and over the years I've learned it off by heart.

I stood outside for a moment, my arms wrapped round myself against the wind. A solitary seagull stood on one of the posts that support the railing that demarcates Marinella's terrace from the pavement, and mewled at me. Taking a deep breath, I walked up the steps and pushed open the door.

It was both a relief and a disappointment not to see anybody I knew inside. Only two of the tables were occupied, one by a couple of elderly ladies taking time over tea and sandwiches and the other by a young touristy-looking couple holding hands but not saying anything to one another. Probably honeymooners. A young waiter I didn't recognize was wiping crockery behind the counter, and another young woman was tidying up at the end of the bar, where the cakes were stored on doilies behind glass. Both were wearing the Marinella's uniform: black trousers, immaculate white shirt, long white apron. The girl's blonde hair was held back with a black velvet Alice band. I used to have one exactly the same.

The young man smiled at me. 'Please sit down. I'll bring you a menu.'

'Thank you,' I said. 'But I'm looking for Mrs Felicone. Angela. Is she here?'

'Is she expecting you?'

'No. But I'm family.' There. I had said it. I had given myself the status Angela never bestowed on me.

'I'll see if she's available.'

'Tell her it's Olivia.'

'Oh.' The young man stopped in his tracks and the girl paused, silver cake knife in hand. They clearly recognized my name. 'I'm so sorry . . .' the boy said.

I gave my widow's smile, a brave little smile of reassurance accompanied by a dismissive 'Don't worry about it' wave of my fingers, picked up the menu and pretended to study it while he trotted off to find Angela.

She came through from the offices at the back almost immediately, her glasses in one hand, the other extended in welcome. She was smiling too, but hers was a forced smile.

'Olivia, what a surprise!' She embraced me politely, a rush of Dior, pink lipstick, heels and hairspray. As always she looked immaculate in a navy skirt and white blouse, with a pale blue cardigan hooked over her shoulders. A string of pearls dangled round her neck.

'How have you been?' she asked, holding me by the shoulders at arm's length so that she could look at me properly.

'Fine,' I said.

Angela steered me towards a table, away from the door that led to the office and the flat which was now Marc and Nathalie's home. I sat down in the chair she indicated.

'We'll have coffee, please, Gavin,' she said to the young man. 'And please bring us a slice each of the orange and rosemary cake. Fabio made it, Olivia, it's delicious. Let's sit here, by the radiator.'

In the face of Angela's exquisite neatness, I felt some-what unkempt. I'd simply fastened my hair back with an elastic band that morning. I was wearing jeans and old brown boots, and a long woolly coat which had seen better days over one of Luca's fleece jumpers. As I hadn't washed anything of Luca's because there were still vestigial traces of his scent in the folds of the clothes, it is a fair assumption that my outfit was grubby. I wished I'd thought to make an effort and put on something special – or at least something clean.

'Well,' Angela said, tapping her spectacles on the table.

I smiled at her, nervously. I realized I should not have come. Angela didn't really care where I was or what I was doing, she just wanted me to stay away from her family.

'So I assume this visit means you're back up in Waters-ford?' she asked after a painful pause.

'Yes. Yes I am.'

'Oh.'

'I just wanted to let you know, that's why I . . .'

'Yes of course.'

Thankfully the young man came over to the table. Like all Marinella's staff he had been expertly trained. He laid out linen napkins, silver cake forks, coasters, three different kinds of sugar and porcelain jars of cream and milk on the table. Then he placed tiny cups of coffee in front of us. He returned a minute later with the cake, the slices lying help-fully on their sides in the centre of the fine white plates.

'This looks lovely,' I said.

'Do eat,' said Angela, pouring cream into my coffee, just the way I liked it.

'So how is everyone?' I asked, my mouth dry and sticky with cake.

'Well, you know,' said Angela. 'No, you wouldn't know. But it's not easy. Maurizio's not been good. Not good at all. Nathalie's been marvellous, of course. She and Marc have taken him out to look at patio heaters. Nathalie says it'll be good for Maurizio to go through some of the familiar motions.'

'Oh,' I said. 'That's nice.'

'That girl has been an angel,' said Angela.

'And Marc?' I asked, moving a piece of cake around my plate with my fork. 'How is he?'

Angela glanced at me. She didn't want to give me anything. Not a crumb of the truth.

'He's fine,' she said. 'He's coping very well really.'

I was shrinking beneath her gaze, becoming less of a person, taking up less space. If Luca had been with me, I would have been all right. Without him, I felt I might disappear altogether. Sensing her advantage, Angela continued along the same lines.

'Nathalie's been an absolute rock to us all,' she said. 'I really don't know how any of us would have managed without her.'

I nodded and spooned crystallized sugar into my coffee.

'She's the best thing that could have happened to this family,' Angela said, just in case I hadn't got the point.

I was trying to be strong, but I knew I couldn't hold out

much longer. The effort of holding back the humiliation was already exhausting me.

'So tell me,' said Angela. 'When are you planning on going back to London?'

I stirred my coffee. 'I haven't any plans at the moment.'

Angela opened her mouth to respond but fortunately was interrupted by a commotion behind us, and a cold draught. Maurizio, Marc, Nathalie and their three little children, their cheeks and noses pink with cold, came into Marinella's.

The two older children ran to their grandmother, shedding scarves, hats and mittens *en route*. Maurizio, who had aged a decade in the two months since the funeral, smiled when he saw me and hobbled over to pat my shoulder. His eyes were rheumy, and had almost disappeared into the hollows beneath his bushy brows. Nathalie, who had the baby in her arms, didn't even bother to pin a smile on her face. Marc was expressionless, although I swear there was a softening of his features when he saw me.

'What are you doing here?' asked Nathalie. Behind her back Marc caught my eye and held it for a moment, and I relaxed.

'I've moved to Watersford,' I said, standing up to kiss the baby's cold little cheek. Two parallel strings of snot ran from his nostrils to his mouth. I wiped them with my napkin.

'Why?'

I hesitated. 'Well, to be near Luca.'

'And is it doing any good, you being up here?'

'I'm not sure, I . . .'

55

'Because really, Liv, I'm sure you'd be better off in London.'

'I've told her the same thing,' said Angela.

'It's not like there's anything for you here, is it? You haven't got any friends.'

'Nat, leave it,' said Marc.

'Nobody wants you. Nobody likes you.'

Nathalie's voice was rising. The other customers were watching us, sensing the possibility of some drama; maybe, if they were lucky, even some violence. The two waiting staff were pretending not to be engrossed, but their ears were clearly pricked too.

Angela couldn't risk a scene. 'Nathalie, would you like a slice of Fabio's cake?'

Nathalie looked at her husband, then at the cake. Her face was white and hard.

'Go on, *carina*, you've been working hard this afternoon, have some cake,' urged Maurizio.

Nathalie glanced back at me.

'I'm not hungry. Besides, Ben needs a bath.'

'No bath. Cake,' said the baby hopefully.

'I'd like some,' said Marc, pulling up a chair and sitting down between Angela and me.

'It's your turn to bath Ben.'

'OK. When I've had something to eat,' said Marc.

'He's cold, Marc.'

'He's fine.'

'Marc . . .' said Maurizio.

'Right,' said Nathalie briskly. 'OK. Come on, kids.'

'Let them stay,' said Marc. 'They can have an ice cream.'

'It'll ruin their appetites for tea.'

'It won't hurt for once.'

'Oh please, Mum,' cried the kids in unison.

'Marc . . .' said Maurizio again.

'Suit yourself,' said Nathalie. 'Don't blame me if they turn out obese.'

Taking the baby, she walked through the café to the door behind the counter and headed off up the stairs to the flat above. Angela immediately scraped back her chair and followed her, not before shooting me a 'See what you've done' glance.

'*Dio mio*,' said Maurizio, unwinding his scarf from his neck and hooking it over a chair. He sat down awkwardly and began tidying the table. 'It's not good,' he said. 'Not good at all. Marc, you should respect your wife.'

'Not now, Pop, please.'

I lifted my little niece on to my knee. She snuggled into my chest, sucking her thumb and rubbing her nose with the silk edge of the scrap of blanket that went everywhere with her. I kissed her forehead. She tasted salty and animal.

Maurizio went to fetch ice cream for the children. Marc helped himself to something from one of the optics at the bar. He came back to the table and placed a glass of Cointreau in front of me and as he did so rested his fingertips on the back of my neck, under my hair where nobody could see them, for the briefest of moments. I could feel each individual fingerprint, each whorl and crescent embedded in my skin. Every nerve ending was concentrated on that few inches of skin from the knobble of my spine to the line of my hair.

'I need to see you,' he whispered. 'I'll come soon.'

I know what I should have done. I know now and I knew then. No harm had been done yet. But I needed to see him too. I needed to be held and touched and loved and reminded of Luca. I needed to be healed.

I stayed another half an hour. I drank some more Cointreau. I played I Spy with my little niece and nephew. When I walked back to my car, in the dusk, I glanced over my shoulder and saw somebody watching me from one of the upstairs windows. In my slightly inebriated state, I couldn't be sure if it was Marc, or Nathalie.

ten

I waited for him. I waited and he didn't come.

The longer I waited, the more time I spent without him, the more difficult it became to think of anything else.

Days later, when I could bear my own company no longer and was desperate for distraction, I set out for a friendly-looking café I'd noticed a few streets away. But I didn't check as I crossed the road and stepped out almost straight into the path of a car. The driver wound down the window and called me a stupid fucking ignorant bitch and made an obscene gesture. That encounter made me feel so hollow and shaky that all I could do was turn round and get back into the flat as fast as I could.

I switched on the TV, fetched the duvet off the bed and lay down on the settee. If Luca had been there, the accident wouldn't nearly have happened. He would have checked the road for me. He used to look after me as if I were something precious, made of porcelain or glass. I'd grown careless of looking out for my own safety because I was so used to my husband taking care of me and keeping danger at bay.

There was a quiz on TV, a terrible, boring quiz. I'd watched it so many times over the past weeks that I knew the patter of the blonde presenter. I said the words with her like a mantra, and after a while I fell asleep, which was a relief because the angry driver was out of my head. I don't know how long I slept but I was woken by my phone. When I picked it up the caller ID showed that it was Marc.

'I'm outside,' he said.

I stood up, the duvet wrapped around me, and crossed to the front window. When I pulled back the net curtain I could see him on the pavement, looking up at me and smoking. Even from this distance it was clear that he was edgy. I opened the window and threw down the keys. A few seconds later there were footsteps on the stairs and the door opened.

'Christ,' said Marc, 'it wouldn't hurt to tidy up in here occasionally, would it?'

'Nice to see you too,' I said, hunkered back down on the settee beneath the duvet, like a convalescent. The relief I was feeling was so overwhelming that I was afraid to let him see my face. I didn't want him to know how much I wanted him. I recognized his mood: Luca used to be the same if he'd had a bad, stressful time. He'd be fractious, he'd try to pick a fight and I knew to be patient and quiet until he had worked it out of his system.

'It's a complete mess.' Marc pulled a face as he picked a coffee mug, which I knew was cultivating mould, off the window-ledge, sniffed it and put it back.

'I'll tidy up tomorrow,' I said.

Marc continued to prowl bad-temperedly, sifting through my stuff. It didn't matter. I had no secrets from him.

He grumbled and nit-picked and carried out some cursory housekeeping of his own. I stayed on the settee, in my duvet, and waited.

After a while, Marc crossed the small room, bent down and smoothed the hair out of my eyes, tucking it behind my ear. I looked into his eyes and felt his mood soften. My breath quickened and my skin grew warm. The ache had become purely physical; it was concentrated in my belly. It was focused on the nearness of his dear face.

'God, you're lovely,' he whispered.

And it happened again, of course it did. We made love, and it *was* love, it was pure and sweet and gentle and urgent and afterwards we were better, both of us. We were better than we were the first time, we were a little more healed, a little more healthy.

Afterwards he looked at me for a long time, going over the shape of my face with his fingers, like he wanted to make a memory. Then he went out and fetched us some wine from the off-licence and some Thai food. I knew he would come back. For once I didn't mind being left on my own.

Sometimes, when I was with Luca, I was so content (not blisteringly happy or dizzy with emotion or madly in love: just content) that I used to feel that if I were to die at that very moment, I would have no regrets. These thoughts would drift into my head when we were in the car together, driving back from the supermarket, say, or when he was watching football on TV and I was reading *Heat* magazine, little fragments of ordinary, mundane life that were insignificant really, but where everything was all right and I felt perfectly safe. The longer we were together, the more content I became. I was a very lucky woman.

Then Luca was gone, and it wasn't the occasional moonlit beach I missed, or the screaming thrill of the terraces, or the birthday jewellery or the rare extravagant gestures and guilty, private pleasures. It was those moments of mundanity and perfect calm.

That evening Marc and I sat together and ate red curry out of tin-foil boxes, drank wine and watched TV. Gradually the room darkened.

Luca was gone, but I was not standing on that precipice dizzily looking down into a vertiginous ravine of fear as I did most evenings. I felt safe.

That was the first time we went to bed and spent the whole night together. I don't know where Nathalie was, I never asked. I was just grateful for the warmth and bulk of Marc's body on the other side of the bed. I delighted in the weight of his arm around my waist, the tickling of his body hair against my buttock, the warm bones of his knees knuckling into the cavities of my legs. He fell asleep like his brother, holding his breath and then releasing it in a series of snores before drifting into baby-like heavy breathing. I knew I wasn't falling asleep with Luca, but I fell asleep feeling almost content.

eleven

Not long after the clocks went forward there was a brief respite from the winter. The air warmed, it was possible to walk without being hunched against the cold, you could hear music drifting into the streets through windows left slightly ajar and washing appeared hung out to dry in the gardens of the houses of Watersford. The birds and insects came out of their shelters, and so did I.

I knew I had to find some way to occupy the times in between seeing Marc. I never have been the kind of person who enjoys her own company. The past weeks had been the only time in my whole life that I had lived by myself, and I had had enough of it. The black dog of misery was getting on my nerves. Besides, my mind needed something to do with itself. Daytime TV was fine up to a point, but you can have enough of Paul O'Grady and *Cash in the Attic*. My skin was bad from being inside too much, my muscles were wasting away, my hair was central-heating dry, my eyes were heavy and dull, and I was finding it difficult to concentrate. I was turning into the sort of person I didn't want to be.

So when the sun came out it felt like a good omen. I

bathed and washed my hair, and then walked the half-mile to the café.

Once inside, I behaved like a normal person. I sat down at a table by the window, which already bore the debris of breakfasts eaten, and ordered scrambled eggs and grilled tomatoes on toast from a friendly, bodybuilder-shaped man with a cigarette tucked behind his ear and a greasy apron. Light was streaming through the glass roof, and 'Brimful of Asha' was playing on the radio.

I picked up a copy of the *Watersford Evening Echo* from a rack by the door and flicked through to the Situations Vacant while I waited for my breakfast. There was nothing in my area of expertise, but then, I reminded myself, I was completely sick and tired of public relations anyway. There were a couple of secretarial jobs which I circled, and a vacancy for a research assistant with good typing skills in the history department of the local university.

By the time I'd copied the contact numbers into my phone my breakfast was ready. The man brought me a mug of tea and food that tasted so good it resurrected an appetite I'd forgotten I had. The eggs were creamy and peppery, the tomatoes sweet and hot. I felt so normal that I even managed a very brief, banal, but good-natured banter with a young woman with a baby who was waiting for her friend at the table next to mine.

I paid and thanked the man, who said he hoped I wouldn't be a stranger, and then I walked out of the café into the warm morning. It seemed a shame to waste my new-found sense of purpose, so on a whim I turned back towards the city centre and followed my feet along the pavements of Watersford's rather grand and leafy suburbs. I wasn't up to a bus just yet.

Watersford's is not a campus university. Instead the different departments are scattered throughout the city, with the majority being clustered in a small area close to the cathedral. It's one of those universities which prides itself on being favoured by the kind of students who have the ability, but not the desire, to go to Oxford or Cambridge. It's the kind of university whose professors are always being quoted in the *Guardian* and whose students quite often turn into peace activists, rock stars or TV ecologists.

I followed the roads uphill towards the city and then, once I cleared the suburbs, it was a matter of heading in the direction of the cathedral spire. Even the walking felt good. Stretching my legs, having somewhere to actually go besides the off-licence and the cemetery, was a pleasant sensation. Soon I was so warm that I took off my fleece and tied it around my waist, baring my arms to the elements for the first time in well over six months. My mind flicked to Luca, walking in front of me along the canal path close to home last summer, sweat darkening the back of his grey T-shirt like a bruise in between the shoulderblades. He stopped at the lock which fed into the River Thames, and stood there, gazing out over the water, his hands on his hips. I caught up with him and he took my hand and our two bare arms touched up to the elbows.

He pointed to the black ribs of an old barge sticking up through the water of the shallows of the river where bits of

rubbish and sticks rippled and when I looked in the direction of his finger he leaned down and kissed me. It was the
day after we'd had the bad news at the fertility clinic. The
doctor had been gentle but brisk. He told us that my body
was not doing its job, that I would never be able to conceive
a child and that there was nothing he or anybody else could
do about it. He gave us some leaflets and told us to go away
and consider the options that remained. In the past I had
wondered how I would feel if it came to this. I had expected
emotional carnage. In the event I felt empty and dry and,
strangely, unsentimental. On the way out of the hospital we
passed a couple with their arms full of babies and flowers
and I felt nothing. No envy, nothing. I had wanted our
babies, mine and Luca's, nobody else's. We paused at the
electric doors which opened out into the hospital car park.

'Shall I get rid of these?' Luca asked. I nodded and he
slotted the leaflets into the bin.

Instead of having a quiet evening discussing egg donors
as the doctor had suggested, we went to Camden and found
a bar and danced and drank into the early hours. I don't
remember how we made our way home, but I do remember
we opened another bottle of wine and grieved a little for
the children we would never have. The next morning we
walked beside the canal and we were all right, I think, both
of us. Luca knew that I wouldn't want to talk about it any
more. Luca was always good like that.

I walked away from the memory and up the steps of the
beautiful building that housed the main university library.

A group of students were sitting on the steps smoking. They looked ridiculously young, like they ought to still be in school. I wondered if they had any idea how lucky they were to be clever and free and alive, or if they were wasting their days by being full of angst and insecurity.

In the cool, dark hush of the library, a blue-haired receptionist directed me to the history department. It was just round the corner, a large Georgian building which must once have been home to a very wealthy merchant. I went inside and asked for an application form for the research post. The young girl behind the desk gave me a pen and invited me to fill it in there and then, so I sat down on a wooden chair and did just that. I was feeling slightly incredulous that everyone was treating me exactly the same as they had done before Luca's death. I felt like a completely different person, but nobody seemed to notice anything strange about me.

'Have you had a lot of applications?' I asked the girl.

She shook her head. 'It's probably not my place to say it, but it's a really boring job and the pay's complete crap,' she said. 'You get more per hour podium-dancing in one of the clubs in town.'

'I think they'd pay me *not* to get on the podium,' I said.

She laughed. 'You'd be surprised,' she said. I wasn't sure if that was a compliment or not.

'So will you let me know? About the job?'

'I expect the professor will be in touch directly if he'd like to see you.'

'What's he like?'

The girl shrugged again and pulled a face. 'He's OK. Old. A bit creepy.'

'Oh. Right,' I said.

On the way back, I was feeling so pleased with myself that I called Marc on his mobile. It was picked up almost at once.

'Hello, it's me,' I said happily. 'Guess where I am?'

'Who is this?'

It wasn't Marc. It was Nathalie.

He must have left his phone on the counter.

I cut the call off straight away and prayed to God that she hadn't recognized my voice.

twelve

My mother, Lynnette and I used to live in one of those narrow, three-storey, stone-built terrace houses that are so prevalent in the north of England in general, and in Portiston in particular. It was, and still is, quite a grand house, although now it's an investment property and, according to Lynnette, belongs to a gay man in London who has made £2 million from buying to let. My mother enjoyed the status endowed upon her by the house. As far as the neighbours and the likes of Angela Felicone were concerned, she had bought the house with money inherited from her late husband. Because it was such a grand house, the implication was that her husband must have been a successful man, an entrepreneur, even.

The house that had belonged to my mother's aunt was well built but not very well insulated. It had largeish sash windows, a small garden at the front where my mother encouraged pot plants to brave the inconsistencies of the saline wind and the temperamental weather, and a long, narrow garden at the back with a washing line strung along it and two long, narrow strips of soil bordering the lawn

which Mum referred to as her 'flowerbeds'. She had difficulty persuading anything much to grow aside from a few
tough, ornamental brackens and after a few years she gave
up trying. The weeds didn't bother to come back.

Lynnette and I had a small room each on the top floor,
in the eaves of the roof. In between our two bedrooms was
the family bathroom. On the first floor was Mum's bedroom, and a large front room which she used as a living
room and which we weren't supposed to use at all. There
was another small reception room downstairs, with a dining
room behind and a narrow kitchen which stretched out into
the back garden.

The house had been furnished by the deceased aunt,
which meant we had the use of good, solid, Presbyterian,
built-to-last furniture. My mother lived in constant fear of
the furniture being damaged, though I can't imagine who
would have grumbled if any harm had come to it.

Normally we were only allowed to eat and drink at the
table in the kitchen, and then only when it had its oilcloth
cover on. On special occasions like Christmas we were pro-
moted to the dining room, but generally Mum preferred to
have the door shut to keep both dust and children out. Both
Lynnette and I had to undergo the indignity of sleeping on
mattresses sheathed in rubber until well into our teens
following a night-time accident I had when I was six, which,
according to my mortified mother, penetrated the mattress
so deeply that the whiff of wee sometimes disturbed her
sleep many years after the event.

Mum was also very hot on manners. Lynnette and I knew

how to ask nicely for things and that it was polite to refuse a second helping of pudding even if we really wanted one. Lynnette would never have dreamed of answering back to an adult, or doing anything to draw attention to herself. I knew how I should behave, but I forgot the rules with a regularity that tested Mum's patience to its very limits.

'Lynnette's such a lovely girl,' Angela Felicone would say to my mother as she paid for our coffee and ice cream at the old-fashioned till on the shiny marble counter at Marinella's. 'I wish I had a daughter like her.'

Angela, glamorous, decorous Angela, would roll her eyes as her sons ran around behind her, shouting, threatening, laughing, making gun noises, pretend-dying, fighting and rolling around on the floor, getting under the feet of the waitresses. It seemed to me that her boys had a good deal more fun than we girls did.

'I don't understand why they don't keep those boys on a tighter leash,' my mother would say. 'They're going to end up in trouble, mark my words.'

But they didn't, none of them. The only child in Portiston who went off the rails was me.

Lynnette was four years older than me. Like me she had dark hair, grey-green eyes, freckles on her face and arms and slightly uneven teeth. Unlike me, she didn't lose things, or break things, or hurt things or spoil things. Lynnette never quarrelled or cried or was unkind. Without trying, she was always popular. She went around with a group of cheerful, sporty girls, did well at school and excelled at music. She was, and still is, kind and clever and beautiful and good.

I am certain she was Mum's favourite. How could she not have been? I would have preferred her if I'd walked in my mother's shoes. Anybody would.

By the time I followed Lynnette up to Watersford Girls' Grammar School, she was already established as the star student. When she turned eighteen, three years later, Lynnette was elected head girl. She played in the school and the county orchestras and had been a runner-up in the regional final of the BBC Young Musician of the Year competition twice. She had unconditional offers from several universities, including Oxford, although she chose London.

Compared to Lynnette, I had little going for me.

Asthma precluded me from playing hockey or netball at any decent level, but I also had an aversion to organized sport. I was also absolutely no good at music. For a little while I had piano lessons, but was constantly being unfavourably compared with my talented sister. I was too lazy to practise the boring scales and exercises, longing for 'Clair de Lune' and 'The Entertainer' but never gaining the proficiency to play either.

Neither was I clever. Not like Lynnette. Although I had passed the 11-plus exam, I was always placed in the bottom third of the class when it came to results. I never won a prize for anything and my teachers made it clear to both me and Mum that they did not regard me as university material.

Yet by my early teens I knew I had something Lynnette didn't have, something quite important. There was something about me that boys liked. They watched me. They jostled me. They pulled my hair and teased me and stole things from me so that I had to wrestle to get them back. I squealed and complained but I knew they were doing this because they liked me, and I enjoyed the attention, and the attention gave me status amongst the girls. As a result, I found subtle ways to encourage the attention. I turned over the waistband of my skirt to make it shorter. I rolled up my sleeves, I polished my lips with cherry lipgloss and thickened my eyelashes with mascara. I started answering back to authority figures. I chewed gum.

Mum knew what was going on. At first she said nothing directly, just watched and worried, but as the months went by she made it clear that she regarded the way I looked and the way I acted as unwholesome and undesirable. She said I was a disgrace, that if I didn't moderate my behaviour I would bring shame on the family and end up alone and unloved. In my opinion it was my only strength, and a talent to be nurtured and developed. So that's what I did.

By this time Mum had a gentleman friend. He was called Mr Hensley and we were encouraged to call him Uncle Colin even though he wasn't a real uncle, as I was always at pains to point out. He was somebody Mum had met through the church and he was the dullest man on the planet. I found him so boring that I'm having trouble now recalling any details at all, save a narrow face, bad teeth, sandy receding hair, a general greyness, and the fact that he always made me feel uncomfortable. He didn't seem to like me very much and the feeling was mutual.

The summer before Lynnette went to university I was fourteen and my best friend was Anneli Rose, who I'd known since the infants' class in Portiston. We were very close, so close that we claimed always to know what the other was thinking. We could make one another laugh simply by exchanging glances and we drove our teachers and the more studious girls in our class mad with our whispering, giggling and exchanging of notes. God knows what we talked about – I can't remember now – but we never ran out of conversation.

Anneli was as popular with the boys as I was. We egged one another on. We were a pubescent double-act of lips and hips and elbows. I was one of the first girls in my year to get a lovebite and I was always being asked out by different boys. I would go to the cinema or to the Wimpy with them. We would hold hands and sometimes I'd let them kiss me, but I never met anybody I really liked. Because I had so many boyfriends, I guess I probably achieved something of a reputation but I wasn't promiscuous, not like the poor girls who traded sexual favours in return for attention from the boys and consequent status from the girls.

At the end-of-term disco, where the girls and boys of Watersford's two grammar schools were finally allowed to mingle, neither Anneli nor I was left standing up against the wall for a moment. I danced with a lot of different boys. I slow-danced to Whitney Houston with a lad called Aiden Tracey. He was very drunk. His breath was hot in my ear and there was a rod in his trousers pressing hard against my belly. We had a kiss. He tasted of Camels and beer. He asked me to go outside with him but I declined.

Mum, egged on by Mr Hensley, disapproved of everything I said, everything I wore and everything I did. Soon, there were so many rules governing what I could and couldn't do that I became an expert in subterfuge in order to get round them.

Forbidden from buying make-up at the chemist's in Portiston, Anneli and I would steal it from the cosmetic shelves in Wasbrook's department store in Watersford after school. (Security tags have made shoplifting so much more difficult for today's teenagers, I sometimes wonder how they manage.) Anneli and I examined and delighted over our booty on the top deck of the bus on the way back to Portiston. When we had one or other house to ourselves, we would practise making ourselves up to look as old and as vampish as possible.

When Anneli's father saw us he said sweetly, 'But why do you put that muck on when you have such pretty faces anyway?'

Mr Felicone put it more poetically. Seeing us posing at a table by the window in Marinella's, he brought over our peach Melbas as we were touching up our lipstick and said he saw no point in gilding the lily. We just sneered and giggled, as teenage girls do.

One day we slipped up. Mr Hensley caught us climbing off a bus wearing baggy but almost transparent cheesecloth shirts and jeans cut off so short that you could see the hems

on the legs of our knickers. Our hair was up in high pony-
tails and we'd both had our ears pierced after convincing
the girl in the hairdresser's that we were sixteen. In Watersford, some much older boys had taken us into a pub and
bought us a cocktail that consisted of cider and Cherry B
and which was quaintly called a 'leg-over'. They had asked
for our phone numbers. It was completely thrilling and we
had been so high on our success that we'd forgotten to put
our decoy long skirts on over our shorts when we got off the
bus.

Mr Hensley was appalled. He made us get into the back
seat of his custard-coloured Morris Minor and drove us
back to my house, giving us a long lecture on the perils of
our 'loose' behaviour, while we squirmed and giggled with
fear and embarrassment and hoped that nobody we knew
saw us.

Anneli's parents were summoned and our behaviour was
the subject of a long, intensely embarrassing discussion, and
we were both grounded for the rest of the summer. We had
to be indoors by eight every evening and we were not
allowed out of Portiston unaccompanied.

Lynnette was unsympathetic when I raged about the
unfairness of the punishment.

'Look,' she said, 'you only have to live here a few more
years. Just do what they say and have a quiet life and then
once you're eighteen you can wear what you want, go where
you want to go, do what you want to do and stay out all night
if you want.'

'But that's more than three years away!'

'Trust me, it'll pass in a second.'

'But what if I die before I'm eighteen and I've wasted my whole life not having any fun?'

'You won't.'

'I might.'

'You won't.'

'But what if I do?'

'You won't!'

'But I might!'

I imagined myself dead (but not disfigured) from an unspecified illness. I saw myself lying on my own bed, on top of the pink nylon counterpane, wearing my Minnie Mouse nightdress, my ankles together, my toenails painted a pretty, sparkly blue, my arms crossed on my chest, my dark hair fanned about me on the pillow, showing off my new gold studs to their best advantage. The image was so moving it brought tears to my eyes. How sorry my mother would be then that she had listened to that horrible, rat-like Mr Hensley and kept me incarcerated in this sober, charmless house in this boring little town.

I wrote the newspaper obituaries in my head. I planned my funeral as a beautiful, artistic production which would show the mourners exactly what a talent they had lost. I would ask for 'Desiderata' to be read aloud by Lynnette and then Anneli could do some ballet. I wanted all my favourite records played, which, at the time, included Culture Club's 'Do You Really Want to Hurt Me?' and 'Like a Virgin' by Madonna, both of which I imagined, with a delicious shiver, would give my mourners something to think about.

I imagined my mother sobbing into her handkerchief. Mr Hensley mortified, ashamed, grim and ashen-faced. Lynnette dwelling on the words of our final, meaningful conversation: 'But what if I die before I'm eighteen . . .' 'You won't!' Hah! That would teach her.

At the time, I thought this was going to be the most boring summer of my whole life. In retrospect it was one of the most charmed.

thirteen

I was watching TV when my phone rang on Thursday afternoon. It was a Watersford number that I didn't recognize but turned out to belong to the university history department secretary. She wondered if I would be available to come for an interview with the professor the following Wednesday at 3 p.m. I asked her to hold on a minute while I checked my diary. I put the phone down and walked round the flat three times, then picked it up and said, 'Yes, I'm free on Wednesday, that will be fine.'

After I put the phone down, I picked up a cushion and danced round the flat in my pyjamas. Then I had an urge to tell somebody my good news. I didn't dare risk calling Marc again, so I called Lynnette. She was still hurt, first because I had moved three hundred miles north without consulting her and second because I had not bothered to let her know that I was all right and not floating face-down in the river.

I put on my brightest voice as I enquired after her and Sean.

'Well, we'd both be a lot better if you were here with us,

Liv,' said Lynnette. 'You shouldn't be in Watersford, it's not the best place for you.'

'But . . .'

'But nothing. The Felicones aren't your real family, we are. We love you and we miss you and we want you here with us.'

'No we don't!' called Sean in the background, not without affection.

'But Luca's here,' I said quietly.

'Liv, Luca's not there. He's in your heart. He's with you wherever you are. And he'd want you to be in London, we *all* know that.'

'Mmmm . . .' I said, non-committally. 'But the good news is that I've got a job.'

'Oh?'

'Well, I haven't actually got it yet, but I have an interview. And it's the first job I've applied for.'

'What about your real job?'

'What?'

'Your real job. Your job at Bluefish Public Relations, Canary Wharf. Your job where everybody knows you and cares about you.'

I didn't know what to say. I had never resigned as such, I had never had a conversation with anyone at Bluefish (they had tried to contact me but I hadn't answered the phone or replied to any correspondence). Lynnette, it turned out, had predicted this.

'I spoke to Amber only last week,' she said. 'She told me she'd be happy to have you back whenever you're ready.'

'I wish you wouldn't interfere.'

At the other end of the phone Lynnette exhaled slowly. 'Liv, it's not interfering. It's just that . . .'

'You know what's best for me?'

'No, no . . .'

'I'm not a baby, Lynnette. Do you know how that makes me feel? You talking to my boss behind my back? Making excuses for me?'

'No, Liv, it's not like that, I just . . .'

'You've always thought I was incompetent.'

'Liv, that's not fair.'

'Life isn't,' I said. 'And *I* should know.'

'Listen to yourself,' said Lynnette. 'You sound like—'

But I never found out what I sounded like. I put the phone down.

Angela called me. She sounded strained. She asked if I was all right. I told her I was fine. She asked me, casually, if I had seen Marc lately. I told her not since the time at Marinella's. It didn't feel like a lie at all. The man who came to my flat three or four times a week was not the same man who lived with Nathalie in the flat above Marinella's.

'Why do you ask?' I asked.

'No reason,' she said, with a tight little laugh.

Marc invited me to Marinella's for a family dinner on Easter Sunday. I told him I thought it was a very bad idea. He said it would be a worse idea if I didn't come because people

81

would wonder why I had stayed away. They would wonder if I had something to hide.

'Oh,' I said.

'It'll be fine,' said Marc. 'Stefano and Bridget are flying up from London and they'll be horrified if you're not there. Pop told Angela that she would be letting Luca down if you weren't made welcome. If she can make the effort then so can you. You must come. If not for yourself, then for Luca.'

'For Luca?'

'Yes.'

There were only a handful of places to eat out in Portiston, so even though Marinella's never served traditional roast Sunday lunches, it was a popular venue with locals and tourists alike. Eating there on a Sunday was always a pleasurable experience. The food was relaxed and hearty, the ambience warm and friendly. Easter Sunday always used to be particularly busy – the first big family calendar occasion of the year, and also the date which unofficially marked the beginning of the summer season, and therefore a day to celebrate.

It was a tradition for the Felicone family to all muck in together on bank holidays. Sons, daughters-in-law, even the grandchildren as soon as they were old enough would help out behind the bar, in the kitchen and restaurant. It made for a great atmosphere, and after the lunchtime rush was over and the last guest had left, Maurizio would lock the doors and the family would settle down to enjoy a meal together. These were always wonderful occasions, even for a black sheep like me. Maurizio knew how to throw a party, he was a generous and congenial host, and he adored his family.

But now things were different. Luca wasn't there. I had never really fitted in and my position was more tenuous than ever. I had been invited to the family party, so I knew that I ought to offer to help out with the lunches. In the end, I decided to call Maurizio to see if he needed an extra pair of hands in the kitchen or the restaurant. I didn't want to turn up in the evening to find that Nathalie and Angela had been run off their feet all day pausing only to bitch about my thoughtlessness in omitting to offer to help. Despite this, I sincerely hoped he would turn me down.

Maurizio was the epitome of kindness.

'How sweet of you to offer, Olivia,' he said. 'But it's a while since you've done any waitressing for us.'

'I could wash up,' I said cheerfully, knowing full well that he wouldn't let me do that.

Maurizio gave a little cough, and said, 'Excuse me, Olivia,' and then I heard a brief exchange in Italian with Angela which I couldn't follow although I picked out the words '*bambini*', 'Nathalie' and '*poveretta*' (poor girl). Angela's voice was shrill, Maurizio's deep and calm and reassuring.

Then Maurizio came back on the line. 'What would help us the most would be if you'd look after the children so that Nathalie could come down and work in the restaurant with Marc,' he said. 'Would you mind doing some babysitting?'

'Not at all,' I said. 'I just don't know how Nathalie would feel about that.'

'Leave Nathalie to me,' said Maurizio.

I put the phone down, wishing I'd never picked it up. The black dog, who had been sitting at my feet listening to my side of the conversation, gave a meaningful sigh and jumped up on to my shoulder. My spine curved, my shoulders collapsed towards one another with the weight of the beast, yet I was soothed by its chin on my clavicle, its deep breathing. Without Luca, I would be the only person at the party who was not linked to the family by parents, siblings, living spouses or children. I didn't really qualify to be there at all.

Easter Saturday night in the flat proved interminable. The good weather had been replaced by a storm of Atlantic proportions.

I had registered at the Watersford Central Library and taken out a clutch of books as I was so tired of TV, but I had overestimated my capacity for concentration. I should, I realized, have stuck to easy-to-read page-turners. A crime novel perhaps, or a friendly chick-lit romance. But I had shied away from detective novels in case I inadvertently happened upon a forensic description of the kind of injuries Luca had suffered, and didn't think I could cope with a happy-ever-after-type plot that featured multiple misunderstandings and orgasms.

Instead I had picked up improving, literary books, which I had neither the energy nor the desire to read.

The books were intended to be an alternative to alcohol as well as TV, but by 9.45 p.m. on Saturday, that 'now or never' time when I either went to the off-licence or I didn't, I put on one of Luca's big old waterproof coats, went out and bought a bottle of Merlot and a litre of gin to replace the one I'd emptied down the sink that very morning in response to a murderous hangover. The woman behind the till recognized me and tried to strike up a conversation. I was appalled that she regarded me as a regular. Surely, surely, part of her training should have been to instil in her a polite blankness when dealing with people who were clearly alcohol-dependent, no matter what their excuses. To shut her up I asked for a bar of mint Aero.

I don't know what was wrong, but I wasn't OK. The flat was, as Marc had pointed out, untidy. Because of its size, it didn't take much to tip it from cosy to claustrophobic. I couldn't open the windows because of the rain and the wind, yet I felt asthmatic and constricted.

Like Sylvia Plath, I am of the opinion that there are few complaints in life that a hot bath can't cure, so I lit half a dozen tealights and arranged them in the tiny bathroom, poured a gallon of lavender and camomile oil into the bath and then turned on the hot tap while I searched for a CD of something guaranteed to relax me. I put Sigur Ros into the machine, but when I tested the temperature of the bath it was icy cold. The pilot light in the boiler had blown out.

By now I had finished the wine and was on to my first glass of gin and lemonade. I caught a glimpse of myself in the window and I looked like a madwoman, a ghost, my hair unkempt, my clothes dishevelled, shadows under my eyes so dark that they reflected in the steamy window glass – oh God, I was a mess. I paced the flat. I drank my drink. I could bear my own company no longer.

For the first time, I felt a bitter anger. It was directed at my husband.

There was nothing else for it but to put on my coat and boots and go to the cemetery. Outside, the wind whipped round my legs, and the knees of my jeans were soon soaked from rain running off my coat. My hair stuck to my head and face and all my exposed skin felt icy, but I didn't care: inside I was burning. I strode through the black streets, yellow streetlamps reflected in puddles rippled by the wind and the wet tarmac reflecting moonlight in explosive fragments. A stream of water ran down the hill from the direction of the cemetery and burbled in overflowing drains which spewed up the water, and as I reached the cemetery boundary the trees were being lashed by the weather, creaking and groaning as if they were being flayed alive.

The gates, of course, were padlocked, bound by a thick metal chain, yet even they rattled and clanged in the wind. I was not deterred. The surrounding wall was six feet high and a little further along the road was a bus shelter, with a bench. It was easy for me, given my anger, to climb on to the back of the bench and from there pull myself up on to the top of the wall like somebody climbing out of a swimming pool. I didn't even notice the shards of glass concreted into the top of it.

There was a drop on the other side, and then I was in the cemetery. There was a light on in the top floor of the lodge. The superintendent and his wife were preparing for bed. Maybe they were brushing their teeth, maybe about to have sex. I wished them well, and scrambled over the graves in the area between the wall and the main path, then jogged up the hill towards Luca's grave, shouting and screaming at him, confident that the noise of the storm would drown out my voice.

'You bastard!' I yelled. 'You said you'd never leave me! You promised, Luca! You promised me! You selfish bastard! You said you'd look after me and now look at me! Look what you've done to me! Look at me!'

There are no lights in the cemetery. The dead need no lights. Yet I could see where I was going quite clearly. From time to time the wind blew the protective sheathing of clouds away from an icy half-moon illuminating the path. And as I walked up that hill, so I began to lose my anger. The further up the hill I went, the calmer I felt. I swear I could feel the dead around me. I was surrounded by them, the kindly, concerned dead, in the air like whispers I couldn't quite catch and glimpses I couldn't quite identify. There are 130,000 people buried in Arcadia Vale and the dear wraiths had been disturbed by my nocturnal ravings and had come to show their solidarity with me. I found it immensely calming.

I held out my own hands as you would if you were walking into a warm, still sea and were trailing your fingers in the water. I walked amongst the dead people; they walked beside me to my husband's grave.

Luca was one of the dead. Luca was not alone.

The alarm, when it shrilled on my phone the next morning, was brutal. I leaned over the bed to turn it off and hurt my hand on the bedside table. There was a maggot of a migraine burrowing away in the optic nerve behind my right eye and I found it hard to open my eyes to locate the phone, which I'd knocked on to the floor.

I hurt my hand again when I picked it up. Squinting, I realized there were ugly gashes on the palm. It was the same on the other hand. The gash on my right hand was so deep and angry it probably should have been stitched.

There were blooms of blood on the pillows. There was blood on the sheets. At the side of the bed, my soaked, torn, muddied and bloodied clothes lay in a filthy pile on top of my wet boots. So the previous night hadn't been a dream. I didn't remember coming home, but I must have found my way back somehow. I must have climbed over that wall a second time. And in less than two hours I was supposed to be at Marinella's to look after my nephews and nieces.

I lit the pilot light in the boiler and ran a bath while the kettle boiled. I took two ibuprofen tablets with a pint of water and bathed, cleaning up my hands as best I could and then sealing the wounds with antiseptic spray. My knees were a mess too but I could hide them beneath a long pink and white gypsy skirt. I put on a washed-out old T-shirt under a cotton shirt with sleeves so long they dangled over my hands, and a pale blue cardigan on top of the shirt.

I dried my hair and used straighteners to tidy it up a bit. I covered the little scratches on my face with foundation, brushed on a healthy pink, artificial complexion, concealed the dark shadows around my eyes, used eyedrops to brighten the whites, curled my lashes, polished my lips and teeth, freshened my breath, scented my wrists and neck, and put on a pair of silver earrings threaded with tiny glass beads and a boho necklace. In the mirror I looked less like the crazy woman of last night, more like Olivia Felicone used to look. I promised myself there and then that I would never let anything like that happen again. Luca was with the dead and I had to leave him be.

Before I left I swallowed a diazepam to stop the trembling and the incipient feeling of panic.

I listened to a broadcast of an Easter service at some cathedral or other while I drove to Portiston. The steering wheel hurt my hands, so I drove mainly with my fingers, changing gear with my fingertips, sometimes forgetting and grabbing the stick, which sent shooting pains from my palms right to the middle of my brain. I practised speaking in a normal tone of voice.

'Please would you pass me the butter, Maurizio? When is it you're going skiing, Carlo? Let me give you a hand with that, Angela.'

On the seat beside me was a bunch of rather sad-looking lilies which I'd bought the day before and forgotten to put in water, and a Happy Easter card for Angela and Maurizio in a yellow envelope. I hadn't signed the card because I couldn't bear not to write *With love from Luca and Olivia,* which is what I always wrote on cards. So I just wrote *Hope you have a lovely day* and three Xs.

At Marinella's, fortunately, everyone was so stressed preparing for the influx of lunchtime visitors while simultaneously coping with an abnormally high number of morning guests that very little attention was paid to me. An Easter

Sunday magical mystery tour bus commissioned by a branch of the Watersford WI had turned up unexpectedly. The tour organizer had not thought to call ahead to check that Marinella's could provide refreshments for fifty-four tourists at the drop of a hat but because it was a bank holiday, and because Angela and Maurizio hated turning people away, they had welcomed the visitors with open arms.

Marc was taking an order from a table of twelve as I went through the door into the restaurant, a napkin dashingly flung over his shoulder as he scribbled on his little pad. My stomach gave a little lurch of desire, which took me by surprise. I recalled the hundreds of times I had come to work at Marinella's as a teenager, and seen both Marc and Luca waiting on tables, just like this. Marc was heavier now, stockier and hairier; he had the profile of a man, not a boy, thicker wrists and a bulge above the hipbone and his hair was receding slightly, but he was still Marc, twin of Luca. He was somebody I had known for such a long time. He caught my eye as I walked past, and I tried to give him a smile, but am not sure if I succeeded.

I went through the bar into the back rooms, smiling hello to Maurizio and Fabio in the kitchen, and up the stairs to the flat. I tapped on the door and it was opened by Stefano and Bridget's daughter, Emilia, who was six.

'Hello, sweetheart,' I said. 'How are you?'

'Hello, Auntie Liv,' said Emilia, reaching up to kiss me. 'What have you done to your hands?'

I gave a self-deprecatory little laugh. I had been practising for this question. 'I slipped and fell down the steps at the entrance to my flat,' I said. 'What an idiot!'

'Poor you!' said Emilia. 'Were you drunk?'

'Emmie!' said Nathalie, coming out of the living room, her face flushed and tight. She had lost a little weight. Well, that wouldn't hurt, I thought.

'But Aunt Nat, you said . . .'

'Enough!' Then to me: 'Are you sure you're up to this?'

'Of course,' I said, smiling and shrugging off my jacket.

'If anything happens . . .'

'You're only downstairs,' I said in a reasonable voice.

Nathalie narrowed her eyes. 'I'm only tolerating you being here for Maurizio's sake,' she said. 'Don't think for one minute this means anything more than that.'

I sighed and stroked Emilia's hair.

'If you don't want me in your home, Nathalie, I'll just go.'

'I certainly don't want you here,' she said in a voice that was almost a hiss. 'Nobody else does either. Did you know that? Even Maurizio doesn't like you, he just tolerates you out of pity.'

I bit my lower lip hard and gave a little shrug which I hoped conveyed the fact that I didn't much care. It occurred to me how satisfying it would be to let the miserable cow know that I was sleeping with her husband, but I didn't. Of course I didn't.

Nathalie turned away from me and straightened her hair in front of the mirror before crouching down in front of her niece.

'Emilia, if anything goes wrong, you come and fetch me straight away.'

Emilia nodded solemnly.

At the door Nathalie turned to me again for one parting shot.

'Just for the record, Liv, Marc can't stand you either. He thinks you're a mess. He despises you.'

'That's what he says, is it?' I asked sweetly.

'Yes,' said Nathalie. 'That's what he says.'

I closed the door behind her and resisted the urge to make swearing gestures at it. This was fortunate, because when I turned to Emilia she was looking up at me anxiously as if she was worried I might do something erratic.

'I don't think so,' I said. 'Come on, Em, let's find your cousins.'

For a pleasant few hours, I sat on the carpet in the living room of Nathalie and Marc's flat, playing Headache with the children while Ben toddled about being cute and funny and trying to join in the games. I began to feel quite relaxed. The diazepam had kicked in nicely and I thought that maybe the day would turn out OK after all.

We ate reheated pasta for lunch and the baby slept for a while in the afternoon while the children and I watched *Shrek* on TV. From time to time, one or other member of the Felicone family put their head around the door, presumably to make sure I wasn't drinking or murdering the children. At dusk Nathalie came back up to the flat, looking frazzled, her hair wisped out of its bun, her apron soiled and her hands sticky, and headed straight into the bathroom to wash and clean up in preparation for the family meal. Behind her was Marc, who swooped into the living room growling at

the delighted children before kneeling down in front of
me, turning over both my hands to inspect the damage.
(Nathalie must have been telling tales.) He looked into my
eyes and I gave a little shrug.

'Don't ask,' I whispered.

I would have done anything for some time alone with this
man.

Marc's eyes held mine for for ever. Then they glanced
sideways, to the four children, who were all gathered round,
watching.

'Pooh! What's that awful smell?' said Marc, a master of
distraction, his gaze sweeping around the assembled children. 'Is it you, Kirsty?' he sniffed in her direction.
'Noooo . . . Is it you, Billy? . . . Uh uh. It must be Emmie? . . .
No, it's not Emmie! Then who is it? It's not Olivia, is it?'

'It's Ben!' shouted the children, jumping up and down,
beside themselves with laughter. Ben, delighted to be the
centre of attention, squealed and bounced on the soles of
his feet.

Marc picked Ben up, turned him upside-down and
sniffed his bottom.

'Pwoar!' he cried, making exaggerated wafting gestures
with this hands. 'This is not going to be pretty, Liv. Why don't
you go down and get yourself a drink and we'll see you in a
minute.'

'All right,' I said. As I left the flat the children were gathered round him inspecting the malodorous contents of
Ben's nappy.

fourteen

Banned from the buses (and our parents weren't above searching our pockets, bedrooms and secret hiding places for cash to make sure we couldn't get into Watersford), Anneli and I were forced to be bored and broke in Portiston. We did once try to hitch a lift into the city, but the first vehicle that stopped contained a large woman with a florid face in a flowery dress with dark sweat stains under the arms who asked us if we realized what we were doing was very dangerous and we might be picked up by a stranger in a white van who would do unspeakable things to us. The second vehicle was a white van driven by an exceptionally leery man with a large, slavering dog and a pornographic magazine in the footwell. So we gave up on that idea.

We had no money, so we spent a couple of weeks on the beach. There were days when it was warm enough to sunbathe, and then we would take off our T-shirts and jeans (the cut-offs had been confiscated, along with our bikinis and other offensive items of clothing) and stretch out on towels in our embarrassing regulation black school swimming costumes, trying to sophisticate the look with pink heart-shaped sunglasses we'd got free with a teen magazine. We rubbed Ambre Solaire into each other's backs and legs. I recall that lovely, cosmopolitan, elegant smell, the delicious oiliness of our hands and the warmth of Anneli's skin beneath my fingers. And then we'd lie, side by side, the only people on the beach, chewing Wrigley's Spearmint and listening to Anneli's portable radio, which brought the world to Portiston beach, and made us realize how much we were missing.

After a couple of weeks of this, we were so bored we thought we would die. We needed money and the only way to get money was to find a job. There were two places in Portiston that offered work to teenagers. One was the newsagent's, which occasionally had vacancies for newspaper-delivery boys and girls. The other was Marinella's. This being literally a stone's throw from the beach, we got dressed and went in. After all, we reasoned, approximately half of Portiston's teenage boys were resident there, even if they were so boring we wouldn't deign to speak to them if they were the last boys on Earth.

Angela was a formidable woman. She had her standards and they were high standards and they never slipped. So when two gum-chewing, slightly grubby teenage girls in wedged espadrilles, jeans and cotton shirts tied above their belly buttons teetered in asking for work, she gave us the most scathing of looks and said, 'Sorry.'

'But there's a postcard in the newsagent's saying you want waitresses,' said Anneli, pushing her heart sunglasses back on to her head.

'And I do. But this is an upmarket establishment with well-presented staff.'

The implication was not lost on either of us.

'We don't always look like this,' I said. 'We've just come off the beach.'

'Yes, Olivia, I can see that,' said Angela.

We were crazy that summer, but not stupid. We went back to my house, knowing it would be empty, and took turns to bathe and wash our hair. Most of my clothes were either on my bedroom floor or scrunched up at the bottom of the wardrobe. It was impossible to work out what was clean and what was dirty. Fortunately for us both, Lynnette's room was a completely different matter. She had a choice of long, formal-ish skirts and clean blouses, all neatly ironed and ranged on hangers. Anneli and I tried them all on. The clothes we didn't like, or that didn't fit, we simply threw on to Lynnette's bed.

Very soon I was wearing a white cotton shirt with a collar and cuffs and a black skirt patterned with tiny daisies. Anneli was wearing a beige shirt with a ruff down the front and a shorter, pencil skirt. We were both wearing new, unsnagged tights from a packet we'd found in Lynnette's underwear drawer, and Anneli, whose feet were the same size as Lynnette's, had purloined a pair of flat, soft-leather pumps. We dried each other's hair with Lynnette's hairdrier and combed it straight and shiny. We put on a modest but effective amount of make-up. We pinned our hair off our faces with Lynnette's kirby grips.

'Now we look like waitresses,' said Anneli as we stood,

hand in hand, admiring ourselves in Lynnette's mirror. Behind us was a scene from a war film: clothes strewn everywhere, drawers upturned, towels and cosmetics scattered about the place. But Anneli and I looked the business. We went back to Marinella's and we got the jobs.

fifteen

Downstairs, the staff had closed the shop, pulled down the blinds and prepared the room for a party.

The tables had been pushed together to make one long table, which was decorated with white linen cloths, fresh flowers, yellow napkins and candles in glasses. Bottles of wine were distributed at intervals along the length of the table which was set for seventeen people, counting the baby. It looked less symmetrical than normal. That was because, without Luca, we were an uneven number.

I greeted Carlo and Sheila and their teenage children. Carlo is the conservative brother. He is completely different from the others, in looks and personality. He is the same height as Stefano, but heavier and fleshier. He doesn't have the same bone structure as the others, his eyes rest on pillows of flesh, there is no clear demarcation between the end of his chin and the beginning of his neck, and his body is corpulent and flabby. Carlo works for the police in an administrative capacity. Luca used to say he was the man who sent tickets to people unfairly flashed driving at just over the speed limit on stretches of road where going just over the speed limit was the only sensible thing to do. Luca used to get a lot of speeding tickets. Carlo is a complete conformist. It is quite incredible that he, and the equally self-contained and repressed Sheila, a small, mousy woman who is a primary-school teacher and an unbridled disciplinarian, ever managed to conceive two children. The children have been, to date, models of good behaviour. Luca used to be convinced this would not last for ever.

'Lauren might look like butter wouldn't melt but she probably sells blow-jobs behind the bike sheds and when Andrew gets hormonal they're going to know all about it!' he had said at Christmas. I had reproached him, for the children are sweet and kind and much nicer than their parents.

'Yeah, but come on, Liv, it's unnatural for teenagers to be sweet and kind, they are supposed to be permanently pissed off and selfish,' Luca said.

'A bit like you?' I said and squealed as he lunged at me. We were in the guest bedroom at Angela and Maurizio's house in Watersford at the time. We were changing our clothes after the traditional family Boxing Day hike up to the cathedral. It was only four months ago. That was the last time, not counting the funeral, that the family was together.

'Olivia?' It was Fabio, standing before me wearing his normal, hard-to-read expression.

I gave my head a tiny shake to dislodge the memory of Luca, and smiled at Fabio, although I didn't touch him. Fabio has some kind of disorder which makes it difficult for

99

him to interact with other people. He doesn't like to be touched except on his own terms.

'Hello, Fabio, how are you?' I said.

'Oh, huh, well, you know, um . . .' said Fabio.

'Am I sitting next to you?' I asked.

'Mama has made a seating plan.'

'Of course.'

As if on cue, Angela clapped her hands. 'Come on, everybody, find your places, hurry up now.'

There was fond laughter at Angela's legendary organizational skills. Maurizio, at the end of the table, put on a Marlon Brando voice and complained that he felt like the Godfather. It was an old joke and it made things feel more normal.

I was placed at Maurizio's right hand, and beside me was Stefano. Lauren was directly opposite with Nathalie to her left. Marc was on my side of the table but at the other end. I couldn't even see him.

We said a quick grace, and were invited to pass round great platters of bruschetta, hand-made by Fabio. This large, lovely boy had been taken out of school at the age of seven because his teachers had classified him as 'subnormal', yet he was a genius in the kitchen. The senior features writer from the *Watersford Evening Echo* had once called and asked if she could come and do an interview with the man she had dubbed the 'Rick Stein of Portiston', and Maurizio had had to keep putting her off because he didn't want her to find out the truth about Fabio. You could just imagine the headlines. Sometimes – often – I hated myself for all the little cruelties I'd inflicted on Fabio when I was a child.

I bit into a mozzarella-and-chilli bruschetta and tasted happiness. For a second I forgot myself and just enjoyed being part of the noisy family group around the table. Then Maurizio touched my wrist and I jumped back into my skin.

'Sorry, Olivia, I didn't mean to startle you. I just wondered if you would prefer red, or white?'

I looked up. From the other side of the table, Nathalie was watching me.

'I'd rather just have water, Maurizio, if that's OK.'

He shook his head. 'No, today it's not OK. I'm requesting the pleasure of a drink with one of my four favourite daughters-in-law. If you're worried about driving home, you can stay here tonight.'

Nathalie pulled an expression which signified this would only happen over her dead body.

Maurizio had a bottle in either hand and was waving them in front of me.

'Red, then, please.'

'Good choice, darling. Good choice.' Maurizio took my glass and filled it. 'And may I say, Olivia, that you are looking particularly lovely today.'

I raised my glass to him. 'And you, Maurizio, are as full of shit as ever.' Nathalie heard that all right. I saw her wince but Maurizio chuckled and gave me a little hug.

I leaned round Stefano to raise my glass to Fabio, who was soaking up the gallons of praise being thrown his way from every corner of the table. At the other end sat Angela, composed and clearly pleased that the whole family had made the not inconsiderable effort to be there. She must have decided to ignore the fly in the ointment that was me.

The children soon forgot that this was a happy-but-sad occasion on account of poor Uncle Luca not being there, and as the wine flowed and the food was eaten, so the babble and chatter of voices around the table became louder, and everyone, even Nathalie, relaxed.

I was glad to be next to Stefano. He's the intellectual brother, a tall, thin man with a big nose, a big smile and a big heart – definitely the most like his father. Stefano has a doctorate from the University of London, and due to our geographical proximity, Luca and I used to spend a lot of time with him, Bridget and the children. Bridget's lovely too. Now a bit of a dreamer with short bleached hair and a nose stud, she used to be quite radical. She has pictures of herself as a student at Greenham Common protesting against the cruise missiles, and was arrested on numerous occasions for trying to protect trees from being chopped down, illegal immigrants from being deported, calves from being transported live, and so on. Stefano adores her, and she him, and the kids are lovely too. As wine was poured, and the waiting staff brought out little bowls of pasta in the lightest, most delicious sauce, Stefano and Maurizio paid me almost undivided attention, and in the enjoyable circle of their dual spotlights, I had no opportunity to remember, or to feel lonely.

By the time the meat was brought out, I was too full to even look at it, and just picked at the communal salad, dark

green leaves polished with olive oil and jewelled with pome-
granate seeds and slivers of orange; it was such a pretty
meal. Then Stefano pushed his glasses up the bridge of his
nose and asked me when I was coming back to London.

'We miss you, Liv. You should come home,' he said.
Across the table I sensed Nathalie stiffen and prick up her
ears.

I twirled a leaf around the prongs of my fork. 'Not yet,'
I said. 'Anyway, the agency called this week. They've found
tenants for the house. I've nowhere to go back to.'

'So?' Stefano shrugged. 'Come and live with us. We'll
abuse you and treat you like an unpaid *au pair*, and you
know how vile our kids are, and nobody ever cleans the
toilet, ever, but we'd love to have you.'

'You make it sound so appealing.'

'Ah, come on, Liv. It's a big house. You could have your
own space. Your own share of the filth and squalor.'

'Thanks, Stefano. I appreciate it, I really do. But I need
to be up here for now.'

Nathalie was pretending to listen to something Lauren
was saying but I could tell from the angle of her head that
she was more interested in our conversation.

'Sure.' Stefano pursed his lips and nodded. 'Sure, I understand. But at some point, Liv, you'll have to draw a line
under this.'

I looked down at my plate and nodded.

'We understand that you have to grieve,' said Stefano,
'but there comes a point where living in the past becomes
unhealthy.'

I drained my glass and helped myself to a top-up.

'There are no happy endings for you in the past. You have to move forward, Liv. You have to look away from here. Get away from here.'

Nathalie's eyes were like little fish darting this way and that.

Stefano leaned closer to me and spoke into my ear. 'Come back to us, Liv. We'll look after you. If you stay here, if you do what you're doing now . . . well, it's not helping anyone. Least of all Marc.'

My heart plunged. My mouth was dry. 'What do you mean?'

'Nothing. I'm just . . . we're just worried. Marc's not coping. He keeps disappearing. He won't talk to anyone. You remind him of Luca, he's told us that. Having you so nearby is just making it worse for him. And you're not coping either, baby. We're worried about you both.'

Stupidly, embarrassingly, my eyes filled up with tears and overflowed at once. I wiped my cheeks with the back of my hand. I shook my head and teardrops fell on the tablecloth.

Stefano put his cool hand on mine.

'I tried to let go of Luca, but I couldn't, I can't,' I said.

'Perhaps you should try again.'

I nodded. I was beginning to feel claustrophobic. It was hot in the room, and somebody had turned the lights down and set up the karaoke machine and the disco lights at the far end of the room, next to the fireplace. Two of the grandchildren were sharing the microphone, doing exaggerated actions and belting out 'Anyone Who Had a Heart', to the considerable delight of their cousins.

'Sorry,' whispered Stefano, covering my other hand with his. 'I didn't mean to upset you.'

I shook my head. 'No, no, you haven't. Really.'

I heard Nathalie, clear as anything, say in an exaggerated whisper, 'There she goes again – the dipso drama queen.'

Lauren, to whom this remark was addressed, flushed and examined her napkin.

I felt Stefano tense beside me. He leaned over the table and said quietly but distinctly, 'Enough now, Nathalie. Leave her be.'

Later, as we cleared the table, Marc asked me what Stefano had said.

'He thinks I should go back to London,' I said. 'Everybody does.'

'No,' said Marc. 'You shouldn't, you can't, not now.'

'He thinks that me being in Watersford is making it harder for you.'

Marc held my eyes. 'You being in Watersford is the only thing that's keeping me sane,' he said. 'You mustn't leave me.'

'It's OK,' I said. 'I won't.'

sixteen

The professor's office was on the ground floor of the history department. It was a large, high-ceilinged room that had probably once been a drawing room. There was ornate cornicing where the ceiling met the walls, and a chandelier caught and threw the sunlight beneath a huge ceiling rose. On the walls were pictures of Watersford throughout the ages. My eye was particularly attracted by a landscape which had been painted when the city was still undeveloped and sheep were grazing where Angela and Maurizio's house now stands.

The professor, once he had shown me in, sat down beside a large, old-fashioned desk which was satisfyingly piled with papers and books. The floor was covered with papers and books too. There was a cork board propped against the desk, and that was pinned three-deep in messages and notes and to-do lists.

There was a second, smaller desk in the far corner of the room, next to one of three tall sash windows. A pile of faded cardboard files stood beside a dusty and bulky old computer.

I sat down, as invited, on a worn, squashy and immensely comfortable cracked-leather settee. There were unwashed mugs on the carpet, which hadn't seen a vacuum cleaner in a good many months if the motes that danced in the light were anything to go by.

The professor coughed, rubbed his cheek and said, 'Yes, well, um . . .'

I smiled, my hands clasped on my knees. I was trying my best to look like a real research assistant. The effect I was aiming for was intelligent and demure with hidden depths.

'Are you interested in history?' asked the professor. He was a tall, dark-skinned, good-looking man some years older than me and he spoke with an American accent.

'Yes,' I said, and then could think of no way of qualifying that statement.

'Good,' he said. 'Well, that's a good start. Would you care for a coffee, er, Miss . . .'

'Felicone,' I said. 'It's Mrs, actually. Coffee would be lovely. Black, please, no sugar.'

'You take it neat, Mrs Felicone,' he said.

'Yes.'

I looked at my hands.

The professor stood up and walked round me to the door. He put his head round and asked the girl at the desk to make some coffee. Then he resumed his position. He seemed to have no idea of what he should be asking me.

'What sort of research do you do?' I asked, by means of encouragement.

'Ahh,' said the professor. 'Good question. I'm writing a biography of Marian Rutherford. Have you heard of her?'

'Oh yes,' I said, on firm ground now. 'The American author. I grew up in Portiston. I know the house where she lived and all the landmarks. We used to have coachloads of tourists turning up every summer to follow the literary trail. They probably still do.'

The professor was leaning back in his chair looking at me, the tips of his fingers touching each other, making a church with his hands.

'So you know the story?'

'I know she came to Portiston at the invitation of her publisher and fell in love with the place and that she set her most famous book, *Emily Campbell*, in the town. I even know the spot where Emily is supposed to have thrown herself off the cliff.'

The professor nodded. 'The eponymous heroine,' he said.

I nodded and made a mental note to look up 'eponymous' in the dictionary.

'Have you read the book?' he asked.

'Of course. And the others. But *Emily Campbell*'s my favourite.'

'Mine too. And can you type?'

'Oh yes, I can type.'

'And do you like to have the radio on when you're typing?'

I hesitated a moment, and then answered truthfully, 'No.'

'Good. Because I don't like any distractions while I'm working.'

At this point the girl came in with two mugs of instant coffee on a tray, and a plate of biscuits. She passed me a mug and offered me a digestive, but I declined. The professor thanked her, broke his biscuit in half and dunked it in his coffee.

'Um,' I said. 'If you decided to give me the job, what would I be doing exactly?'

'Typing up my notes. Putting them on the computer. I'm afraid I prefer to write with a pen.'

'Oh.' I smiled and nodded.

'A tiresome habit but you can't take a computer to bed with you, or have it with you on the train, or sit with it on the clifftop.'

I thought it would be impolite to point out that you could, actually, if you bought a laptop.

'So there wouldn't be any actual research for me to do?'

'I think,' said the professor, 'that if you read the advertisement carefully, you'll find that I'm looking for a research assistant, to assist me in my research.'

'Of course,' I said.

'I could have advertised for a copy typist, but I thought that would attract the wrong type of applicant.'

'Mmmm,' I said non-committally. I sipped at my coffee. It was scaldingly hot, but weak.

'Well, it sounds as if you have all the necessary qualifications for the post,' said the professor. 'To be honest Miss, er . . .'

'Felicone.'

'Miss Felicone, I find these interviews tiresome. Would you like the job?'

'Well, yes, I . . .'

'Monday through Friday, nine until four. I'd like you to be punctual, please. The pay is standard university rates. I have no idea what that is but it won't be much. You'll have to turn off your phone and I'm not very good company. People find me unsociable.'

'I really don't mind unsociable.'

'Good. I'll get Jenny to put something in the post then,' he said, standing up and reaching out to shake my hand.

I stood up. His hand was cool and dry. It was an academic hand, skin like the pages of a well-thumbed book. He took off his glasses and gave me the briefest of smiles.

'Now if you'll excuse me,' he said, and returned to his work.

Marc and I drove out to the coast in my car. We took a flask of coffee, a blanket and our coats, and drove to the end of the road. We climbed down a steep, shingly path to a little pebble-beached cove we'd discovered many years earlier with Luca. We knew there was a cave beneath the cliff. The waves were foaming and spuming, clacking and turning the pebbles, seagulls screamed and dived and the clouds raced across the sky. Marc and I lay on the blanket at the entrance to the cave and took off our boots, our jeans and our underwear and had exhilarating, joyful sex, and afterwards I lay on my back laughing up at the sky while he, somewhat bashful in his fisherman's sweater and thick grey socks, sat beside me, his wide, dark-haired thighs next to my narrow, pale ones, and took photographs with his phone of the seals basking out on the rocks.

'People used to think that seals were the souls of the dead,' said Marc, turning his windswept head towards me. 'It's something to do with the noise they make, or the way they lie on the rocks.'

'They look fat and healthy enough to me.'

'Bit sad, though. Those eyes.'

'They're probably bored of the sea. It's a bit monotonous if it's all you have to look at day after day.'

'And an uninterrupted diet of raw fish.'

'Ugh.'

'And the weather.'

'Poor seals.'

'It's not much of a life for them.'

Marc turned, and took a photo of me.

I swept the hair out of my eyes and opened my mouth to protest.

'It's OK,' he said. 'I'll delete it straight away.'

'Delete it now.'

'OK, OK.'

'Marc . . .'

'All right, I've done it, it's gone.'

He leaned over me and kissed me full and warm on the mouth. His lips were salty and dry. I wriggled back down again and he smiled and shook his head and put his cold hand between my legs. I was shivering. I wanted more. I drank him in.

This sweet oblivion, this thing we had, I could pretend it was a survival tactic but that wasn't the truth so much any more. It had become more than a balm for the raw wound of grief, more than a way for us to comfort one another. That day, the day we went to the coast, I felt something I hadn't felt in months. For a long time I couldn't remember what it was I was feeling, but later, back at the flat, as I washed the sand out of my hair, I worked it out. I had, for a few moments at least, been happy.

seventeen

That first summer I worked in the restaurant, I fell in love with the Felicone way of life. I had always found it attractive and glamorous, now I found it utterly beguiling. Compared to my mother, with her flat shoes, large ankles, short salt-and-pepper hair and martyred expression, Angela was like a queen, or a film star. Petite, elegant, blonde, her nails were always beautiful and she always smelled expensive and she always smiled, even when she was telling you off. Maurizio had a neat little beard and what he called a 'high' forehead which was really where his hair was receding, like Mr Hensley's. Unlike Mr Hensley, though, Maurizio laughed a lot. He also sang a lot, and kissed a lot, and quoted poetry a lot. And he shouted a lot too, but nobody minded because his explosions of bad temper were always exclusively verbal and over in moments. He praised me and Anneli expansively with dramatic gesticulations. He made us taste titbits from the kitchen, and gave us doggy bags to take home filled with all manner of delicious little leftovers. I loved the cooking smells, the bustle and business, the banter, the music on the radio, the attention to detail, the vivacity of the place. Being at Marinella's was like living life in colour.

Home was less black and white than grey. Lynnette's departure to university was imminent, and the thought of me being there with just Mum and Mr Hensley was getting me down. At home, we only ever ate English food. That was white bread and butter, Heinz tomato soup, gristly pork sausages, and dishes made with mince. Occasionally, for a treat, we'd have spaghetti hoops, which I loved. Mr Hensley usually ate with us in the evenings. He tucked his serviette into his collar and made us say, 'For what we are about to receive, may the Lord make us truly thankful.' He always praised Mum's cooking effusively. He didn't like Lynnette or me to speak until we were spoken to, yet, despite his skinniness, he was a greedy eater who often spoke with his mouth full. He made grotesque chewing noises when he ate. He repulsed me.

I couldn't bear the thought of Mr Hensley getting his hairy white fingers on the Marinella's delicacies. Anything in the doggy bags I didn't eat on the way home, I fed to the seagulls.

When Anneli and I started at Marinella's, Stefano was at university and Carlo was already working in some kind of law-enforcement capacity at Watersford and going out with Sheila, so we rarely saw the older boys.

Fabio was at Marinella's all the time. He stayed in the kitchen, cooking up his cakes and pastries with intense concentration. He only had to be shown how to do something once, and then he would reproduce the recipe exactly time and time again. Eventually he learned the confidence to adapt the measurements and to experiment with ingredients of his own, but at this time he was still a year younger than us, and still getting used to being 'different' from the other boys his age with their loud, leery ways. He needed to be nurtured and protected like a greenhouse flower.

Also living in the flat upstairs and helping out with the business were Luca and Marc and a pasty, lumpy girl who had come to live with the family. Her name was Nathalie Santo.

Marc told us that Nathalie's mother had been Angela's cousin and best friend. She and Angela had gone to school together, and their families had holidayed together. The two women had always promised one another that, if anything happened to one of them, the other would step in and care for the children. Nathalie was an only child. Her father had passed away years ago, and now her mother had died of cancer. Angela had reassured her cousin, when she was on her deathbed and in front of the whole family and the priest, that Nathalie would be loved and protected and be made part of the Felicone family. Angela promised her dying cousin that no harm would ever come to Nathalie, that nobody would ever be allowed to do her wrong and that she, Angela, would make sure Nathalie made a good marriage. The cousin was reassured. Angela was a woman of her word; she knew her daughter was in safe hands.

When she moved into the Felicone household, Nathalie was treated with the utmost respect and consideration. The twins had been told they had to be very kind to Nathalie.

They were not to tease her, frighten her or be boisterous around her. It was strange for them to have a girl in the flat. I think they were intrigued and curious. But Nathalie was clever. She did not put her underwear in their laundry basket. She kept her secrets to herself.

I thought it was quite a romantic story, and was a little jealous of Nathalie, but we didn't see much of her in those days. After the initial novelty of her joining the family had worn off, the boys didn't talk about her so I didn't pay her much attention.

Now I know how grief feels, I think I should have been kinder.

The twins were two years older than Anneli and me, and both attended the Boys' Grammar School. We hadn't had much to do with them for several years, although obviously we'd seen one another around town and we travelled to and from Watersford on the same bus on school days. Luca was the leader, the confident, more boisterous one. He was the one who smiled at the girls, who gave lip to the bus drivers, who was reputed to get into trouble at school and always got out of trouble through sheer charm. He was the one who drove his mother to distraction, whose shirt was always loose from his trousers, whose tie was always askew, whose hair was too unruly, whose smile was too wide, whose eyelashes were too long, whose body had grown so quickly that he wasn't used to it yet, the long, bony limbs, the neck with its tendons and its voicebox. He was the pin-up of our year.

Marc was shorter and less lanky, always two steps behind Luca, swimming in his wake but enjoying the ride. He was the cleverer twin, not just academically but socially. Because Luca 'did' while Marc 'watched', it was Marc who worked out the cause and effect of actions. He knew what made people tick. Luca used his charm instinctively, Marc was more sensitive. He was a nice boy. His teachers liked him. He had a lot of friends who were girls. A lot of these girls were just trying to get close to Luca.

The first summer at Marinella's, Anneli and the twins and I enjoyed a good deal of light-hearted, flirtatious banter and messing around. We girls weren't allowed up into the flat. After work, if the weather was fine, we would go on to the beach with the twins, and play football or frisbee. Anneli and I would change into our jeans, roll up the legs, and splash about in the waves, and the boys would throw the ball at us, bouncing it off the water and our knees and making us wet. We squealed and insulted one another; it was all quite physical, but innocent too.

Nathalie was older than us; I don't think we ever considered her at all. We never invited her to come to the beach with us. It never occurred to us that she might be lonely, or unhappy. She spent all her time at Marinella's or in the flat. Angela kept her close and nursed her through her grief. The pair became almost inseparable. Angela thought it best if Nathalie had something to do, to keep her mind occupied. She showed her how to balance the books and taught her the skills she would need to manage the staff and suppliers. Nathalie was enrolled on a marketing course at Watersford Technical College so that eventually she could help expand the business.

Even after she'd settled in, Nathalie rarely spoke to Anneli and me, except to tell us what to do, or to reprimand us for lateness, slovenliness or some other lapse in standards. Behind her back we called her a stuck-up cow. She was probably just trying to please Angela. She was probably just shy.

In September, we gave up our jobs at Marinella's to go back to school and Lynnette left home to go to university. I don't know who was sorrier to see her leave, me or my mother. We saw her off at Watersford Station together. The three of us sat miserably in the canteen waiting for the train and drinking tea so weak that I made a joke and said the water couldn't have had a meaningful relationship with the teabag. Nobody laughed.

Mum had bought us each a Danish pastry as a treat, but they weren't nice, sweet, juicy pastries like the ones in Marinella's, they were dry and hard and the pastry fell away in lumps from charred currants. Whatever had been used to glaze the pastries stuck to our fingers like glue.

Lynnette was anxious to be away, but also anxious about leaving. She was wearing an old pair of favourite jeans, a wide leather belt and a polo-necked black sweater for reassurance. Her hair was pulled rather severely away from her face in a French plait. She had a little make-up on, and flat-heeled pixie boots. She looked very pretty. If I looked at her for too long I felt my eyes prickle. I didn't want her to go because I loved her so. I didn't want her to go because

I didn't want to be left behind in that gloomy house, alone with my mother.

As for Mum, she was brittle-cheerful. She babbled on about Lynnette's wonderful opportunities, the people she would meet, the books she would read. At least once a minute she made some subtle allusion to the fact that she had never enjoyed such opportunities. I would have ignored them, they were so irritating, but Lynnette, eventually, put her smooth hand on Mum's and said, 'I know, Mum, and you know I appreciate all the sacrifices you've made to give me this opportunity.'

Mum's eyes filled with grateful tears and Lynnette smiled and looked humbly down at her half-eaten pastry and I, slouched in my chair chewing bubblegum, rolled my eyes and dreaded the next few months.

It was a relief to us all when the train's arrival was announced, and we went out on to the platform and helped Lynnette on to the train with her remarkably small amount of luggage.

'Promise you'll call me at least once a week!' said Mum.

'I will,' said Lynnette, leaning out of the window looking flushed and excited. She beckoned me over and I stood up on tiptoe to kiss her cheek. 'Keep your chin up, Liv,' whispered my sister. 'Just remember, everything changes. No matter what's going on, even if it gets really tough, remember it won't last long.'

'I don't want you to go,' I cried, tears now running down my cheeks.

'Oh, come on,' said Lynnette. 'You have complete access

to my bedroom, my clothes, my records. It's what you've wanted for years.'

'No!' I sobbed. 'No, I thought it was what I wanted, but . . .'

Lynnette, sensing histrionics, put a finger to her lips. 'Write to me, Liv. Tell me what's going on. And Liv, please, please, don't do anything I wouldn't do.'

'I won't,' I sniffed, backing away to make room for my mother who was coming in for another embrace with her good daughter.

And I meant it. And for a while, at least, I kept my promise.

eighteen

I arrived on time for my first morning at work at the university. On time, and relatively bright-eyed and bushy-tailed
which, for me, was an achievement. The previous Saturday
I had caught the bus into Watersford and bought myself a
slim-fitting brown skirt which came down to my ankles and
looked great with my boots, and a couple of V-necked tops.
The brown, I thought, was fashionable but with a hint of
the musty academic about it. I had straightened my hair,
painted my nails the palest pink and equipped my handbag
with practical items like a purse and a little wallet of tissues.

I knew that I had fallen on my feet with the university
job, and I didn't want to mess up. I couldn't have coped with
a regular office job, with all the accompanying gossip and
politics, and I was certainly not up to anything that involved
'client contact' or would have required any kind of charm
on my part. Instead I had the benefit of being in one room,
with just one other person, and a self-confessed unsociable
person at that. The work could hardly be easier, and
although I would be spending my days doing straightforward, brainless copy typing, at least it was on a subject I knew

a little bit about, and in which I was interested. I had filled in the relevant forms and submitted them to the university and my wages would be paid directly into my bank account. I didn't need the money, but it was still gratifying to think that I had turned the tide of creeping inertia that had infected me since Luca's death.

Every child in Watersford is taught about Marian Rutherford and her influence on nineteenth-century literature at some stage during their school career, and those of us lucky enough to hail from Portiston couldn't escape having Miss Rutherford's talent drummed into us at every available opportunity. There's even a literary festival in the town every August when visitors come from all over the world to walk in her footsteps, drink wine with authors, poets, retired politicians and celebrities of varying stature, and listen to lectures about her work. I had suggested to Luca on more than one occasion that we attend one of the festivals because I was genuinely interested in finding out more about Portiston's only really famous daughter (adoptive daughter, to be accurate). Luca said he suspected my motives. He was sure all I really wanted was to rub shoulders with the likes of Jo Brand and Alan Davies, whom I had a crush on at the time. He may have been right. He usually was.

I was at the foot of the steps that led to the door to the history department building by 8.50 a.m., in plenty of time for when Jenny turned up to unlock at nine.

'You're early,' she said.

'The professor asked me to be punctual,' I replied.

'Mean old hypocrite! He's rarely here before ten. Come on in, I'll get the kettle on.'

I felt slightly awkward sitting in the reception hall drinking tea with Jenny, who claimed she had been at a party all night and was wrecked, when I should have been getting on with my typing, but the door to the professor's office was locked and there really was nothing I could do but sit and wait for him.

Jenny was twenty and had very short hair and a boyfriend called Yusuf who was studying medicine but who liked to DJ. She also had an infected belly-button piercing, and was one of those girls who never run out of things to say, which made her easy company. She told me the ins and outs of her life, the row she'd had with her flatmate after her flatmate had borrowed her best Kookai top yet again and then sworn she hadn't only Jenny had found it in the laundry bag so the cow was so lying, and I drifted off into a place in my mind where I could sit and wait with Luca. While I daydreamed, Jenny moved on to talking about the professor and I listened half-heartedly. She wasn't a particular fan of his, although his faults seemed relatively minor to me. He was 'a bit grumpy' and had no sense of humour (according to Jenny) and was something of a recluse.

'Apparently,' she said, 'he didn't always use to be like that, but then his wife left him or died or something and he went all weird. He gives me the willies, know what I mean? And it's not just me. There've been four or five people doing your job and they've none of them lasted more than a couple of weeks. The last one was only here for three days.'

'I thought he seemed very nice,' I said, which I thought was adult of me when Jenny was trying to make me into an ally for her gossiping. However, I didn't have time to revel in my maturity, because then the professor did turn up, and with him a sort of black cloud of bad temper which he asked me to ignore because it was normal for a Monday morning.

He unlocked the door to the office, which seemed to have accumulated even more piles of paper since my last visit (perhaps it had been tidied for interview purposes), and asked if I knew what to do with the computer. It looked like a fairly basic PC and it only took me a couple of moments to establish that it was plugged in and to locate the on/off switch.

'Are you in business?' the professor asked as the machine booted itself into life with the sort of mechanical surliness that my car demonstrated on its rare outings.

'I think so,' I said.

I clicked on the username 'Assistant', and sure enough, there was a handful of files with 'Rutherford' in the title.

'What would you like me to do first?' I asked.

'Any of those,' said the professor, indicating a haphazard pile of cardboard files on my desk. 'They're all full of notes which need to go on the computer.'

I opened the top folder. Inside was page after page of handwritten notes. The writing was small and spidery. There were multiple crossings-out and amendments, and cross-references marked with stars and numbers, with the

124

reference sometimes being found several pages later, and sometimes appearing not to exist at all. In the first folder, there were probably forty sheets of paper. There were seven folders on the desk.

I glanced over to the professor. He was sitting at his desk with his back to me, a gesture that precluded conversation, stroking his chin and reading a typewritten document. I guessed it was the work of one of his students. He appeared to be engrossed. As I watched, he tapped a pencil against his teeth, and then he leaned over the desk and made some sort of note in the margin of that document. He appeared to be oblivious to my presence.

I started to type in the notes.

Deciphering the handwriting was a task in itself. I soon realized that if I was ever to finish even one folder then I would have to allow myself a margin of error and guess at some of the words. It was unlikely the professor would remember exactly what he had written, and surely he wouldn't have the time or inclination to go back through hundreds of sheets of paper checking for accuracy. As long as I was careful with dates, places and real names, I thought I could afford to be more relaxed about general pieces of information.

It was like a puzzle and pretty soon I found myself immersed in it. I was concentrating so hard that I forgot where I was, and I didn't even notice Jenny opening the door and bringing in coffee.

'How are you getting on?' she asked quietly, placing a mug on my desk.

'OK,' I whispered. 'I'm quite enjoying it.'

'It won't last,' she said.

The professor cleared his throat. 'Miss, er . . .'

'Mrs. Mrs Felicone.'

'You are entitled to a break. Perhaps you'd like to sit in the garden while you drink your coffee?'

'No, I'm fine here, thank you,' I said.

I had just discovered that Marian Rutherford was buried at Arcadia Vale, in a grave marked with a fine white headstone adorned with garlands of lilies and ivy. The lily-of-the-valley symbolized purity and the ivy, immortality and friendship. It was, according to the professor, an elegant and aesthetically pleasing memorial and one which seemed to suit well the character of the person to whom it was dedicated. I was interested to find out more.

The silence between us was comfortable. In fact, all things considered, we seemed to be working together well, the unsociable professor and the bereaved copy typist, until just before I was due to finish, when the mobile phone in my handbag rang. I had forgotten I'd brought it with me. It seemed an age before I managed to silence it, and in that time the professor had expressed his crossness via a series of minor actions, including thumping the document he was working on on to the desk, taking off his glasses, sighing, standing up and pacing the room.

'I'm sorry,' I said. 'It won't happen again.'

'Please make sure it doesn't. I find those things really irritating.'

'Sorry,' I said.

'I don't mean to be difficult,' said the professor, taking of his glasses and rubbing his eyes. 'But I cannot concentrate if there's a danger of a phone going off at any moment.'

I smiled. 'Fair enough.'

'So I'll see you tomorrow, Miss . . . er . . .'

'Please,' I said, 'call me Olivia.'

nineteen

The following summer, Anneli and I went back to work at Marinella's. This time, Angela and Maurizio didn't advertise the waitressing posts; they just asked us back, which was completely thrilling. It made us feel like part of the family. We had spent the last weeks of term very much looking forward to a summer spent in the company of Luca and Marc, now sixth-formers and, therefore, even more glamorous in our eyes. However, when we reported for work the first week of the school holidays, to our disappointment the twins weren't there. Fearing that they were losing their Italian language and sense of culture, Angela and Maurizio had dispatched them to Naples to work in the office of Maurizio's cousin's agro-tourism business.

It was a shame because we had hatched what we thought was a brilliant plan. We had decided we would each go out with, fall in love with and marry one twin. We would be married on the same day in the same church and share our reception. We would both move into Marinella's, and sleep with our respective twins in adjoining rooms. We would not just be best friends, we would be sisters-in-law. We could have parties together. We could have babies together. It would all be wonderful. We would be together for ever with our wonderful twin husbands.

But the twins were in Naples and we were in Portiston with the sour-faced Nathalie telling us what to do. She was, if anything, a little heavier and a little plainer than she had been the year before. She was probably only about twenty but she seemed like a grown woman to us, a grown woman who wore dull clothes and didn't wear make-up, didn't watch TV or listen to pop music, who had no interest in fashion or gossip or any of the other things with which Anneli and I were preoccupied. She was a barrier between us and the Felicones. Yet one thing was clear: Angela and she were closer than ever. Almost like mother and daughter.

twenty

'Where have you been?' Marc came into the flat on a wave of April warmth and gathered me into his arms like the hero of an old Broadway musical. I allowed myself to be gathered, and relaxed into his embrace.

'I've missed you,' I breathed into his ear.

'But where have you been? I've kept calling.'

'I've got a job.'

'Oh. Great.'

'I thought you'd be pleased.'

'I would have been. Doing what?'

'At the university. Typing.'

'Well, thanks for letting me know.'

'Oh Marc, how can I?' I said, pushing him away. 'How can I phone you up and talk to you? I don't know when you're on your own; I don't know if Nathalie's going to pick up the phone; I have no right to call you.'

'You're my brother's wife. You can call me whenever you like.'

'It wouldn't be right,' I said. 'Because I'm not just your sister-in-law, am I?'

Marc held up his hand in a 'stop' gesture. I took a deep breath and paused. We stared into each other's eyes for a few seconds.

'I keep calling,' said Marc, 'and you never answer.'

'I have to switch the phone off at work,' I said, slightly tetchily. 'I finish at four. If you call after that then I will answer.'

We both knew that four o'clock was the time when people started piling into Marinella's during the holiday season and, consequently, the time when both privacy and time became more limited.

'How have you been?' I asked gently. He didn't look so good. He had lost weight, his face was gaunt and the skin around his eyes was puffy and dark.

Marc rubbed his eyes with the heels of his hands and shrugged, a gesture of such despair that I immediately went to him, put my arms around him and held him close.

'It's all right, darling,' I whispered. 'Don't worry, it's all right.'

'No, it's not,' he said, pushing me away. 'Nothing's right, everything's wrong. The universe is perverted. My life is all wrong.'

'Are you free this afternoon?' I asked.

He nodded.

'Then let's go to our beach.'

We drove up the coast. We walked on the cliffs where tiny flowers were peeping into the sunshine, as if they couldn't believe their luck. Though the clouds were still chasing one another across the sky, the sea was blue and glorious and hundreds of small white seabirds were swooping and calling below us, making me feel dizzy. Gorse bushes, their backs bent over against the sea wind, were in flower and if I closed my eyes so that I was looking through the lashes, the whole world was blue and green and yellow.

On the cliff path we stopped and kissed and the universe righted itself. Marc smiled at me.

'When it's just us,' he said, 'you and me, then everything is bearable. I feel there is a point in carrying on.'

'I know.'

'Away from you, all I have is missing Luca.'

'I think,' I said carefully, 'that what we do for each other is fill the space where Luca should be.'

'I think,' said Marc, 'that it's more complicated than that.'

We walked down the steps cut in the cliff to the beach. Somebody else had been there. There were the remains of a fire on the shingle at the entrance to the cave, and discarded Stella cans inside. We made love with the utmost gentleness. On the island, the lugubrious, sad-eyed seals gazed towards the mainland where we sat holding hands, two human beings who didn't matter very much at that moment in time, except to one another.

twenty-one

The third and last summer that Anneli and I went to work at Marinella's, we found out that Luca and Nathalie were officially a couple. They went out on dates. They had performed a passable foxtrot at the annual Portiston and District Trading Association dinner and dance. I couldn't believe that Luca knew how to foxtrot. The thought made me queasy. After we were married, I could never get him to talk about what happened on these dates, but you can bet that the relationship progressed very, very slowly.

I don't know for sure. We didn't talk about it because it was a part of his life Luca preferred to forget, but I'm certain Angela was pulling Luca's strings. She can't have forced him to go out with Nathalie, but she probably brainwashed him into thinking it was a good idea. Nathalie had a good business brain and Luca was showing signs of being a talented chef. The two of them had the potential to forge a partnership as successful and strong as Angela and Maurizio's. If Luca married Nathalie, then all the promises Angela had made to her cousin would be fulfilled. Her favourite son and heir apparent to Marinella's would be forging a matrimonial and commercial partnership with her almost-daughter. It was perfect. Luca never liked confrontation and Angela never backed down. If his mother told him that he should take Nathalie out, it would have been impossible for him to refuse without upsetting the whole household. And perhaps he liked Nathalie. Perhaps, for a while, Luca thought Nathalie was what he wanted. Going out with an older woman certainly raised his status in the teenage male pecking order another couple of notches, though his ego didn't really need boosting and heaven knows he can't have been getting much action.

Angela was very protective of Nathalie. Because Nathalie wasn't like the other girls in Portiston, she decided it was the other girls who were at fault. She judged us by Nathalie's high moral standards and found us lacking. Fairly early on in the summer that last year, Anneli and I were called into Angela's office and given a dressing-down. She had been watching us. She didn't approve of the way we conducted ourselves outside work and scolded us for walking provocatively along the seafront, our arms entwined, each of us enjoying the stares we attracted although we scowled at anyone who looked at us. She told us that unless we shaped up, she wouldn't tolerate us working in Marinella's. She said we reflected badly on the business.

Anneli and I had long since abandoned our original plan of marrying one twin each. What was the point of dreaming when Luca was spoken for? I suspected that Anneli was still sweet on Marc. She pretended that she wasn't but I was forever catching her looking at him through her lashes, and once, after we'd been drinking cider on the front, she wrote his name in pebbles on the terrace outside Marinella's. I'd been hanging around with a nineteen-year-old called Georgie, with whom I was a little bit in love. Georgie was a drama student at Manchester University and he had a holiday job working the Seal Island ferry, which belonged to his uncle.

We worked harder than ever that last summer. We were rushed off our feet serving *gelati*, toasted sandwiches (this was before anyone in the UK had heard of panini), iced drinks and pots of tea to people sitting inside and outside the restaurant. There were always long queues at the counter, where we were occasionally asked to deputize if neither Luca nor Marc was available to scoop one of twelve different flavours of ice cream into the deliciously crisp and sweet home-made cones.

As soon as one table emptied we had to clean it, dust away the scraps beneath it, wipe and prop up the menu, and show any waiting clientele to the vacant seats. We made a small fortune in tips. Even if the weather was bad, the restaurant was always busy. In rain, those who could came inside for tea and cake. Those who couldn't fit inside huddled beneath the large green, red and white canopy over the terrace where they were sheltered from the worst of the weather. At the end of the working day our feet hurt, but we were generally happy.

On what Maurizio called 'the last day of summer' – the final Saturday before school restarted – there was a party for the family, staff and suppliers of Marinella's.

The restaurant closed at 6 p.m., and we were sent home to change into our glad-rags.

I went back to Anneli's house to prepare for the party. My mother was already in mourning for Lynnette's imminent return to university and grey Mr Hensley would be with her, making things worse. I couldn't bear the long looks of silent reproach we'd have to endure. It was easier, and more fun, at Anneli's.

In her bedroom, a chaos of pink and yellow Flower Fairy wallpaper covered with posters of Duran Duran, we made each other up, and tried on every single item in Anneli's wardrobe, aiming to find outfits that made us look the same, but different.

In the end Anneli wore a cute little pair of cut-off jeans with a tight black shirt and I went for a leather-look skirt worn with a black halterneck shirt and a very old, lacy cardigan. The effect was designed to be soft punk. We covered ourselves in perfume – I can't remember the brand but it had a lovely sherbetty smell, like the taste of Love Hearts. We both looked and smelled pretty good.

'Liv, can I tell you something?' asked Anneli as she ironed my hair. I was in an uncomfortable position, my head on a towel on her pink carpet, the rest of me curled in a foetal position so that she could have the best access to my hair.

'You *do* fancy Marc!'

'Oh all right, I do.'

'I knew you did, I knew it I knew it I knew it!'

'Nobody likes a bighead, Liv.'

136

'Yes, but I knew, didn't I! It's perfect, you two will be perfect together!'

'So what should I do?'

'You should tell him, of course.'

'What, really?'

The iron was uncomfortably close to my ear as Anneli hovered above me to look at my face to see if I was serious.

'I think he likes you too,' I said. 'I've seen him looking over when he didn't think anyone was looking.'

'Are you serious? Really? What, really looking at me?'

'Anneli, you're burning my cheek.'

'Oh, I wish you hadn't told me. I won't know what to say.'

The room was beginning to smell of singed hair. Anneli smoothed her hand over her work. 'Your hair looks lovely, Liv. It's perfect.'

I looked at myself in the mirror above Anneli's white and gold dressing table. My hair did look good. I gave my friend a quick hug and we swapped positions so that I could iron hers.

It was impossible to escape the house without saying goodbye to Anneli's parents, who were watching *The Generation Game* on TV. Anneli's mum gave us a half-hearted smile and told us to have a nice time and make sure we were back before midnight. Her dad looked at me and said, 'Is that a skirt, Olivia, or a pelmet?'

'Oh ha ha, Dad, you're so funny,' said Anneli, leaning over to kiss his cheek. She was positively glowing with anticipation. 'See you later!'

*

137

The party was already in full swing at Marinella's. Karaoke hadn't yet arrived in Portiston, yet the spirit of karaoke was born there. Maurizio was on the 'stage' at the fireplace end of the restaurant with a microphone, singing along with Gene Pitney at the top of his voice and telling the story in hand gestures too. He waved when he saw us and we waved back as we headed for the bar.

The room was full. There were some young people, like us, who worked in Marinella's or were family friends, but most of the guests were older. Whiskery brewery representatives rubbed shoulders with clean-shaven bank staff. The fish lady was dancing with the sanitary-ware man. Everyone was having a great time.

Luca and Nathalie were sitting together stiffly at one of the tables, like a couple posing for an old-fashioned photograph. Luca looked strangely tidy. I actually didn't recognize him at first. He was wearing a pair of dark trousers and a pressed shirt that was open at the collar where his Adam's apple bulged. His hair had been combed and flattened, somehow. He looked rather like his brother Carlo – a sort of Stepford son. Nathalie was, for once, wearing something feminine. It was far too old for her, a sort of floaty two-piece in green and black. On her feet were long black shoes with a pointed toe and a squat heel. They weren't talking to one another. They just sat, and watched the party.

Marc was having fun. He was dancing with Fabio and a couple of children who belonged to the newsagent up the road, doing the same exaggerated actions as his father and miming along to the words.

Annoyingly, Angela was standing at the bar, dashing any hopes we had of being served anything alcoholic. Luckily Marc had planned for this contingency.

After he'd finished his dance he came over to us, out of breath and laughing, and we talked for a while about this and that and he topped up our glasses of fruit punch with something or other he'd stolen from the cellar, which made our heads buzz. And then Maurizio called all the males in the house to the centre of the dance floor, where he told them to take off their socks and shoes and roll up their trousers to the knees. Anneli and I were helpless with giggles as the businessmen of Portiston, as well as the Felicone boys, did exactly that. Then Maurizio told them there'd be a prize for the best surfer, and played 'Surfing USA'. All the shopkeepers and suppliers, the accountant, the solicitor, even the vicar was there, their hairy, bony, white male legs bare beneath their trousers, swaying and balancing like they were real surfers. It was so funny we were nearly crying. I happened to glance over at Nathalie; she wasn't even watching, but was deep in conversation with Angela.

When it was over Maurizio asked the assembled womenfolk who should win the prize and Anneli and I jumped up and down and shouted, 'Marc! Marc!'

'Hey, what about me?' asked Luca, bounding up to us, his shirt all out of his trousers, his tie askew and his hair back to its normal dishevelled state.

'Sorry,' I said with a tiny sneer. 'But your brother was better.'

Luca gave us an Italian double-raised-palm gesture of confusion and disbelief and hopped off back to Nathalie, shoes in hand. Marc showed us his prize, a bottle of Aloha sun cream.

'Thanks for your support!' he said, looking vaguely embarrassed.

Anneli looked at her feet and twisted a strand of hair round her finger.

I must have been a little drunk. 'Why don't you ask Anneli to dance?' I said.

'Liv!'

'Go on,' I said. 'She'll say yes.'

Marc blushed and shuffled his feet back into his shoes. But he did ask her and she did say yes and they went, hand in hand, to the dance floor. And that was how Anneli and Marc started going out with one another.

I looked across to Luca. He was sitting between Nathalie and Angela, drinking from the rim of a bottle of beer. I caught his eye but he looked away.

I was bored by the party. I found my coat and slipped away and met Georgie off the late ferry. We sat in the dark on the pebbles. He rolled a joint and held it to my lips and I breathed in and burned the back of my throat, and then he lay back and sang 'Stairway to Heaven' while I gave him a blow-job and marvelled at the twinkling of the lights in my inky black mind.

twenty-two

Every day I learned a little more about Marian Rutherford and nothing at all about the professor. I liked being in the large office with him, though. It was quiet but it was companionable. The only sound, generally, would be that of my fingers on the keyboard and him turning the pages of whatever document or book he was reading. We were comfortable with one another, like an old married couple who had run out of things to talk about years before. Some mornings he would come in to unlock the door and then go straight off to lectures or seminars with his students. Other days, if he didn't have to see anybody, he would let me in and then disappear to work from home. He said it was easier to concentrate there. I imagined a big old house, semi-derelict, with wall-to-ceiling books, a couple of mangy cats sleeping on the windowledges, and the professor scribbling away at a desk like a character from Dickens.

Working gave my days a purpose, and because picking apart the professor's writing was so difficult, I had to concentrate and that meant there was no room in my mind for other thoughts. I approached my job rather as I would have approached evening classes in my previous life – as a welcome distraction from reality and as a means of relaxation. I am a fast typist but it was taking for ever to work through the notes. The professor never asked how I was progressing, or looked over my shoulder. I was certain he didn't check the computer when I wasn't there. I was glad that he trusted me.

When he wasn't around, Jenny often came in to chat with me. She'd curl her knees beneath her on the leather settee and tell me about Yusuf and the noodle bar and her kleptomaniac flatmate. She was very entertaining and I enjoyed her company. Best of all, she wasn't the slightest bit interested in me. If anyone had asked her, I doubt she'd have been able to tell them anything about me, except perhaps my Christian name.

There were dozens of different editions of Marian Rutherford's books on the shelves in the office, but I didn't dare touch them. Instead, I went to the Central Library and ordered them, one at a time, to read in the flat. I started with *Emily Campbell*, which I'd read at school (or not read most of it, if I'm honest) and then again some years back after I'd found a copy on the second-hand bookstall at the market near our London home. The story is set in Portiston, with no attempt to disguise the town or any of its landmarks. Its heroine, Emily Campbell, was a daughter of the town, a charming, headstrong and selfish girl torn between her longing to escape what she regarded as the suffocating constraints of her life, and the desire to live and die amongst the people she knew and loved. This conflict is epitomized in the characters of the two men who love her, the handsome, faithful but unambitious Jude McCallistair and the driven but slightly dangerous John Perriman.

As in all good tragedies, it is a fatal flaw in Emily's character – her inability to act logically instead of impulsively – that leads to her own undoing. Without giving away the plot, it's a well-known fact that, in summer, you'll see queues of tourists waiting to have their picture taken at the place on the clifftop above Portiston town where, in the book, Emily threw herself to her death on page 414.

What I had never known, until I started transcribing the professor's notes, was that in real life, from that point on the cliff, you can see into the back garden of Andrew Bird's house. He was Marian Rutherford's friend and publisher and the reason she came to Portiston in the first place.

The professor and I exchanged polite but brief pleasantries, but that was as far as our relationship went. I didn't mind, because it was so peaceful being with him in the office, both of us sheltering under our separate umbrellas of anonymity, but I did want to talk to him about *Emily Campbell*. There were some loose ends in the plot that frustrated me, and I wasn't sure if I was missing something. I decided I would find a moment, a coffee break when he wasn't immersed in work, in which to broach the subject. In the meantime, in order to find out about the professor himself, I waited until the day when he told me he was going home to work and wouldn't be back until midday, which also happened to be a day when Jenny had called in sick ('Babe, I'm puking my guts up, been on the Bacardi all night, just tell him it's women's problems and he won't ask any more questions'). Alone on the ground floor of the university history department, I took the opportunity to examine the contents of his desk.

twenty-three

By the autumn Anneli and Marc were an item of sorts. However, in my opinion, their relationship was moving exceptionally slowly. They had held hands and kissed (without tongues), but that was all. Marc hadn't asked for any sexual favours whatsoever. In fact, Anneli reported, he was a perfect gentleman. That was how she liked it for, despite our predilection for dressing like temptresses, Anneli was at heart a traditional girl who had made her mind up that she wouldn't go all the way with someone until she was certain that she'd found the right someone. She wasn't sure Marc was that person.

She and Marc had been to the cinema, and they spent some time together at weekends, either listening to records in the bedroom Marc shared with Luca, or watching TV with Anneli's parents round at her house. On the bus into town they sometimes, but not always, sat together and sometimes they would walk together, although Marc never put his arm around Anneli's shoulder, which would have bothered me if I'd been her, but she didn't seem to mind. She didn't want me to feel left out so usually she walked with me anyway.

Anneli was a very good friend to me.

Once I asked her if she loved Marc and she said, 'Oh Liv, I don't know!'

'How can you not know?' I would persist. 'Either you love him or you don't; you must know.'

'Well, do you love Georgie?'

'It's not that kind of relationship.'

'Well, maybe ours isn't either.'

I was, in my defence, only sixteen, and most of my education about life and sex came from teen magazines which were, in those days, still massively biased towards a romantic view of the world.

'If you don't know,' I said, 'then you can't love him.'

'Well, does it matter?'

'Of course it does! If you're going to spend the rest of your life with him . . .'

We had this sort of conversation many times. But the occasion I remember most clearly happened early the following year. It was the school holidays and Anneli and I had arranged to go swimming in Watersford Public Baths. Marc turned up with Luca, but no Nathalie.

At the time it never crossed my mind to wonder why Nathalie didn't come; I was just glad she hadn't and assumed she was working. It must have been a Saturday. Probably she just didn't much like swimming. The public baths with their busy changing rooms and loud children wouldn't have appealed to her. To be honest, she wouldn't have looked great in a swimming costume either.

Away from Nathalie, Luca reverted to his normal, boisterous self, breaking just about every swimming-pool rule in the first five minutes as he hared out of the changing room, ran along the side of the pool yelling the *Dam Busters* theme and then dive-bombed Anneli and me at the deep end. We screamed and shrieked as our hair and make-up were drenched in the cold, chlorinated water while Luca resurfaced next to us, shaking his head like a dog, his long black hair spraying droplets of water all over us again. Marc returned to his traditional role as the quieter, more thoughtful twin. He stood at the side, his arms crossed over his chest, holding on to his shoulders and laughing. I noticed, I remember, how white his feet were, his slender ankles and his long, thin toes.

We swam and played for a while, annoying the other swimmers with our noise and our physicality. The boys swam beneath our legs and then stood up, lifting us on to their shoulders, and then we raced, all of us squealing and laughing. Sometimes they'd tip us into the water backwards, sometimes we would dive in forwards. Luca would ping the back of our costumes. He had a beautiful body, the wide-shouldered, slightly triangular upper-body shape of a male athlete – slim hips, slender, racehorse legs. Marc was attractive too but he was darker, sturdier and shorter. Our games involved a good deal of body contact. It was fun, it was exciting, and it wasn't entirely innocent. I told myself it was just playing, but when I was sat on Luca's bony shoulders, his wet black hair fanning out on my wet, white thighs, I would be lying if I said I did not enjoy the moment. I enjoyed being that close to Luca. I was very glad that Nathalie wasn't there. She wouldn't have joined in anyway.

Anneli and I got out first because we were cold. We changed in adjoining cubicles, stamping out of our wet costumes and pulling dry clothes awkwardly over our still-damp bodies. Teardrops of cold water followed one another from the rat's tails of my hair down my chest. I only had one towel and it was too small and old to be of much comfort.

While we waited for the boys we sat in the little cafeteria which looked out over the pool, sipped hot chocolate out of the machine and shared a carton of chips which we dipped into a communal pool of ketchup.

'I think Luca's really nice,' I confessed.

'It's a shame he's taken,' said Anneli.

'Maybe Nathalie will cheat on him or move to Australia or die or something,' I said hopefully.

'I don't think she'd be that obliging,' said Anneli, twirling her chip round in the ketchup. 'I think she really loves him.'

'Why do you say that?'

'It's just the way she looks at him. When they're together she's always sort of next to him. She notices him all the time.'

'It sounds a bit obsessive.'

'It's actually quite nice.'

I shrugged.

'Nathalie's all right when you get to know her, Liv.'

'Yeah well, I don't really care about Nathalie,' I said. 'What about you and Marc?'

Anneli gave a little sigh, and put down the chip she had just picked up.

'I don't think I love him and I don't think he loves me.'

'Are you sure?'

She nodded. 'I can't imagine going shopping with him or having children with him or having holidays with him, or growing old with him.'

I rolled my eyes. 'That's all boring, middle-aged stuff, Anneli! What about the wild passionate stuff?'

She shook her head. 'Nope, I can't imagine any of that either.'

'Just because you can't imagine it doesn't mean it can't happen.'

'I know it's not going to happen.'

I tipped the last dregs of chocolate into my mouth and licked my lips.

'What are you going to do?'

'I'm not going to do anything. I don't have to do anything. We both know where we stand.'

Anneli was – is – a cleverer girl than me. If only I could have been more like her the next few months of my life would not have been such hell.

twenty-four

'So what did you find?'

'Huh?'

'In the weird professor's desk.'

'He's not weird, Marc, he's just quiet.'

'Always a bad sign.'

We were sitting in the café, eating teacakes. Outside was a thunderstorm. The sky was dark grey although it was only early afternoon and rain was streaking down like bullets, puncturing the puddles on the pavement and roads in a million different places. Every now and then lightning would jag across the sky and the café lights would flicker, and then there would be an aural torrent of thunder, like a reverse crescendo, which rattled the windows and my nerves.

'I didn't find anything much. Just a lot of clutter, lots of bits and pieces.'

'Come on, Liv, there must have been something that gave you a clue about the man.'

I shook my head and licked butter from my fingers. I was ashamed of my prying and I didn't want to exacerbate my disloyalty and my nosiness by sharing what I'd found with

anyone, not even Marc. When I knew more about the professor, then maybe I would be able to explain why, in the
right-hand-side drawer of his desk, hidden beneath a diary
dating back to 1989, there was an empty scent bottle, a
scuffed, pale blue leather baby shoe and a postcard with
a picture of Madrid by night on the front, and nothing at
all on the back.

'There was just paperwork, exam guidelines, pens, sta-
tionery, stuff like that.'

'No secret diary?'

'No.'

'No revolver?'

'No.'

'No stash of hash?'

I giggled. 'No.'

'No saucy letters from besotted students?'

'Stop it now.'

'No women's underwear?'

'Shut up, Marc.'

'I'm just showing an interest in your career.'

'Yeah, right.'

'And did you know that what you just said is the only
example in the English language of two positives being used
to denote a negative? I heard it on Radio Four.'

This was something Luca did. All the time, he would
hear something on the radio, or see something on TV, or
read something, or somebody would tell him some quirky
fact, and he would file it in his memory and regurgitate it

at an appropriate moment. It amused me. I found it endearing.

There was a flash of lightning and Marc's face gleamed electric-white for a tiny second. I felt the beginning of a headache in my temples. As if he sensed my discomfort, Marc leaned over the table and stroked the side of my face very gently with the backs of his fingers. I closed my eyes and leaned in to his touch.

He whispered something. I wasn't sure what he said, but before I could ask, the café's bodybuilder chef brought two mugs of tea to our table.

'How're you doing, baby?' he asked. Over the past weeks we had become friends, this muscled, tattooed man, and I. He didn't know the details, and was too sensitive to ask, but he knew I'd had some kind of a bad time. He gave Marc a sidelong glance as if to enquire if this man were the root of my troubles.

'This is Marc, my brother-in-law,' I said.

'Pleased to meet you,' said the chef, wiping his right hand on his apron and offering it to Marc.

'Marc runs the restaurant in Portiston, Marinella's,' I ventured.

'Oh yeah? I know it. On the seafront? Bet that's a little goldmine,' said the bodybuilder.

'It's not bad,' said Marc.

'Double negative denoting a positive,' I pointed out.

Marc's face relaxed into a smile and then he laughed, out loud. The chef looked perplexed.

'Sorry,' I said. 'It's just something we were talking about.'

'Yeah, well, I'll catch up with you guys later,' he said.

We sat in silence, holding hands. Outside rain streamed down the window-glass; inside the panes were steamed up so it was hard to make out the details of the faces of the people who rushed by, chins down, hands in their pockets, hurrying for shelter. I licked the sugar from my lips, which were still a little swollen from our love-making earlier. I wonder if it showed. I wonder if the chef knew what was going on.

I saw Marc's eyes flicker upwards to read the clock behind me. He would have to go soon, in order to fulfil whatever obligation he had used as his alibi for this afternoon. I tried to look as if I hadn't noticed, but loneliness came at me in a rush. The tea had gone cool and anyway it was too milky and the storm which had previously been thrilling was now simply enervating.

'God, I'm tired,' I whispered, longing for my bed and the oblivion of sleep, and I remembered, with a rush of pleasure, that there was plenty of alcohol in the flat, a nice glass of red wine to start maybe and then gin and lemonade to send me to sleep, and I wondered if Sundays had always been like this and of course they hadn't.

When Luca was alive, Sundays were our best days. Our lazy, lie-in-bed days, our coffee and chocolate-spread-on-toast days, our sleepy amble-round-a-market-or-a-park days, our hands-held days, our snoozing-in-front-of-the-TV days. Sometimes we talked of what it would have been like if we had had children. We imagined taking them to do entertaining but educational things, but probably we would have been useless parents. We were too disorganized, too selfish. In my heart I knew that no Sundays could be better than the ones we shared, just Luca and I. The only thing that spoiled them was the prospect of Monday on the horizon. Still, we drank wine on Sunday evenings, in celebration of the weekend and in preparation for the week that was to follow. Luca said it was a waste to have a hangover on a weekend; he said you might as well have it during working hours, not in your own time.

Luca worked in a restaurant in Covent Garden. He enjoyed the buzz and the business, and the banter with the clientele. There was none of the rigmarole associated with being part of the only restaurant in a small seaside town: none of the community politics, or having to remember everyone's name and what was going on in their lives so that you could make polite, friendly chit-chat. Instead, Luca revelled in the anonymity of the big city, and the variety of people he met, and their different tastes and languages and manners. He got on well with the owner and knew how much the mark-up was on each dish, and his ambition was to open a place of his own. A café with food, not a restaurant, somewhere that did good-quality sandwiches, soups and salads at lunchtimes, and simple early suppers in the evenings to attract the working crowd, not the drinking crowd. He had his eye on a fish-and-chip shop that we knew was coming up for sale not far from where we lived, in Bow. What with the Olympics coming and everything, he thought it was the perfect venue for his enterprise. He was going to call it 'Liv's'.

'Liv?'

'Sorry, what?'

'I'm sorry but I have to go.'

'Yes, of course. Of course you do.'

I stood up and unhooked my coat from the back of the chair. Marc helped me into it, kissing my hair as he did so.

'This is crap,' he said.

'I know.'

'I'll sort something out,' he said. 'I'll take you away for the weekend. We'll go somewhere nice, away from here. We'll go somewhere where we don't have to keep looking over our shoulders or watching the clock.'

'That would be nice.'

As we went out into the storm, I glanced over my shoulder and saw the chef watching us. He was rubbing his chin with his fingers. I wondered what went through his mind as Marc and I, our fingers trickling apart like they were playing scales on a piano, turned in opposite directions out of the café.

twenty-five

April turned into May, a pretty, fertile May when everything turned green at the same time and the honeyed smell of the blossom on the city hedgerows was as intoxicating as the sunshine. The pavements around the university buildings were speckled with pink petals and students displayed their bellies and the edges of their underwear, innocent and optimistic as the baby birds which squawked in their nests in the eaves. The office workers packed sandwiches to eat in the departmental gardens at lunchtimes where the young people sunbathed and talked on their mobile phones and canoodled, their fingers hooked into the waistbands of each other's jeans.

In the evenings, in my flat, I longed for a garden. I wondered what was happening in the yard behind our house in London. Last summer, it had been full of pots. Luca had grown potatoes, peppers, tomatoes, basil, coriander and courgettes. I had grown freesias, geraniums and roses. It had been a horticultural division of labour and gender: he did practical plants, I did pretty ones. He cultivated the vegetables and then he cooked them. I forgot to water mine.

If it hadn't been for Luca, my roses would have been destroyed by greenfly.

'Look at them, Liv,' he said, combing a baby rose leaf between his thumb and forefinger. 'It's crawling with greenfly. Imagine how that must feel to this poor plant.'

His fingers were stained green and grungy with crushed insects. I imagined being the rose, the irritation, the pain of these little creatures burrowing and scurrying and chomping into my new buds. What a slow, miserable death that would be. Shamed into action, I became obsessive about wiping down the leaves myself, ridding my plants of pests. By July, my roses were lovely.

There were tenants in the house now. It was unlikely that they would bother with my plants. I couldn't really expect them to water them, feed them, and wipe the greenfly from their leaves. Lynnette would call round and retrieve the pots if I asked her, but she wouldn't nurture them as we had done. Why should she?

Lacking a garden, but craving fresh air and flowers, I went to the cemetery, which was lush with new growth. As I walked the path up the hill millions of tiny insects clouded before me and the birds sang in the trees like it was the first spring ever. I felt like lying down on the grass beside Luca's grave and enjoying the late-afternoon sun. The grass was golden with buttercups and tiny purple flowers like pansies, and it looked dry and friendly and comfortable. The cemetery was full of people though, living people, and I thought I might alarm them if I lay down. So I stood, for a moment, hoping the sunshine was permeating the soil down to where

Luca lay, and then I changed the water in the pickled-onion jar and threw away the carcasses of the poor dead flowers that had been turning to slime inside it and replaced them with yellow tulips. The flowers, I knew, wouldn't last long, but the yellow petals on the greening soil of the grave would be pretty. The general effect was one of colour and optimism. I smiled, pleased. Luca's grave looked like an Impressionist painting.

Afterwards I went to the café for a glass of wine and a plate of bread and olives. The café was loud with made-up women in high heels, heady on hair gel and the prospect of a night out. The chef slipped me a smile and a bruschetta.

Some evenings I drove to Portiston and wandered along the beach, watching the sun fading over the sea. I remembered somebody, Maurizio perhaps, holding me by the shoulders as a child and telling me to listen for the hissing sound when the hot sun dipped its toes into the cold water. The sunlight disappeared from Seal Island and the constant cloud which shrouded its nightly departure was, according to the voice in my ear, the steam sent up from the bubbling, boiling water. Now I sat on the pebbles and threw stones into the darkening water. Each time I went to Portiston, I intended to go into Marinella's, but each time I changed my mind. I couldn't bear the thought of looking into Nathalie's distrustful eyes. Portiston made me feel more alone, but I could not stay away.

twenty-six

When she left university, Lynnette found a job with a music-publishing company in London, and after that she only came back to Portiston for the occasional weekend, and she was different, completely different.

Her visits were ever shorter and sweeter, and when she left, the tall old house felt empty, bereft and miserable. She had started mentioning a man, Sean, and I think both Mum and I knew that soon we would lose her to London for ever.

When Lynnette was there, our home was not exactly full of chat, but it was livelier and more colourful. I had somebody to talk to and a reason to be at home. When Georgie came to Portiston during the university holidays, I also had a reason to be out.

The year I turned seventeen, we couldn't keep our hands off each other. We had the best time. He would sound the horn as the ferry approached the beach, and I would make up an excuse (where necessary) and run down to meet him. Once the incoming cars were unloaded, there was nearly an hour before the return journey. While the outgoing cars queued in the car park, Georgie and I would hide beneath the ramp and have urgent, exciting sex. We littered the beach with our condoms, like some kind of pale, fragile sea creatures, vulnerable and slimy, washed up on the pebbles. God, I really thought I loved Georgie, the oily ferry smell of him, the gap in his teeth, the way he spat into the waves, his thin, feral body, his narrow face. In the evenings, he wanted to go to the pub, but none of the pubs in Portiston would serve me because the proprietors had all known me since I was knee high and, being good Christians, respected my mother's views on alcohol. So instead I rode on the back of Georgie's Yamaha into the countryside, and shivered as I drank cider in shabby pub gardens. I ached for him when we were together and when we were apart.

And then the academic holidays were over, and Georgie was gone. When he left, I lapsed into a sullen bad temper, missing the sex and the dope and the motorbike and wrapping myself in the oily denim jacket he had given me.

My mother no longer suffered from migraine. Instead, she filled her days with church business and Mr Hensley. She was a member of various committees and societies. She helped with the flowers and organized coffee mornings to raise funds for the new roof. Laboriously, she made tapestry covers to replace the worn fabric on the hassocks. At least once a week a group of elderly women and men, all of them older than Mum, would arrive at the house to drink milky coffee and eat water biscuits while they worked their way through an agenda or agreed upon a rota for some church chore or other. Mr Hensley liked to preside over these meetings, but I don't know why the committee put up with him.

Everything about him irritated me: the way he rocked on his heels, the way his trousers were shiny at the knees and just a little too short so that when he sat down you could see the ginger hairs on his bony little ankles, his big, flappy ears, his red turkey-skin neck, the officious and nauseating way he was constantly clearing the phlegm from the back of his throat, spitting it into his handkerchief and then examining the contents.

It made me feel queasy just touching anything he had touched. I was sure he was not the sort of man to wash his hands after he'd been to the lavatory. I began to make an inventory in my head of everything Mr Hensley had handled, even the furniture he had used, and I avoided contact with polluted items. Because I could never be certain if cutlery was clean, I only ate food that I had prepared, or that I could eat with my fingers. As a result, I lost weight. I knew I looked good skinny. I longed for Georgie. I wanted to see myself reflected in his eyes.

Mum was, I think, as happy as she had ever been, even though it was perfectly obvious that she missed Lynnette dreadfully. Every time my sister left, Mum would spend two days cleaning her room, washing the curtains and bedclothes and generally making it as nice as possible for when Lynnette came back.

I never exactly felt like she resented me, but I knew she would be happy when I, too, flew the nest. But we were all right. As long as I behaved reasonably sensibly, left the house looking presentable and didn't give her cause to worry about what the neighbours might think, Mum and I could rub along together fine.

The regularity of our domestic routine left when Lynnette did. Mum didn't bother making meals for the two of us, for which I was relieved and grateful. I didn't feel hard done by; instead I was happy to see to myself, making my own sandwiches, grating my own cheese and heating my own cans of tomato soup, washing all the implements and crockery before I started to erase any trace of Mr Hensley's fingerprints.

She lived her life and I lived mine.

Apart from the church meetings, our house was a quiet house. Mum sometimes listened to Radio Two (Terry Wogan made her smile) but she had an aversion to both teenagers and what she termed 'modern' music. So I never had friends back, and tended to creep around in my socks while Mum was at home.

It was a different matter when she went out. Then I would turn the radio up good and loud, and dance in the living room, choreographing my own steps, swinging and twirling and jumping on and off the furniture.

I would run upstairs and try on lots of different clothes. I would pin my hair up, pull it back, plait it, loop it, knot it, make bunches, straighten it, wave it and make kinks in it. Then I would experiment with make-up and pull faces at myself in the mirror. Sexy faces, pouty come-hither faces, angry faces, fuck-off faces, bored faces, tragedy faces and lunatic faces. Then, dressed like a rock star, I'd fly downstairs again to turn the music up even louder and pogo to some retro punk while I made myself something to eat in the kitchen. I was always hungry when I was on my own; I couldn't eat a thing when Mum and Mr Hensley were in the house.

Sometimes, I would spend hours on the phone talking to Anneli, lying on my stomach on the hall floor, swinging my feet and sharing secrets. I told her what I had done with Georgie and she was horrified, and thrilled, in equal measure. By now, her relationship with Marc had become, by mutual agreement, a close friendship and nothing more. Yet still she was welcomed backstage at Marinella's as if she were one of them, and she told me what was going on in the family, how the plans for Carlo and Sheila's wedding were progressing, how Nathalie and Angela were thick as thieves, whispering and plotting. They were delicious conversations.

My favourite pastime outside school was my diary. It wasn't a proper diary, but a blue hardback notebook full of lined paper. I wrote in it religiously. Some days there were just a few words. Other days, I spent ages recording a complete, illustrated account of events, thoughts, feelings, even song lyrics. If I had had the slightest idea of the trouble this would lead to, I wouldn't have bothered.

twenty-seven

'How are you getting on?'

The professor was looking, for him, almost cheerful. He was jingling his car keys and obviously had news to impart. It was a Wednesday afternoon.

'Fine,' I said. 'The more I learn, the more I'm enjoying this.'

'Would you buy it, if it were a book?' he asked.

'Of course,' I said. 'And I'd give it to all my friends for Christmas.'

'Good, good.'

'I'm sure it would be a bestseller.'

'All right, don't over-egg the pudding. Where are you up to?'

'Well, it's not exactly in order, but I'm up to the bit where Marian Rutherford comes to England to visit her publisher.'

'You come from Portiston, don't you?'

I nodded.

'So would you mind driving me there this afternoon? I need to take some pictures of the publisher's house.'

It was a lovely day, warm and balmy, and I could think of

few things more pleasant or relaxing than a drive to the coast. I knew where Andrew Bird's house was. I could make myself useful.

The professor asked me to drive his car. I had been expecting something old and characterful. In fact, it was a red Toyota Celica.

'Wow,' I said.

The professor scratched behind his ear, a sure sign that he was pleased.

'My students refer to it as my MLC turbo,' he said.

'Sorry, I'm not very good at cars.'

'Mid-life crisis,' he explained. 'I bought it after my wife left me. I think they thought I was trying to pull,' and he gave a long, low chuckle that was so infectious I started laughing too.

'I haven't driven anything like this for ages,' I said. In fact, in the wake of Luca's accident, driving anything apart from my beloved Clio made me feel uncomfortable.

'You'll be OK, she's easy, a piece of cake,' said the professor, folding himself somewhat awkwardly into the passenger side. 'I need to be able to jump out as and when to take pictures.'

'You'll have trouble jumping out of that seat, if you don't mind me saying,' I pointed out. 'You're almost lying down.'

He smiled. 'Well, we're not in a rush, are we?'

We weren't. I drove at a speed that seemed, even to me, embarrassingly slow and was very careful, braking if anybody showed any signs of imminently stepping off the pavement, or turning into our path. Yet if the professor was aware of my caution, he didn't show it. He just put on his spectacles and examined the papers on his knee and occasionally said, 'Hmm, yes,' or similar. By the time we were out on the Portiston road, I was enjoying myself.

We stopped on the crest of the hill which overlooked the town. You couldn't see much of it from this point, just the ferry terminal where Georgie and I had loved one another all those years ago, and the roofs of the houses and shops at the top end of the town, and the church spire.

'This is the only road in and out, so Marian Rutherford must have approached this way,' said the professor. 'I need a photograph.'

He undertook the laborious business of extricating himself from the low seat and then faffed around for some time with the camera.

'Olivia,' he called after a while. 'Do you know anything about digital cameras?'

Sometimes, I swear I thought this technological naïvety of his was an affectation. I squinted up at him through the windscreen.

'I can't make it work,' he said helplessly.

It took me about thirty seconds to show him how to operate the device, and then I breathed the air and enjoyed the view down to the sunlight on the waves, and the white birds which ballet-danced in the sky around Seal Island while he took his pictures.

'So how long did you live in Portiston?' he asked, back in the car.

'All my life until I was eighteen,' I said.

'Then you left for university?'

I smiled, and manoeuvred the car round a hairpin bend with which I was intimately familiar.

'No, no, I didn't go to university.'

'Oh.'

He didn't ask any more, and there was a longish silence as we drove down into the town. I had no intention of filling it.

'So where now?' I asked as we pulled into the main street. 'Andrew Bird's house?'

'You know where it is?'

'Of course I do. Every primary-school-age child in Portiston knows where it is. Honestly, professor, it's about the only famous building in the whole town.'

'There's also that very unusual art deco restaurant.'

I ignored this.

'It's listed, you know. If there's time, we could go in for a snack.'

Andrew Bird's house was one of six fine Regency buildings in the terrace at the northern end of the beach. If Marian Rutherford had crossed the Atlantic expecting a romantic encounter with her long-term, long-distance literary correspondent, she was to be disappointed. As we sat in the car outside the house, the professor read Miss Rutherford's own description of the publisher, who had probably suffered a stroke while she was *en route* from America.

'She called him a "poor bent, pale, old creature, wheezy of chest and rheumy of eye, more slumped than seated in a bath chair in the shade of a fine plum tree where he could enjoy the scent of the roses",' said the professor.

'Not exactly a sex god, then.'

'No. She was sure that he didn't even know who she was and, apparently, confused her with his servant girl and scolded her for asking him questions.'

'Oh dear,' I said. 'Poor Marian.'

'Oh, I shouldn't feel too sorry for her,' said the professor, opening his car door. 'If she hadn't come to Portiston, she would never have written her best works and she wouldn't have found her true love.'

'I thought she died a spinster?'

'Ah hah,' said the professor, giving me one of his rare and beautiful smiles. 'You haven't reached the end of the story yet.'

Andrew Bird's former residence had a long, narrow front garden mostly laid to tarmac, and a blue plaque on the wall beside the front door, but it was now, like its neighbours, a bed-and-breakfast establishment. The landlady had been expecting us and was proud to show us all the Rutherford/Bird memorabilia she had collected over the years. As well as several valuable and rare first editions in a glass-fronted bookcase, she had framed photographs on the walls of the long, narrow hall, from celebrity attendees of the literary festival.

I drank a cup of tea in the kitchen and listened to the landlady's anecdotes while the professor took his photographs in the garden where the two literary giants first met. I looked through the kitchen window, past a ledge where plastic flowers jostled for space with vases of pencils and novelty memorabilia, and watched him as he nosed about, clearly enjoying himself, examining the contents of the flowerbeds and then looking up the cliff which towered above the garden. I suspected he was wondering if any of the existing plants had witnessed the arrival of Marian Rutherford. I couldn't see anything that looked like a plum tree.

When he had finished we drove back into the town and the professor took photographs of the pretty little house that Marian had lived in, on and off, for the rest of her life. Now the Rutherford Museum next to the fudge shop on Church Street, this was where she had written her best-loved and most famous novel. This took some time, because we'd happened on one of the rare out-of-season days when the museum was open. The curator, a fierce and fearsome woman called Miss Scritch whom I remembered from my schooldays, saw us malingering outside and emerged, anxious to find out exactly what the professor was up to and to put him right on several important facts.

'Just wait,' said the professor, back in the car and rubbing his hands with delighted anticipation. 'Just wait until the book comes out. She won't like it one bit.'

'You have a shocking revelation?'

'Yes,' he said. 'There's some work to be done, but I believe I do. Now, do we need to rush back or can we go and have a look at this restaurant? I'll treat you to a coffee.'

I had been hoping he'd forgotten.

'I'll take you down there,' I said, 'but you'll excuse me if I stay in the car.'

The professor glanced at me sideways. He could have asked any one of a million awkward questions, but all he said was, 'Well, we should be getting back anyway. I have more illegible crap to write in order to keep you employed putting it back into English.'

I smiled at him.

That was what I liked about being with him. He let me be. And I never asked him any questions either.

twenty-eight

When Lynnette was at home, she used to be in great demand as a babysitter. This was because her reputation for honesty, reliability and common sense travelled before her. In a small town like Portiston, everybody is connected to everybody else in one way or another and everything a person ever does or says is stored in a kind of communal memory bank, to be retrieved at the appropriate occasion. So after Lynnette had looked after our immediate neighbour's granddaughter one Saturday night, and coped admirably, this achievement was duly noted and soon whenever anybody needed a babysitter Lynnette would get the call.

Once she had left for good, there was a big babysitter vacancy in the town. It was a vacancy that I was keen to fill.

I had learned from Lynnette that Portiston's parents were exceptionally grateful to anyone who was kind to their children and simultaneously managed to get them in bed, and asleep, before the parents came home. I also knew that the parents felt disproportionately guilty if they weren't back at the time they said they'd be. If they promised to be home by 11.30 and didn't roll in until 1 a.m., then they were likely to double or even treble the agreed fee. These unexpected bonuses happened quite a lot.

Unfortunately, my reputation in the communal memory bank was nowhere near as glowing as my sister's. While a little of her glory inevitably rubbed off on me, there were still doubts about my moral fibre. However, needs must, and soon the young parents of Portiston realized that any babysitter was better than no babysitter and I gained much useful employment during the winter months before Marinella's reopened full-time and I could go back to the job I liked best.

I had three or four regular clients, but there was one family I particularly liked.

The Parkers lived in one of the big new detached houses that were clustered around the road out of the town. They were brick-built, with bay windows at the front, integral garages and paved driveways. They were the very height of luxury and sophistication and didn't leak, let in draughts, creak and groan or smell slightly musty, all of which were common phenomena in the older houses in the rest of town.

The Parkers' house was also beautifully furnished. The carpets were thick and soft, the complete opposite of the dusty, threadbare versions we had at home. Their settees were big and soft and squashy, their bathroom was warm and scented, the central heating was so efficient that there were none of the cold and warm patches with which I was familiar: you didn't have to huddle round the fire in the living room to feel comfortable, everywhere was warm. The children could pad around in their pyjamas even in the middle of winter.

There were two little Parkers, Jessie and Cal, and a third on the way. The children were adorable little poppets, all big eyes and dark lashes and silky hair. I, of course, always arrived at bedtime when they were bathed and smelled of baby shampoo and Johnson's powder. They would snuggle up, one on either side of me, on the cushions of the voluptuous settee, dressed in flannelette pyjamas, Jessie's with pink bunnies and Cal's with yellow ducks. Sleepy-eyed, their thumbs clamped between their little rosebud lips, they would gaze at the pictures in the book as I turned the pages and read them a story. When I took them up to bed, there was never any complaint or rebellion, but then their bedrooms were each so beautiful, warm and welcoming that it was small wonder really.

Mrs Parker was, at least in my eyes, the embodiment of femininity. I aspired to be like her, while not exactly wanting to be her. She was small and curvy and very pretty. She had the nicest nails I'd ever seen and her honey-coloured hair was always shiny and smooth. She had a collection of shoes in her wardrobe, and the most beautiful clothes. It was impossible to imagine Mrs Parker shaving her armpits or plucking her eyebrows, yet she must have done so because she was always so immaculately groomed. She once confided in me that she got up before her husband every morning so that she could wash, clean her teeth and do her hair and make-up.

'It never does to be complacent when you're a woman,

Liv,' she used to tell me. I wasn't quite sure what she meant by this but I never saw her in a bad mood; she was always smiling and patient and kind. Mrs Parker used to buy shop cakes and leave a selection out for me. We never had these sorts of cakes at home and to me they were sophistication on a plate. Mrs Parker used to say, 'Call me Annabel,' but I never did, although I rolled the name around on my tongue and practised it.

It was Mr Parker, however, who charmed me most. He would have been in his mid-thirties, I suppose, and he wasn't like the other men I knew. The male teachers at school were all, to a man, ugly and vaguely unsavoury. They had hairs in their nostrils and the veins bulged on the backs of their hands and they were either bony and knobbly with dandruff flakes on their shoulders, or sallow, moist creatures with bellies that tested the seams of their pullovers. The only other grown-up men I dealt with regularly were the awful Mr Hensley, Maurizio, and my friends' fathers.

Mr Parker was not like them at all.

He had the widest smile, which he used as a gift to bestow on anybody who wandered close enough. He laughed easily and often, tipping back his head and chuckling, so that his Adam's apple bobbed up and down in the most fascinating way. He lacked any of the disgusting physical habits that so often put me off grown-up men, like sticking their fingers into their ears and probing, or scratching their crotches. Most importantly of all, when his attention was focused on me, he had a way of making me feel like I was the only person in the world.

I knew he flirted with everyone and I also knew that he could be cruel. This was a combination that made him devilishly attractive. It was the secret of his success. I had heard him on the telephone, one moment friendly, the next ruthless, without ever changing the timbre or tone of his voice. He worked in the entertainment industry and there was a gold disc framed in the downstairs cloakroom. It was rumoured that Mrs Parker had once been a singer and that she had had a number-one record in the charts back in the early seventies, but I never found out if that was true. Mrs Parker used to scold Mr Parker when they came back tipsy and he launched into one of his charm offensives.

'Now, William, don't tease the girl, she doesn't know how to take it,' she would say, fishing in her purse for the money to pay me.

'But Olivia, you are, without doubt, the best and most beautiful babysitter in the entire UK,' Mr Parker would continue. 'No, I take it back, in the entire northern hemisphere.'

'William, stop it. Now is ten pounds enough, Liv?'

'It's plenty, thank you, Mrs Parker.'

'No, it's not enough. Not for an exceptional babysitter like Liv. Give her another fiver.'

I would shake my head and Mrs Parker would roll her eyes and sigh as if she was bored with this routine. I would shut the door behind me and walk back down the hill into Portiston with his glorious adjectives still ringing in my ears.

If it was raining, Mr Parker would drive me home in his Range-Rover, even if he had had a few drinks.

'The bastard police won't be out in this, they'll be sitting in the station with a cup of shitty coffee and the *Sun* crossword,' he would say. He pronounced it 'poe-lease', with the emphasis on the first syllable. I took to imitating him.

The car was always already warm from the Parkers' journey back from wherever they'd been, and it smelled intoxicatingly of alcohol and cigars and Mrs Parker's perfume. I knew what it felt like to be Mrs Parker as I sat beside him, up high, in the dark, watching the familiar road go by in the glare of the headlights. I used to feel sexy and adult. I would glance at his handsome profile illuminated by the blue dashboard lights, and wondered what I would do if ever he were to put his hand on my thigh. Just the thought would make me tingle with anticipation. I sort of knew that one day he would.

In the car, Mr Parker would ask me about my life.

'So do you have a boyfriend, Liv?'

'Yes. He's at university.'

'What do you do for male company when he's away?'

'Nothing.'

'You don't have a part-time boyfriend for when the real boyfriend's not around?'

'No.'

'Why not? A beautiful girl like you. I thought you'd be beating them off with sticks.'

I would blush in the dark and pull my skirt down a little.

'It wouldn't be right.'

'Bloody hell, Liv, it doesn't have to be right! You should be out having fun while you have the opportunity.'

'I am. I do. But there aren't many lads in Portiston. And hardly any nice-looking ones.'

'What about that tall Italian kid? I've seen him watching you.'

'Luca?'

'That's him. He's got something about him.'

I giggled and shook my head. 'He is nice, but he's already got a girlfriend.'

Mr Parker swung the car round into our road and said, 'So?'

When I was babysitting at the Parkers', after the children had gone to sleep I would creep into the main bedroom. It was quite the loveliest room I could imagine, papered in pale apricot with a slightly darker carpet and a huge bed which was always covered with a silky cream bedspread. There was a large dressing table against one wall with three oval mirrors, a walk-in wardrobe divided into separate areas for Mr and Mrs Parker, and an *en suite* bathroom complete with a huge bath sunk into the floor. One whole wall of the bathroom was mirrored. I would unscrew the lids from the bottles of oil and scent beside the bath and sniff them. It was the scent of money and London and glamour, the scent of Mrs Parker with her little ankles and painted toe-nails and sparkling jewellery.

I sat at the dressing table and patted my cheeks with her powder puff and sprayed each side of my jawline with her perfume. Her lipstick was red and glossy and made me look pornographic. I put on her earrings and pulled faces at myself in the mirrors, pretending I was being photo-graphed by the paparazzi.

I didn't dare get into the bed, but I did lie down on top of it and close my eyes and imagine I was married to Mr Parker.

'Are you coming to bed, darling?' I would whisper. For some perverse reason I preferred to think of him coming to bed in one of his ruthless moods.

I looked in the drawer of the bedside cabinet at Mrs Parker's side of the bed. There was a Danielle Steel novel, cotton-wool pads, Oil of Ulay cream and a book about preg-nancy which had interesting pictures of the various stages of foetal development. I didn't look in Mr Parker's drawer. I was a bit scared of what I might find and that somehow he would know what I had been doing.

I was completely besotted with the Parker family, and naturally they began to feature prominently in my diary. In retrospect, I put in far more detail than was necessary.

One night, Mr Parker did put his hand on my thigh in the car on the way home. He did it casually, in a friendly sort of way, so I really wasn't sure if he meant anything by it. I didn't react, but I couldn't hear anything he was saying, all I could feel were those strong, warm fingers gripping my leg. He stopped the Range-Rover a little way up from my house and said, 'How about a kiss?'

It wasn't like kissing Georgie. It was a grown-up, gentle, accomplished kiss which turned me on like nothing I'd ever experienced before and at the same time he was brushing my nipples really gently with the back of his hand. I made a little noise, a groan, and he moved away and laughed and said, 'Hot to trot, aren't you?'

I honestly didn't know what he meant.

It went on from there. I recorded it all dutifully in my diary. I hid the diary beneath my mattress. It never occurred to me for a second that anybody else would ever look at it. Let alone my mother.

twenty-nine

'Liv? It's me.'

   'Marc . . . ?'

   'Sorry to wake you.'

   'What's wrong? Is something wrong?'

   'Not really. I just . . .'

I dropped my head back on to the pillow. 'Marc . . .'

The phone transmitted the clicking of a disposable lighter as, twelve miles to the east, Marc struggled to light a cigarette.

   'I couldn't sleep.'

   'No.'

   'I had this dream.'

   'Of Luca?'

   'We were kids again.'

   'Was it a good dream?'

   'Oh yes. We were playing football on the rec. Luca was bossing everyone around . . .'

   'As he did.'

   'Yeah. He was an arrogant fucker sometimes.' Marc took a long drag on the cigarette. 'And in the dream I told him

I thought he had died but he was there and he just laughed and told me not to be so stupid, and everything was OK, everything was normal. So I felt this relief. I thought the dying bit was the dream and then . . .'

'You woke up?'

'Yeah. And I tried to wake Nathalie to get her to talk but she just . . .'

There was a long sigh, and a pause, in which I imagined the sleepy-eyed Nathalie turning her unfriendly, bulky back on Marc and his tears and how lonely that must have felt for him. My heart went out to him, but I said, 'It's not her fault, Marc.'

'But I need to talk about him.'

'It's my fault,' I said, feeling my eyes burning.

'No, it's not your fault. We should be together. If we were together now, everything would be better.'

He exhaled again, and his breath was shaky. 'I heard you were in Portiston today.'

'We were taking pictures for the professor's book.'

'Why didn't you come into Marinella's?'

'You know why.'

'I would have seen you. At least that would have been something.'

I rubbed my eyes, exhausted.

'Next weekend,' he said, and I imagined his face wreathed in smoke, his dark, shadowed eyes and the stubble on his jaw, 'I'm supposed to be going to Ireland for a stag party. If it's OK with you, I'd like us to go away together.'

'The whole weekend?'

'Yes.'

'I don't know, Marc. What if—'

'Please. Please say you'll come with me. For my sake. For Luca.'

'All right,' I said.

We talked for a while longer. Marc said he felt calmer. We said our good-nights, we whispered endearments. It was so late that there was already the faintest whiff of light in the sky beyond my curtainless window. I reached under my bed for the bottle of gin, poured an inch or so into my glass and swigged it down. I knew I would suffer at work in the morning, but I wanted something to take the edge off my guilt so that I could go back to sleep wrapped in the arms of the promise of a whole weekend without loneliness.

thirty

It was the start of the first term of my last year at school. The day my suspicious mother found my diary and read the detailed, descriptive and highly romanticized account of my affair with William Parker, Anneli and I, together with the rest of the sixth form, were meeting the local authority's careers-information officer. Anneli planned to go to university to study medicine. She wanted to go and work in Africa for Médecins sans Frontières or some other such charity. Nobody believed my grades would be good enough to get me into university, but that didn't matter because, inspired by Mr Parker's glamorous anecdotes about the entertainment industry, I'd set my heart on a career as an actress.

Watersford Girls' Grammar was an institution that was justifiably proud of its academic achievements, and its ongoing campaign to achieve equality in the workplace for women, encouraging its students to go out into the commercial world and break down glass ceilings, explore new avenues and prove that anything our male counterparts could do, we could do better. Nobody was particularly

impressed when I, who had never shown the slightest interest in staying behind after school to support the activities
of the drama club, announced that I wanted to be a star of
stage, screen and TV (but not necessarily in that order). It
was an ambition that was regarded as letting the side down
somewhat.

While Mum was sitting on my unmade bed, reading
about exactly what Mr Parker had done with his tongue, I
was sitting in a dusty, high-windowed office with Miss Keane.
She was trying to persuade me that the entertainment
industry was a ruthless and cruel place, and one that was
extremely difficult to break into if you didn't know the right
people.

'There's no course you can take that'll get you a job on
Neighbours, Olivia,' she said. 'You'll have to try and find a way
in at the bottom and work your way up.'

'OK,' I said.

'And only the most talented people ever make it to the
top,' said Miss Keane. The intimation, which wasn't wasted
on me, was that I wasn't one of those people.

'I don't want to discourage you, Olivia, but you're going
to find it difficult. Why don't you take a secretarial course,
and then you could always go into the BBC via that route?'

Mum was always telling me I should do a secretarial
course. I ignored her too.

I had absolutely no idea that anything was wrong as Anneli
and I left school that day. We stopped at the baker's and
bought an iced doughnut each, and a can of Coke to drink

on the bus on the way home, and then idled towards the bus stop, looking in shop windows, talking about this and that. Anneli had had a more constructive careers interview than I had. Miss Keane had given her the names and addresses of several major international medical charities. There was a possibility of her even being sponsored through university. I was glad that she was so happy. I was proud of her.

We sat downstairs on the bus. In the sixth form we were allowed to wear our own clothes, and we didn't like to be associated with the younger kids, especially not the raucous, ebullient Portiston gang who monopolized the upper deck of the bus and the back seat and who bounced and chattered and squealed as they ate their post-school crisps and apples. That bus was like a mobile canteen. I pity whoever had to clean it.

We got off in Portiston as normal, and parted at the junction by the newsagents' with a little hug. Then I headed for home.

I didn't even realize anything was wrong when I went through the door.

'Hello-o, I'm back!' I called, dropping my bag by the front door, kicking off my shoes and hanging up my jacket.

I wandered through the hall and into the kitchen in my socks, and then stopped. Mum was sitting at the kitchen table, a cup of tea in front of her. Her face was haggard, the skin stretched tightly across her bones. Her lips were pursed and tight at the corners. Beside her was Mrs Parker, hugely pregnant and white as a sheet. There were dark mascara smudges on her cheeks and a menthol cigarette was burning in the ashtray beside her. Mr Hensley stood at the window with his back to me but I could tell by the set of his shoulders and the angle of his horrid little head that something terrible had happened.

For a moment I thought somebody had died, but if that was the case, why was Mrs Parker sitting in our kitchen? I looked from Mum's face to Mrs Parker's. She was staring at the cup between her palms, resolutely not looking at me. I hadn't done anything wrong, had I? I racked my brains and then I saw the diary on the table and the shock hit me like a slap across the face.

'You haven't been reading my diary, have you?' I yelled at Mum, simultaneously horrified and furious. 'That's private! You have no right!'

Of course I can see now that that was completely the wrong thing to say.

My mother slowly raised herself to her feet. She was trembling with anger. I had never seen her in such a state.

'How could you, Olivia? How could you behave like that? Setting your sights on a married man! I am so ashamed of you.'

'Oh no,' I cried, making involuntary rubbing-out gestures with my hands. 'No, no, I didn't!'

At this Mrs Parker let out a sob and put her head down in her arms. Shudders ran along her shoulders. She was making a thin, wailing sound. Mum put one hand down and stroked Mrs Parker along the curled vertebrae of her spine.

'Have you no shame?' asked Mr Hensley. 'You evil little harlot!'

'Oh no,' I cried again. 'No, I'm not, I'm not!'

'How can you stand there and deny it?' he continued. 'It's all here, you've recorded your own salacious confession.'

'No!' I clasped my hands now and shook my head. I was desperate for a way out of the situation. I wasn't thinking about myself, I was thinking about Mr Parker, about what he'd say when he found out what had happened. 'I made it up,' I cried. 'It's not true, none of it, it's all fantasy!'

'I knew you'd say that,' said Mum. 'But it's not made up, is it? Because you have every detail correct.'

Mrs Parker raised her head, tear-smudges all across her cheeks, and said: 'I knew he was seeing someone, I just knew it. But I trusted you, Olivia. I was kind to you.'

'Oh Mrs Parker, I would never do anything to hurt you!' I cried. 'Honestly I wouldn't!'

'You're just like your father,' said Mum. 'You disgust me.'

I was crying now. I was desperate. 'I made it all up! Mr Parker never touched me. Never.'

Mrs Parker opened her handbag and pulled out a handkerchief. She wiped her face, still gulping. I looked frantically from her to my mother.

'You have to believe me! You can't tell Mr Parker. He never did anything!'

'The thing is, Olivia,' said Mrs Parker, becoming more composed, 'that my husband has something of a track record with silly little girls like you. You're not the first and you won't be the last.'

'Oh God!' cried my mother, turning her head away.

I was beside myself. A hideous shame at the thought of these two women and Mr Hensley reading the more purple extracts from my diary was now paling into insignificance beside the thought of what would happen if Mr Parker were to discover some of the words I'd used to describe him.

'It happened last time I was pregnant,' said Mrs Parker sadly. 'Then it was some young slut at the office. It's just unbearable that this time it's somebody I know and trusted and liked.'

I really wanted to apologize. I would have done anything to make things better, but I still thought it would be best if I could convince the woman that it was all made up. 'Mrs Parker, please,' I begged her with my voice and my eyes, 'please believe me. None of this is true.'

Mrs Parker just shook her head sadly and blew her nose. My mother stretched out a hand and placed it gently on her forearm.

'I'd heard rumours about you and that ferry boy. I heard you slept around, but I didn't believe them,' said Mrs Parker.

'I haven't slept around,' I said miserably. 'I haven't slept with anyone.'

'May God forgive you,' said Mr Hensley.

'I never will,' said Mrs Parker.

'Go to your room, Olivia,' said Mum, her voice icy. 'I don't want to breathe the same air as you right now.'

My fate was sealed. And so was my reputation.

thirty-one

The plan was this. I was to make my own way to the airport. One of the family would be dropping Marc off. We would meet in Pret A Manger on Friday evening, and we would both catch the flight to Shannon. We would find a bed-and-breakfast and spend Friday night and most of Saturday together. On Saturday evening Marc would go to the stag night, as arranged. He had to go because Nathalie would be at the wedding and the event would almost certainly be discussed. He would 'lose' the rest of the party as soon as they were drunk enough not to notice his absence and come back to me. We would have all Sunday to ourselves until the flight back in the evening. I would have to hang around the luggage carousel until Marc had left the arrivals gate in case anybody was waiting to meet him off the plane. After a reasonable amount of time had elapsed, I too would be free to leave and find my own way back to the flat. The fact that there would be nobody to meet me was almost enough to stop me going in the first place. The thought of coming out of the gate on my own, walking past the expectant faces of the people waiting for their loved ones, and then working out which was the appropriate bus to catch, felt as desirable as the prospect of driving the Clio at 80 mph into a solid brick wall. A car crash of loneliness was how I imagined it.

But then, I reasoned, a weekend with Marc would fill me up with enough positive emotion to make the ending irrelevant. Like the poem that says that death is the price we all have to pay for the privilege of being alive. So all week I looked forward to Friday, sometimes forgetting to lose myself in the professor's terrible, spidery handwriting, sometimes even missing a footnote or an amendment.

On Thursday the professor, who was nowhere near as self-absorbed as his reputation would have you believe, asked me if anything was wrong.

'No,' I said. 'No, nothing's wrong.'

'Only you seem a little out of sorts.' He turned to smile at me over the top of his glasses.

'It's just, I'm just – I'm going away for the weekend.'

'Is that a bad thing?'

'No, no. Only I'm, I mean we're going to Ireland and I don't like flying.'

'Oh,' said the professor. 'I see.'

Two minutes later I knocked one of the files of loose notes off my desk. The sheets of paper fluttered and slid over one another until they settled on the dusty carpet like flat, dead fish on the seabed.

'Oh God,' I said. 'I'm so sorry.'

'Worse things happen at sea,' said the professor.

I bent down and began to gather the paper together,

tucking my hair behind my ears, conscious of the red rash of embarrassment that was creeping up my neck like a bloodstain.

'I can't believe I did that,' I said.

'It's all right,' he said. 'It's just paper.'

'But it's all in a mess.'

'There's no harm done,' said the professor, who was crouching down to help me. 'They weren't in any particular order. It doesn't matter how we pick them up, they won't be any more random than they were before.'

'I'm not usually that clumsy,' I said. 'I must be more nervous than I thought.'

'That often happens before one does something one isn't sure about,' he said.

I glanced at him. He wasn't looking at me.

'After Elaine, my wife . . . after she was gone, I used to worry about things that never worried me before,' he said.

I hoped he wasn't going to become emotional and tell me everything. I was curious about his missing wife, but in a detached way. I did not want to become the professor's confidante. Still he kept going.

'It was completely unexpected, you know. She gave no indication that she was unhappy with me. I didn't know, for some time, where she had gone. I didn't know if she was alive or dead.'

'How awful.'

'I was so adrift. I wanted to drift away from everyone. But that was wrong. People need people, especially when their ties have been cut. It's easy to feel that the pressure of their concern is unbearable when in fact it is the only thing holding you together.'

I nodded.

'If you ever need anyone to talk to . . .' he said.

'Thanks, but I'm fine,' I said.

The professor pushed his glasses back up his nose and there was an awkward silence.

Then he cleared his throat and passed me several pieces of paper, and our fingers touched. I didn't mean to but I flinched. I pretended nothing had happened but sat back on my heels and turned my face away from him to gather the papers behind me.

The professor stood up and put his hands in his pockets, jingling his loose change.

'Perhaps I'll go and ask Jenny to put the kettle on,' he said.

Oh God, I thought, I can't go on like this.

It was all right though. He didn't try to break through my defences again. By the time he returned with a lukewarm mug of tea for me that was so milky it was undrinkable, I had almost succeeded in losing myself in the life of Marian Rutherford, who on one sheet was a young woman exploring the town of Portiston and getting to know its inhabitants whose friendliness she found 'intoxicating' and on the next was in late middle age and working on her last book.

thirty-two

It didn't take long for the story of my affair with the married Mr Parker to get round Portiston. It took a little longer for me to work out why conversations stopped when I walked into a shop and people suddenly became very interested in displays of envelopes or sink unblocker.

Mr Hensley told me, as we sat around the kitchen table eating our Sunday lunch in an atmosphere so strained and unhappy we could have been on Death Row, that prayers had been said for me at church. I was too humiliated to ask if I had been referred to by name. Even if the priest had been kind enough to spare me that particular punishment, everybody would have known whom he meant. Mum, who was building up to her own great confession, made it clear (although not in so many words) that she wished I'd never been born. My life was a straitjacket of shame and I could see no way out of it.

Then, to top things off, I had a letter from Georgie, who told me he was sorry but he wouldn't be coming back to Portiston to work the ferry any more. He had been offered the role of bass guitarist with a promising new rock band.

He wrote that he loved me and that he would never forget me and that one day he would write a song called 'Ferry Girl' in memory of the times we shared. I went down to the seafront and watched the ferry lights as it cut its course through the waves to the island and drank a bottle of sherry. Then I was sick on the pebbles with their tarry, seaweedy smell. I wondered why Georgie hadn't asked me to join him; that would have solved all my problems. (It turned out that he was courting the band's punky girl singer. They later married and lived happily ever after, which was nice for them but not so good for me at the time, given my situation.)

Some good things happened. I had a postcard from Lynnette which simply said: *Nothing matters very much and few things matter at all.*

Anneli refused to bow to pressure from anyone to renounce me as a friend. I heard her hissing in the ear of one girl who had curled her lip at me, 'You're just jealous because no man will ever look at you.' Anneli's parents were nice too. Her dad gave me a (very paternal) hug and said, 'Chin up, Liv, in a couple of weeks they'll have somebody else to talk about. You're just experiencing one of the downsides of living in a small, boring town.'

For some reason their forgiving kindness was harder to shoulder than other people's cruelty.

In due course Mum received a letter from school. She and Mr Hensley made an appointment to see the headteacher. I was spared the ordeal of being present at the interview, but had to wait on a seat in the corridor outside the head's office. The head's secretary was kind to me. She brought me out a glass of water and asked if I'd rather sit in her office than in the public corridor, beneath the smug boards listing the names of successful scholarship students. Lynnette's name was on the boards in gilt letters twice, once for being Head Girl and once for winning a music prize. My name too had made it on to a school wall, only the wall was the lavatory wall and my name was written in permanent marker.

I declined the secretary's offer. I thought it would be worse to be in her office, with her feeling sorry for me, than out in the corridor. The secretary's eyes were so full of pity that I knew something serious was going to happen.

Little girls, eleven- and twelve-year-olds, filed past me in a navy-blue rush of giggles and whispers and scabby knees and sticky fingers and I tried to smile at them in a patronizing manner, like I was about to go in to the head's office and get an award or something.

Eventually I was summoned. The office was huge. The mullioned window gave on to a rosebed outside and the smell of pig shit which the gardener had laid around the base of the plants hit me first. Light was streaming through the windows in oblongs and the air was cloudy with dust motes.

Mum had been crying. Her eyes and the rims of her nostrils were red. She was dabbing at her nose with a screwed-up handkerchief. Mr Hensley sat beside her, his face set like concrete, his stupid hairy ears sticking out of his stupid shiny head. On the other side of a great, old, wooden desk was the head. I'd hardly had any dealings with her close up, never having either excelled at anything or been particularly badly behaved in my time at Watersford Girls' Grammar School. She was probably only in her fifties although, at the time, I regarded her as an old woman. The skin on her face and neck was soft and jowly. Her silver hair was set solid, like the hair of a woman in an oil painting. It moved as a unit, not as thousands of individuals. I can't remember a word she said, but the long and short of it was that I was being expelled. Mr Parker, apparently, was close friends with the chairman of the governors. He had given a generous donation towards the construction of the new science block. My indiscretion was public knowledge and couldn't be ignored, blah blah blah. Mum sniffed and swallowed bravely, Mr Hensley stared, the head asked me if I was ashamed of myself and I nodded.

I was only two terms away from the A levels that might have opened up some doors for me. The headmistress had indicated, kindly, that there might be a possibility of taking the exams as an external candidate if we could organize some private tuition, but I think we all knew that was not going to happen. My education was over.

On the drive back, while I sat hunched and tearful in the back of Mr Hensley's beige Morris Minor (the scene of so much humiliation), Mum told me about Dad. She told me how his lasciviousness had destroyed her once and now I was following in his footsteps.

'You mean my dad is still alive?' I asked, shocked and incredulous.

'I have no idea,' she said. 'And no wish to find out.'

'You had no right to tell us he was dead!'

Mr Hensley turned round and said, 'Don't you speak to your mother in that tone of voice.'

Mum stared straight ahead. 'I knew you were going to turn out bad right from the beginning,' she said. 'You were such a difficult baby, such a fractious child.'

I wasn't listening any more. I leaned my head against the window and watched the leaves of the bushes go by and I swallowed all the questions that were bubbling up from my stomach and decided that I would go and live with Dad. There was absolutely no reason for me to stay in Portiston any longer. There was nothing to keep me.

I never heard from or saw any of the Parkers again. Somebody told me they went to live in Edinburgh.

thirty-three

I went to the café to wait for my taxi.

'Going anywhere nice?' asked the bodybuilder chef. I only had a small bag with me but I kept checking my handbag for the ticket receipt and my passport.

'I'm going to Ireland for the weekend.'

He put my coffee down on the table and scratched behind his ear with his pencil.

'A dirty weekend?'

I smiled. 'No, nothing like that.'

'But you're going with the brother-in-law?'

I looked up at him. There was nothing judgemental in his expression, no malice. He was just asking what he thought was an obvious question. I looked away and stirred my coffee. It smelled divine.

'None of my business,' he said. 'Just that you're not the sort of woman who deserves to be waiting for a taxi on her own.'

'It's complicated,' I said.

'It always is.'

I concentrated on the consuming task of sugaring my

coffee, and a few moments later the chef returned with a little slice of perfect treacle tart. He set it in front of me like a gift, together with a pastry fork and a napkin. I felt at home.

'Can I sit down for a moment?' he asked.

'Of course.'

'Mind if I smoke?'

'No.'

He retrieved his roll-up from behind his ear and struggled to light it, his hands cupped round it, striking the flint of the disposable lighter again and again. When it caught, he inhaled gratefully and I inhaled the scent of the tobacco, as familiar to me as the smell of my own shampoo.

'My husband used to smoke roll-ups,' I said.

The chef raised an eyebrow. 'Filthy bloody habit,' he said.

'He died,' I said.

'Of smoking?'

'No, no. It was a motorway crash.'

'Shit. I'm sorry. Life's a bastard, isn't it?'

'Sometimes.'

'So whereabouts in Ireland are you going?'

'Shannon.'

'It's beautiful. You'll like it. They know how to enjoy themselves in Ireland. They're not dour like the miserable buggers over here.'

I sipped coffee froth from the spoon.

'My husband was a chef too,' I said.

'All the most alpha males are.'

'He was going to open his own restaurant in London.'

199

'What sort of place?'

'Well, like this really. Only more Italian. He wasn't going to do cooked breakfasts.'

'Try the tart.'

I forked off the tiniest sliver of the tart and tasted it. It was heavenly, butter and caramelized breadcumbs with the sweetest toffee aftertaste.

'You like it?'

'It's lovely.'

'Good. It's nice to . . .'

'What?'

'Oh, nothing.' He stabbed out the centimetre of cigarette he had left between his yellowed fingertips on the glass ashtray.

'I was going to say it was nice to see you smile and then I thought that sounded like some kind of sad-act chat-up line.'

I couldn't help myself. I smiled again and took another, larger mouthful of the tart. The chef stood up and wiped his hands on his apron.

'Make sure he takes you to the Cliffs of Moher. If you're staying in County Clare, that is. They're amazing. You'd like them.'

'OK,' I said. 'Thank you for the tart, and, you know, everything.'

He shrugged. 'No worries.'

And then the taxi arrived and I went to the airport for the secret assignation that would launch my first and only weekend with my beloved brother-in-law, Marc.

thirty-four

It was early summer. I had just turned eighteen. It should have been the best time of my life, only unfortunately no new scandal had broken and I was still the town pariah. I went to Marinella's to see if Angela would give me a job, naïvely assuming that, because I'd done a good job for the Felicones in the past, she might be prepared to overlook my indiscretion. The bell tinged as I opened the door, and the first person I saw was Luca, who was standing behind the bar wiping glasses.

He was twenty years old, still lanky, with big hands and shoulders and a slender throat, and a shadow of acne around his jawline. His hair was shoulder-length, black and silky, and his smile, oh God, was a smile a girl would die for.

'Liv!' he cried, and my heart flipped and then danced because he was so clearly pleased to see me. I had entered the restaurant hopefully, but still with the downcast air of the penitent which I assumed was appropriate for somebody in my position. Now I perked up a bit.

Luca vaulted the bar – if Angela had seen him she'd have

been furious – and in two strides I was in his arms and my feet had left the floor.

'Boy, you have been one naughty girl!' he said, paraphrasing one of our favourite Beatles songs.

I was so relieved by his reaction, and it was so good to see a genuinely friendly face, that I hung on to Luca's neck and put my face on his shoulder, breathing in his hot young-man smell, and stayed there for as long as I could, which was only about a second because Nathalie came into the restaurant and coughed pointedly.

I let go of Luca and he let go of me, but he was still grinning slightly wolfishly.

'It's our local celebrity,' he said to Nathalie, somewhat unnecessarily. Nathalie looked at me. There was no kindness in her eyes. They were cold and her face was expressionless.

'What can we get you?' she asked, producing a notepad and a pencil. I glanced to Luca for help. He bit a little piece of his lower lip between two canine teeth.

'Um, actually, I came in to see Angela,' I said. 'I wanted to ask about my job.'

Nathalie's expression didn't soften. 'We don't have any vacancies at present,' she said.

I tried to adopt a friendly but humble expression. I still wanted to be an actress and had practised.

'I don't mind what I do, Nathalie. I'd be willing to—'

'There are no vacancies,' she said.

'Oh come on, Nat,' said Luca, 'there must be something we can give Liv. She's an old friend of the family. She's worked here lots of summers.'

Nathalie gave Luca one of her looks. 'What's that got to do with anything?'

'Well, we should at least ask Pop if he needs a hand with anything.'

Nathalie rolled her eyes, very quickly, so that you couldn't be sure if she'd done it or not, but I didn't like her patronizing Luca in this way, and little hackles of anger began to strain at my shoulderblades.

'Don't worry, Luca,' I said sweetly. 'I wouldn't want to put Nathalie to any trouble.'

'Hold on a minute, I'll go and ask him myself,' said Luca, and he disappeared into the back of the restaurant.

Being alone with Nathalie was uncomfortable. She had a way of imparting her mood to the whole room, and the atmosphere was so chilly I was practically shivering.

'So, how are things with you?' I asked.

'Very good,' replied Nathalie, straightening the cutlery in the trays by the counter. 'You know that Luca has asked me to marry him?'

'No,' I said. 'No, I didn't know that.' I swallowed. I felt dizzy. 'Congratulations,' I said.

'Thank you.'

'Have you set a date yet?'

Nathalie smoothed her skirt. 'Christmas,' she said. 'It won't interfere with the business, and we'll have snow on the hills for the photographs.'

'Lovely,' I said. 'Just perfect.'

Nathalie looked at me without smiling. As always, she was neatly turned out, but in a suit that probably came from

Country Casuals. Her hair was cut in a bob which didn't flatter her heavy jaw. Her skirt stopped just below the knee. She was wearing tan tights and flat shoes.

There was a hole in my black tights, and I hitched down my skirt to try to cover it. My T-shirt was dark green, with a black Blondie print on the front. I could see the outline of my nipples through the fabric. Standing this close to Nathalie, I felt naked. I sat down at one of the little circular two-person tables by the window, crossed my legs and rested my chin on my hands. I swung my foot and gazed at the door, waiting for Luca to come back.

It only took a couple of minutes, and he emerged from the office with Maurizio in tow. Nathalie melted away, a satisfied, Cheshire-cat smile on face. She knew what was going to happen because she and Angela had already guessed that I would come looking for a job, and had prepared themselves for this eventuality.

'Olivia, *carina*, you're looking as beautiful as ever.' Maurizio came over to me, put his hands on my arms, just below my shoulders, and leaned down to kiss me on both cheeks in a waft of garlic and wine. 'But I have bad news,' he continued, pulling a comic-tragic face and holding his hands to his heart. 'There is no work here; we have too many sons to do the jobs that need doing, we don't need any extra help.'

Luca said, 'Pop, you're always saying we're understaffed at weekends . . .'

Maurizio held up his hand. 'But your mother interviewed this week for the position.'

Luca opened his mouth but before he could say anything I stood up and pulled down my skirt. 'Well, thanks for letting me know, Maurizio. I assume you won't be needing me in the summer either.'

Maurizio did his Italian, palms-open gesture of helplessness.

Luca was doing an exaggerated, open-mouthed mime of incredulity. 'Liv is one of us, Pop. You can't do this!'

'It's OK, Luca,' I said. 'I completely understand.'

My pride was in tatters. I turned and went out of Marinella's, wondering if I would ever go back. I was halfway along the seafront, seagulls keening above me, waves commiserating at my feet, wiping my nose with my forearm, when Luca caught up with me.

thirty-five

The bed was wide and low with a pale green candlewick spread and the room smelled of air freshener. There was no TV or kettle but the landlord brought us a tray of tea and biscuits. We sat on opposite sides of the bed, our feet on the practical carpet, and drank our tea like strangers thrown together by circumstance.

We had driven out of Shannon Airport in a hired Ford Focus and I had watched the countryside of Ireland go by while Marc drove. We'd stopped at several bed-and-breakfast establishments, but all had been full until this one, a large, modern bungalow, painted what Marc had dubbed 'Clare yellow' because so many of the buildings favoured this particular colour. The bungalow was so new that there were still piles of bricks and other construction detritus stacked up on the tarmacked drive, which had space for several cars.

The landlord was a young man with a nice face and a kind manner who practically tripped over himself trying to make us feel welcome. I wondered if we were his first customers. Later, we heard a baby crying in the bowels of the bungalow, and then the sound of singing as its parents tried to quiet it, obviously anxious it didn't disturb us. I wanted to go and tell them to let the baby cry, we didn't mind, but Marc said that would only draw attention to the fact that we had heard it. So I stayed by the mirror, applying my make-up, warm with anticipation because Marc and I were going out for a meal together and I hadn't been out for a meal since Luca died, and I loved the whole drama of going out to eat.

Marc was in the shower, and warm steam heavy with the apple fragrance of my shampoo billowed into the bedroom through the open door. I opened my eyes wide to comb mascara on to my lashes, and smiled at the result. So many times lately I'd looked in the mirror, or caught sight of myself in shop windows, and I hadn't recognized myself. But that evening, I looked like Olivia Felicone, green-eyed, brown-haired, wide-mouthed Olivia, wife of Luca Felicone, top chef and self-confessed sex god; he who never tired of telling me how lucky I was to have him. So when Marc came out of the bathroom, naked, rubbing his hair with a blue towel, I said, 'Luca, you're right, I am lucky,' and didn't even notice that the man I was with was not my husband.

He came over to me and kissed my neck.

'It's me,' he whispered, 'Marc. Sorry.'

I swallowed.

'Oh Marc, I'm sorry. I just forgot . . .'

'What did you forget?'

'That I wasn't happy.'

'Maybe that's the same as actually being happy.'

'Yeah,' I grinned. 'Yes, you're right. Maybe it is.'

*

I was wearing a blue shirt and black jeans with a gold necklace that Luca had given me for Christmas. Marc put on his normal, scruffy clothes, his jeans and his baggy sweatshirt, and rumpled his damp hair with his fingers and pronounced himself ready. He had lost weight too, and that made him look more like his twin. Together we fitted. In the mirror we looked like a proper couple.

Marc wanted to drink, so we left the car on the drive and walked back along the lane to a pub that we'd passed half a mile or so back. There was a river in the valley below us, and lights twinkled in houses and bungalows and pubs as far as the eye could see. Marc hooked his arm over my shoulders and kept me warm against him. From time to time he kissed my head. Distantly, imprecisely, it occurred to me that perhaps his feelings for me had nothing to do with Luca, but I batted the thought away like a moth. We were partners in grief, that was all. We were helping one another through the worst time in our lives.

There was music in the pub. A couple of handsome, middle-aged men were playing guitar and a young boy tapped a drum between his knees. One of the men was singing and the other was harmonizing and some of the clientele were joining in.

It was late but we were starving hungry so we ate hot sardines on toast, and I, not liking the taste of Guinness, drank whisky and lemonade until my head was full of music and laughter and I did pretend Irish dancing with a man with a huge belly and a straggly grey beard while people clapped and I laughed so much I almost collapsed. Marc was watching me, like Luca used to, with his pint in his hand and an amused, slightly indulgent expression. Then the music ended and the man, whose teeth were bad and whose breath was sour, made a toast to us. He asked our names and I said Olivia Felicone and Marc said Marc Felicone so he made the toast to Mr and Mrs Felicone, and of course, that was right, that was who we were.

With one arm around each of us, his right arm looped around my neck so that he could still drink our health, he said, 'May the most you wish for be the least you get.' And while I tried to work that out in my head, everyone was smiling and we bought a lot more drinks and honestly I have no recollection at all of how we got back to the bed-and-breakfast that night.

thirty-six

Luca and I walked up the cliff path into the woods, and we stopped at the point where Emily Campbell is supposed to have thrown herself to her death and we gazed out to sea.

By the time we reached the top of the hill, I was out of breath and warm. I told Luca exactly what had happened. How it started when Mr Parker put his hand on my thigh. How I had, in the diary, embellished the truth to make it sound more romantic and more meaningful. I told him about coming home to find Mum and Mrs Parker with the diary and what they had said. I told him about being expelled. Apart from Lynnette, he was the only person I told who believed my version of events instantly and absolutely and without question. Lynnette had been sympathetic and appalled. Luca was neither. Quite the opposite. When he'd heard the whole story he laughed and laughed like it was the funniest thing ever.

'Oh that's terrible, Liv! Confessing every detail of a crime and then getting done for it because they uncovered the confession, not the crime!'

'Shut up,' I said.

'It's a classic!'

'Shut up, Luca. It's not funny.'

'It is! It's so funny I'm going to piss myself.'

'You are pathetic and disgusting,' I said, and I turned my back on him, but only because his laughter was infectious and I didn't want him to see me smile. I wiped my eyes with the hem of my sleeve and tried to suppress a little bud of laughter that was opening up inside me.

'Jesus Christ, it's fantastic. So was Mr Parker any good in bed, Liv?'

'Stop it!' I cried, turning round to slap him, but the bud had turned into a great blowsy rose of laughter and I put my hands over my mouth, but it was no good, I couldn't contain it. The two of us collapsed on to the grassy bank and rolled around laughing.

When we were exhausted, we lay together side by side, on our backs, and I looked up at the blue, blue sky and the white clouds and the gulls and all my problems turned to nothing.

'People are mean,' said Luca, taking my hand. 'They're making such a big deal of this because their own lives are so dull and boring. You've just given them something to gossip about.'

'That's what Anneli's dad said.'

'He's right. In another week or another month they'll have moved on to their next victim and they'll have forgotten all about you.'

'What about poor Mrs Parker?'

'She said he'd done it before and she stuck with him. If

he's done it before then he's going to do it again and she must know that. That's her choice. It's not up to you what she does.'

'You're right!' I said, sitting up and looking down at Luca, who was squinting into the sun. 'I've kept worrying about her but you're right, thank you. I'd never have worked that out!'

Luca looked pleased with himself. 'Ah well,' he said. 'Some of us have it and some of us don't.'

I smiled at him. 'Bighead.'

'And you know what they say about lads with big heads . . .'

'Ah, stop it, Luca Felicone.'

'I'm only telling it as it is.'

I shook my head and stood up, brushing down my skirt with my hands, and then walked over to lean on the safety fence that protected the cliff-edge. There was a Samaritans notice and a phone number for anyone who felt inclined to follow in Emily Campbell's fictional footsteps. The sun was on my face. From here, I could look down at Portiston and see what a small town it was. Just a tiny little insignificant part of the world, that was all, a place of no consequence to anyone. I made a mental note to myself to find my copy of *Emily Campbell* and see what was going through her mind just before she jumped to her death.

'It's nice up here, isn't it?' said Luca, coming up close behind me.

I sensed danger. I had the teenager's animal instinct for sex. I knew he wanted to kiss me and more. Part of me thought that after everything I was going through on account of sex, the last thing I needed was Luca Felicone's hands slipping beneath my T-shirt, lovely as the thought of his fingers on my breasts was. And another part of me thought that seeing as everyone thought I was a marriage-wrecking slut anyway, what did it matter if they did?

At the last moment I turned to face him, smiling as if I hadn't been aware of what was about to happen.

'Why are you marrying Nathalie?'

He paused. 'Oh. She told you.'

'Well yes, of course she did. I sort of knew it was on the cards but . . .'

Luca sighed and looked down and his face went into shadow, hidden under his hair, just the tip of his ear visible in the soft dark waves. Little bits of grass and twig were caught in his hair. He picked up a pebble and rubbed it in his hands and then flung it over the fence. It didn't make the sea but bounced on the rocks beneath us.

'It seemed like the only thing to do,' he said. 'Get engaged. That's what they all wanted.'

'What about what you wanted?'

He shrugged.

'What *do* you want, Luca?'

'Oh, I'd like to go to London. Have my own business. The usual.'

'So why don't you?'

He shrugged again. 'I can't, can I? They need me here.'

I looked at him. Surely he didn't feel trapped in this town.

'You mean you feel like there's no way out of your life?'

'Do you know a way?' he asked.

I shook my head. 'But there must be one. More than one. Especially for you.'

'Carlo and Stefano have both left and Pop and Mama need somebody to run the place.'

'It doesn't have to be you.'

'Who else?'

'Marc? Fabio? Oh come on, Luca, there's no law that says you have to stay here all your life if you don't want to.'

'There's family, and that's worse than the law.' He scratched his head fiercely with the fingers of both hands, a nervous habit I remembered from when we were children.

'They can't make you do anything you don't want to.'

Luca picked a catkin off a tree that overhung the path and began to pull it apart.

'For the last couple of years everyone's been talking about me and Nathalie getting married and running the business. Everyone, not just Mama and Pop. There's all this expectation, you know?'

I shrugged.

'You don't understand what it's like to be in my family, Liv. Everyone is expected to do their duty, do what's right by the family.'

'You're not a prisoner, though. You could go to London if you really wanted.'

'No,' said Luca. 'Nathalie wouldn't want to go to London. She likes it here. She says she never wants to leave

214

Marinella's. She says it's the only place where she's ever been happy.'

I thought Nathalie had a funny way of being happy but I didn't say anything. Maybe she *was* happy when I wasn't around. Maybe she was the life and soul of the party. We were silent for a moment. I moved a pebble around with the toe of my shoe.

'I'd go to London with you,' I said. 'If you weren't engaged.'

There was a heartbeat's pause. Then Luca said, 'Yeah, but who'd want to go to London with a marriage-wrecking little slut like you?'

'You'll regret that, Luca Felicone!' I cried, lunging at him. We tumbled on the ground and mock-wrestled and chased each other all the way back down the hill towards our insignificant little town and at the bottom of the hill we struggled to say goodbye.

I think I knew then what was going to happen. I think we both did.

thirty-seven

Breakfast next morning was served in a sunny little annexe overlooking the valley, which was gloriously lush and green in daylight. Summer-yellow sunshine was streaming through the glass roof and on to three small tables, two of which already bore the debris of breakfasts eaten.

We sat at the third. I drank the small glass of orange juice in one swallow. Marc, fondly, passed me his too.

'I am never drinking again,' I said.

'You should have stuck to Guinness. I feel fine.'

'Nobody with a hangover likes a smug breakfast companion,' I warned him.

A young blonde woman with a kind, round face came over and wished us good morning.

'What can I get you?' she asked.

'Full cooked for me, please,' said Marc. 'And paracetamol on toast for Liv.'

'Ha ha,' I said. 'I'd just like some tea, please.'

'Were you down at the pub last night? It's great on a Friday, isn't it?'

'Liv did a tribute to *Riverdance*,' said Marc. 'It was unique. Unforgettable. The regulars will need counselling.'

The woman laughed and disappeared to fetch our breakfasts. I groaned and put my head in my hands. My fingers smelled of soap and sex.

'What time do you have to be in Limerick?'

'We're meeting at four. I'll have to leave here after lunch, I guess. We've got a few hours, we could go for a walk.'

'OK.'

'Will you be all right here, on your own this afternoon?'

'Of course I will.'

'I don't want to leave you.'

I gave a little 'So what?' shrug. Marc reached across the flowery cotton tablecloth and squeezed my hand.

'It's lovely being here with you, Liv.'

That little moth of unease flickered into my field of vision again, but I ignored it. The young woman came back with a tray of tea and milk and sugar and we set about the business of breakfast and everything was all right.

thirty-eight

I didn't know how to tell Lynnette about our dad probably still being alive. I was still having difficulty coming to terms with the fact that anyone could have told such a terrible lie, especially my God-fearing, gossip-fearing, holier-than-thou mother. It was also weird that she didn't appear to feel the slightest remorse about what she'd done. She held tight to her conviction that she had taken the only reasonable course of action, that she was the one who had been wronged and that any good mother would have done the same.

Later on, I would have more sympathy with her position, but at the age of eighteen, I was furious and sad. Unless something had happened to him in the meantime, I had a living, breathing father and my immediate instinct was to start searching for him. Then I realized that if he'd wanted contact with us, he could have come looking. Surely we wouldn't have been *that* difficult to find. He must have known some of Mum's relatives, they could have pointed him in the right direction. And what if he had come and Mum had sent him away again? What if he'd been told that we were dead? There were so many questions and, because Mum wasn't speaking to me, no way of finding the answers.

With no school to go to, and because there was no work in Portiston (and even if there had been, nobody wanted to employ me), I had too much time on my hands. Anneli was studying for her A levels, and though she never turned me away, I knew it was unfair to burden her with my boredom. Sometimes I drifted amongst the streets and paths like a wraith, my eyes cast modestly downwards, my posture that of the penitent, but that was only when Mum and Mr Hensley were at home watching TV or holding one of their meetings. The house seemed increasingly joyless and grey. It was too quiet. Nothing ever happened. Nothing changed. It was always the same: cold meat on Monday, mince on Tuesday, shepherd's pie on Wednesday, sausages on Thursday, fish on Friday, cheese sandwiches on Saturday and a cut of meat on Sunday. Mr Hensley's shiny suits, his carbolic attitude and Mum's pursed lips, her unflattering, self-cut hair, her ageing face devoid of make-up and pleasure. They deprived themselves of the smallest treats – 'Would you care for a biscuit?' 'I'd love to, but I won't.' 'There's a programme you might enjoy after the news.' 'But look at the time, it's nearly ten, I must be going' – and were constantly competing to see who could be the most humble, the most self-denying and self-deprecating. Nobody ever ate the last potato out of the pan because that would have looked greedy. Delicious morsels of food were thrown away. Sunsets were missed because there were dishes to be washed and every mealtime felt like a rush to see who could start clearing away first. They denied themselves anything that could be regarded as an extravagance (I don't mean real extravagances like holidays, but simple things like a bar of chocolate or a pot of hand cream). People who spent their money on such fripperies were discussed in disparaging tones. There was nothing pretty in our house, nothing that didn't have a practical purpose. Except, I suppose, me.

Eventually I got my life back on track. I applied for, and was given, a job at Wasbrook's department store in Waters-ford. I loved it from the start. Mondays to Saturdays, I caught the early-morning bus which travelled the single road out of Portiston and took me into the city. I loved going round to the back of the grand Wasbrook's building and in through the staff entrance by the delivery bays where the lorries reversed. I enjoyed saying good-morning to the Sikh security man who was called Garth and who always offered me a fruit Polo. I soon learned to associate work with a stickiness between my back molars. I liked the cloak-rooms, where I had my own locker, and where the female staff gossiped and laughed and shared things. It was like being part of a flock of highly scented birds. My colleagues took me under their collective wing. They showed me how to tie my hair back so that I wouldn't get into trouble, they told me to ditch the sparkly nail varnish and go for some-thing simple and pale instead, and they advised me to invest in a pair of low-heeled shoes for the benefit of my feet. They didn't know me but they seemed to like me. In the canteen at lunchtime we ate cheese-and-pickle baps and the women made fun of the men and talked about sex and contraception and stuff like that in a completely uninhibited and thoroughly educational manner. They swore a lot. They were the kind of people my mother and Mr Hensley would have called 'crude' but they were generous and loyal and kind. At work, in my blue skirt and cardigan and my white blouse, amongst my new friends, I was perfectly happy. It was just the going home I dreaded.

As a general assistant, I was moved about Wasbrook's from department to department. I never went on the cosmetic counters where the girls with flawless complexions traded, or anywhere else that required specialist knowledge, but started to learn a little about a lot of things. Soon I could demonstrate how food mixers worked and advise parents-to-be on the pros and cons of different kinds of pushchair with equal confidence. I knew which ribbons went with which fabrics, and which hats with which gloves. No question fazed me. If I didn't know the answer, all I had to do was ask.

I saved as much money as I could, but Mum was, quite reasonably, taking board out of my wages, there were bus fares to pay and I needed money for drinks with my friends in the White Hart after work. I realized it would take for ever to save up enough for lodgings of my own in Watersford, and this thought depressed me. When the landlord of the pub asked if I'd like to help him out a couple of evenings a week, I agreed gladly. That kept me out of home too, and it was fun. The landlord and his wife were jolly, friendly people, the money was good and I was popular with the punters, who were always telling me to get one for myself.

I thanked them, and put the money into an empty pint glass under the counter to take home and add to my kitty.

In the pub I kept male admirers at arm's length. I was especially careful not to flirt with anybody old enough to be my father, just in case he *was* my father. It was a good game. There were men I hoped were my dad, and men I hoped weren't. I longed for Lynnette and the chance to share my secret.

Life was looking up, and I was becoming more independent, and the day when I moved out of Portiston and into Watersford was drawing closer by the minute. Then one day in October, when I was working in the bridal department, Angela came in with Nathalie.

They were looking for a wedding dress. They headed straight over to the display and touched the satin on the dummy's skirts, and smoothed the sequinned net of her train. For once Nathalie seemed quite animated; her eyes were bright as she and Angela cooed and admired the dress. They didn't notice me.

I was working with an older woman called Jean, a nice woman.

'What is it, Olivia? You've gone white as a sheet,' she said.

I chewed my lower lip and nodded over towards Nathalie and Angela.

'Those two. I'd just rather not serve them.'

Jean squeezed my elbow. 'Don't worry, chicken, I'll look after them. You go and tidy up round the bridesmaids.'

Gratefully I went over to the bridesmaids' displays and started rearranging tiaras and fake bouquets quite unnecessarily in order not to hear what was being discussed some twenty feet away amongst the wedding gowns. Even so, Angela's clipped voice travelled and the bridal phrases, light and shiny as the materials of the dresses, shimmied over to me: words like princess, beautiful, appliqué, petticoat, tiara, dreams, happiest, day, of, your, life.

Any bride-to-be who came into this part of Wasbrook's invariably stayed for several hours, trying on different dresses and shoes and veils and jewellery, and Nathalie was no exception. I kept myself hidden, finding bits of paperwork to do, organizing the tiny drawers of pins and silk flowers. After a while my attention was distracted by a miserable, heavily pregnant young woman and her mother, whose expression of tight-lipped martyrdom so resembled my own mother's that I felt completely at home.

My pregnant lady was in one of the luxurious changing cubicles with their little gilt chairs and flattering lighting when Nathalie came out of the other. She looked, to me, like a man in drag in a shepherdess-style dress with a froth of skirts, a deep, heart-shaped neckline and old-fashioned ribbon-and-lace sleeves. It was a shame she was so round-shouldered and so flat-chested. The dress didn't fit right but both Angela and Jean clasped their hands to their chests and sighed when they saw her. Angela fished in her handbag for a tissue and dabbed at her nose. Nathalie twirled clumpily round in front of the huge, ornately framed floor-to-ceiling mirror with its permanent, elaborate silk flower displays and then stopped when she caught sight of me reflected in the background. There was nothing for it but to go over.

'You look lovely, Nathalie,' I said, smiling like an adult, like we were on equal terms, like I didn't care about the way she had talked down to me in the past, like I didn't care she was marrying Luca Felicone.

'Thank you,' Nathalie said graciously, but the smile had died on her lips and the light had gone out of her eyes. 'Do you work here?'

I nodded. 'It's a great job.'

'Are you training to be a manager or something?'

'No. I'm just an assistant.'

'Oh. Right.'

'Horses for courses,' said Angela. 'I'm glad to see you're sorting yourself out at last, Olivia. Your poor mother.'

The pregnant woman's mother's ears pricked up. She was pretending to study the Pronuptia brochure.

Now that I was out of Portiston, in my own territory, I felt more than a little irritated by Angela's tone. Jean came to stand beside me in a supportive manner. Waves of warm Lancôme washed soothingly over me.

'So, are you all ready for the wedding?' she asked Angela. 'There's always so much for the MoB to do.'

'I beg your pardon?'

'MoB. Mother of the bride.'

Angela and Nathalie exchanged coy glances, but they didn't correct Jean.

'We want it to be really special,' said Angela. 'For

224

Nathalie and for Luca, of course. We're so proud of both of them.'

She bestowed one of her best smiles on Nathalie. The bare skin on Nathalie's chest, shoulders and neck flushed a furious red.

'Ahhhh,' said Jean, smoothing an imaginary wrinkle out of Nathalie's skirt. 'How lovely for you all.'

'Is Luca looking forward to the wedding?' I asked.

Nathalie looked at her feet. Angela bustled.

'Of course he is. Oh, he pretends he's not interested, but deep down he's as excited as we are, isn't he, Nathalie?'

'He thinks weddings are female territory,' said Nathalie.

'They're all like that,' Jean piped up. 'My husband couldn't be doing with any of the preparations but you should have seen him on the day. He had the time of his life. And we've been married thirty years.'

I smiled at Nathalie. 'Let's hope you and Luca last that long.'

She opened her mouth but before she could speak my pregnant bride-to-be came out of her cubicle. While Nathalie looked like a character from a pantomime, my poor lady looked like something out of her own worst nightmare. It was nothing short of sadistic to make the poor girl marry in such an advanced state of indignity, let alone in a white dress that hung off her shoulders but strained at her waist.

The mother pulled a face. 'Not what I imagined,' she said. 'You'd better go up another couple of sizes.'

The daughter shuffled back into the cubicle. I saw

225

Nathalie and Angela exchanging amused, patronizing glances. I had had enough of them.

'That was a lovely surprise to see you both. Please give my love to Luca and Marc,' I said briskly, and turned to the martyr-faced mother of my bride, hoping to persuade her very subtly that they'd all have a much nicer wedding if they waited until after the baby was born. I thought it might take my mind off Luca. It didn't.

thirty-nine

When Marc was gone to meet his friends in Limerick, I had planned to go for a walk on my own. In the event, however, I just lay on my side on the green candlewick bedspread and watched the pattern of sunlight dancing the shadows of leaves on the wall in front of me until I fell asleep.

I had a nightmare and woke sweating and cold and confused. It took me a moment to work out where I was. The sun had gone down. It was dark. I had a shower. I wrapped myself in towels and moisturized my face, and then I stood at the window and, for a while, gazed out over the valley, where the lights twinkled just as they had the night before. Then I settled myself into bed, leaning up against the pillows like an invalid, opened the bottle of wine that Marc had left for me and drank from a china teacup while I watched a film with Cary Grant on TV.

While I lay there, alone, miles from home, the situation I was in became clear to me and I knew exactly what I must do.

No matter how painful it was, no matter how lonely I was, no matter how much I cared for him, and he for me, there was only one reasonable course of action to take.

I resolved to end the affair with Marc.

forty

Luca and Nathalie were due to marry on Christmas Eve. I had not been invited to the wedding, but Mum was doing the flowers at the church. She went for an audience with Angela to discuss the colour of the bridesmaids' dresses et cetera, and returned full of outrage at the opulence of the wedding, the amount being spent, the downright extravagance of it all. She was, at the same time, full of grudging admiration for Angela for the way she had organized everything down to the last little detail.

'You should see the bridesmaids' headdresses, Olivia, they are exquisite, like little Roman tiaras woven with silk flowers and silver and purple ribbons cascading down the back,' she said. And then in the next breath: 'Heaven knows how much they cost, it's an obscene waste of money.'

'Did you see Luca?' I asked. I was peeling potatoes for dinner, my sleeves rolled up to my elbows, my hands white in the cold sink water. The pan was already boiling on the hob, steaming up the kitchen window so that I couldn't see out to the wet orange and brown of the fallen leaves in the autumn garden.

'I saw one of them but I can never tell those boys apart,' said Mum, sitting on a kitchen chair and rubbing her foot. 'Did you get the sausages out like I asked you?'

It must have been a Thursday.

I nodded. The sausages were on a plate, pricked and waiting to go into the frying pan.

'Nathalie's a lovely girl,' said Mum. 'She reminds me of Lynnette.'

'Excuse me,' I said. 'She's not fit to lick Lynnette's boots!'

'Well, Lynnette does have a better figure,' conceded Mum, 'but Nathalie's been through so much and still she always puts other people first. She's such a help to Angela, you know. Such a hard worker and so reliable. Angela says she doesn't know what they'd do without her.'

I pulled a face and carried on scraping.

'Angela says Nathalie's the daughter she never had. She says Luca and her make the perfect couple.'

'Good for them,' I said, draining the water and scooping the poor pale potatoes out with my hands. They were like little naked dead animals.

'Angela says it couldn't have worked out better. Nathalie and Luca can take over the business and live in the flat, and she and that husband of hers are going to take things a bit easier. Perhaps even move to Watersford.'

'Lovely.' I was halving the potatoes, slipping them into the bubbling water.

'Did you salt the water?'

'Yes.'

'Are you sure?'

'Yes.'

'Because Colin will be here shortly and you know how he likes his potatoes properly cooked.'

I rinsed my fingers under the tap and collected the peelings from the drainer.

'How did Dad like his potatoes, Mum?'

She ignored me.

'It's going to be the most beautiful wedding, you know. Ostentatious, but beautiful. Of course Angela said I must go back to Marinella's for a glass of champagne after the service. The whole place is going to be decorated in silver and purple and green. There'll be a huge Christmas tree outside with lights, and flowers tied to all the railings, and they're having a proper Italian opera singer. Such dreadful extravagance.'

'Big wow,' I said. I lit the gas for the frying pan and melted a triangle of lard and by and by the conversation turned to something else and by the time we sat down to eat Mum and Mr Hensley were happily assassinating the character of the Sunday-school teacher and I was left alone to dwell on my personal collection of 'what if's' and 'if only's'.

It was late October and Anneli was back from university for the weekend. She seemed scruffier and less well kempt than before, and was full of stories of her new life and her new friends, but I could tell from the look on her face that she was pleased to see me. We spent a whole day in her bedroom while she talked about living in hall, and what it was like getting to know all those new people, and how her room-mate was the daughter of a really famous liberal film star, and how it was really quite frightening and how she really really really wished I was there with her. And so did I. I'd forgotten how much I missed my best friend. Anneli knew how desperate I was to escape Portiston.

The first evening Anneli was back we went for a walk along the seafront but it started to rain so we went into the Black Swan and drank a couple of beers and I told her about Luca and Nathalie's wedding and she rolled her eyes and said, 'That's a marriage that's never going to work.'

I asked her why and she said that her mum was friends with the woman who did the laundry for Marinella's and she had told her that ever since Luca had got engaged he'd been walking round like a condemned man.

'Mum says you should never fight destiny,' said Anneli. 'Which isn't exactly a scientific term but I do know what she means.'

'What does she mean?' I asked, blowing out cigarette smoke through puckered lips, an affectation Anneli had adopted and which I had immediately copied.

'You know, you should always take the path of least resistance, that crap.'

I stared at her blankly.

'Oh, you know, Liv, if it doesn't feel right, then don't do it.'

'You mean Luca shouldn't marry Nathalie?'

'Of course he shouldn't. It's basically an arranged marriage. It's ridiculous in this day and age.'

'Hmmm,' I said. 'But I was there when Nathalie was choosing her dress and she seemed quite happy about the whole thing.'

Anneli stubbed out her cigarette into the Courage ashtray on the wooden table between us.

'Nathalie doesn't know any better. She's got this romantic notion in her head that she's heading for happy-ever-after because Angela promised her that's what's going to happen. I feel sorry for her. She'll be the one who ends up getting hurt.'

'Shame,' I said.

'I know you don't like her, Liv, but she's a nice girl really. She's just a bit scared of you.'

I actually coughed at this. I coughed and spluttered and attracted bad-tempered looks from the elderly incumbents of the Black Swan.

'She's scared of me? Why would she ever be scared of me? She looks down her nose at me, is what Nathalie does.'

Anneli shook her head and drained her glass.

'No, she's afraid of what you might do.'

'Why? What could I ever do that might hurt her?'

Anneli shrugged. 'I dunno.'

We changed the subject. A couple of our old schoolfriends came in and we chatted with them, but all the while we were drinking and laughing I was aware of a tiny little seed of potential in my mind. A dream that I had long ago put to sleep rubbed its eyes, yawned and came back to life.

The next evening we went to Romeo and Juliet's nightclub in Watersford. We didn't know – how could we? – that Luca was going to be there.

forty-one

Marc was contrite.

'I'm so sorry, darling, so terribly sorry.' He was holding my hand between his knees under the breakfast table. Sunday morning, just a few hours to see the Cliffs of Moher and then back to our real lives. I was tired and missing Luca. I extricated my hand and stirred sugar into my tea. There was a light drizzle outside.

'I just couldn't get away. They weren't as drunk as I thought they'd be. Steve kept checking heads to make sure nobody got separated from the group. I couldn't get away.'

'Whatever,' I said. I really didn't care.

'Oh, don't be like that.'

'No, I didn't mean . . . I meant I really don't mind.'

'All I wanted was to be here, with you.'

'It doesn't matter, Marc. Honestly it doesn't.'

'Is something wrong? Did something happen?'

'No.'

'Is everything all right?' It was the young landlord bringing us a rack of toast triangles, his eyes dark-rimmed from working so hard and the baby and all.

'It's all lovely, thank you,' I said.

'Any plans for this morning?'

'We're going to see the Cliffs of Moher.'

'Ah, you'll love it there, it's a lovely spot. You get a few tourists, mind.'

'We're used to those,' said Marc.

'It's a shame you can't stay longer. You'll have to come again.'

Marc beamed. 'Oh, we will, we will, won't we, darling?'

I smiled feebly. 'Maybe.'

That morning I was overcome with fatigue, the old torpor had returned. While Marc paid for our lodging, I slipped back beneath the sheets of the wide, low bed and drifted off again. When Marc came back he climbed back into bed with me and made love to me, his hands cold, his breath loud and hot in my ear. I just lay there, gazing over his wide, pale shoulder, waiting for him to finish. He groaned and sighed and covered my face in kisses but I didn't believe him when he said it had been lovely and amazing. I had felt nothing. No relief, no escape from grief, no shallowing of the well of loneliness. I lay on my side, staring at the wall, while Marc packed and tidied the room, and then he helped me out of the bed and into the hire car like an invalid. I was supposed to read the map, but I couldn't be bothered. Instead I watched the countryside through the drizzle, the rocks and moors, the ancient monuments and the modern bungalows set out like miniature ranches with their electric gates and topiary. I was missing Luca. I was missing Luca with every breath and every heartbeat and every blink. Marc had turned on the radio and there was a phone-in about why fewer people were going to church on a Sunday in Ireland, yet all the churches we passed were surrounded by flocks of parked cars, the bulky, macho four-by-fours of prosperous family men and women. Marc was driving carefully and that was irritating me. I craved the thrill of Luca's recklessness, his habit of taking corners too fast and too sharp, rocking the car, the way he would take his hands off the wheel and steer with his elbows while he lit a cigarette or consulted a map, or shift his hip to fetch his mobile out of his back pocket. I remembered how Luca would turn up the radio to any song he liked (and his tastes were eclectic and multiple) and tap his head in time to the music. If it was a rock song then his head would be going up and down, his hair all over his face. That wide, wide smile, those eyes.

'What are you smiling at?' asked Marc.

'Oh, nothing.'

'You were thinking of Luca?'

'Yes.'

Marc put his hand on my thigh in a companionable fashion, and I relaxed a little and cried, quietly and without fuss. It made me feel a little better.

The Cliffs of Moher were reached via a path which cut through a green, bosomy swathe of the westernmost few acres of Ireland. At the side of the path were people selling CDs of Gaelic music, knitted jumpers and hats, all manner of jewellery and little pieces of artwork painted on to shiny grey slate.

The rain had stopped and the sun had come out. There was a good breeze. We walked along the path hand in hand and then to the viewpoint where the Atlantic wind blew away my despair and I inhaled and held the hair back out of my eyes and gazed out over the sheer, dramatic cliffs, so different from Portiston's own miniature version. Marc put his arms around me and I leaned back against him, feeling safe again.

We climbed down on to a shelf of rock which jutted horizontally from the cliff-face. The sea was a long, long way below. I stayed away from the drop, keeping my palms flat against the warm grass growing out of the side of the cliff. I didn't dare go even a yard closer to the edge; the very thought made me dizzy. Marc, like all the other young men, seemed drawn to the edge; it was probably some kind of display of machismo, for the rim of the shelf, where I stood, was fringed with anxious-looking women while the men sat at the edge, dangling their legs over the side. One little push, the tiniest tilt, and they would have been lost.

The light of the watery sun on the sea was scorching my eyes. Marc was just a silhouette against the light. He was one of thirty or forty silhouettes, I wasn't even sure which one he was. So I turned away and climbed back up on to the grassy path and pulled myself to my feet.

I looked straight into the face of Mrs McGuire, the cleaner at Marinella's.

She was standing on the path, not six feet away from me,

snug in a long coat, sheepskin boots and a headscarf, and
her arm was looped through that of a younger version of
herself. She looked slightly perplexed and I realized that
she recognized me, but couldn't place me. I turned away
quickly, but not fast enough, for Marc was already behind
me, one hand on my waist, his voice in my hair.

I didn't speak, just turned and walked away from him
and Mrs McGuire.

I kept my back to them, walked away back up on to the
path, and then, going as fast as I could, headed south. After
about half a mile I stopped and sat down, my chin on my
knees, looked out to sea and waited for Marc. He came soon
enough.

'Did she recognize me?'

'I don't think so,' said Marc. 'But it was pretty bloody
obvious we were together. Shit.'

He picked up a pebble and lobbed it out over the cliff-
edge. I had a vague memory of Luca doing something
similar a long time ago.

'What can we do?'

'Nothing. Nothing.' He delved into his pocket and
pulled out his cigarettes. 'Do you want one?'

I shook my head. Marc sat down beside me, and I cupped
my hands around his to help him keep the match alight
long enough for the tobacco to catch. He took a long drag
and looked out towards the horizon.

'Funny to think that if you jumped in now you'd have to
keep swimming until you reached America. Maybe that's
what we should do.'

I smiled, picked at the grass.

'She's bound to say something, Marc. To your mother, if not to Nathalie.'

'I know.'

Marc blew a gust of smoke into the wind. It blew back in my face. He leaned over and kissed me. 'Of all the dramatic cliffs in all of western Ireland . . .' he said.

'Don't joke about it. Aren't you worried?'

'Of course I'm bloody worried. But it could be worse. Mrs McGuire doesn't know you. I'll just say you were a friend of Steve's or something. I'll say we were just messing around. I can talk my way out of this.'

'Oh. Right.'

'Well I can't tell the truth, can I?'

'It's a sign,' I said. 'It's a sign that we must stop this, now. Before anyone gets hurt.'

'It's not a sign,' said Marc. 'It's doesn't mean anything. Don't get paranoid.'

I knew though. I knew that somehow or other Mrs McGuire would be the undoing of us.

forty-two

Romeo and Juliet's was the place to go drinking and dancing and pulling in Watersford. At one time it had been the old Top Rank, and probably before that it had been a dance hall or a bingo hall or something. The club was over some of the post-war, less nice shops in Watersford, in a non-residential district where there was nobody to be disturbed by hundreds of drunk young people spilling through the streets shouting and laughing and arguing and having energetic, standing-up sex into the early hours. Inside drinks were expensive and hard to come by (the queues at the tiny little bars were extensive) and, as we couldn't rely on being bought drinks straight away, Anneli and I had come prepared with several glasses of Bacardi and Coke in each of our bloodstreams and a quarter of vodka tucked into the waistband of my skirt. It didn't show beneath my winter coat. The doorman looked in our handbags but wouldn't have dreamed of body-checking. Not in those days.

Girls were allowed in free before 10 p.m., so at 9.55 we tripped through the external glass doors and then climbed the carpeted stairs with golden ropes looped along the flocked walls on either side, feeling like princesses. We exchanged our coats for raffle tickets in the cloakroom which was to the side of a large, open lobby area at the top of the stairs, and then followed the noise through swinging double doors into the club itself. Inside it was dark and warm and packed and throbbing with sound so dense it was like a physical presence. The dance-floor was already heaving – predominantly with girls taking advantage of the ten o'clock rule. The boys would come later, once the pubs closed. Anneli and I went to the ladies' and shared a cubicle where we had a wee and a large swig of neat vodka each. It burned my stomach and made Anneli retch and giggle. We had to queue for the mirror to put on new lipstick. There was a huddle of bare arms and hair and perfume. Everyone was drinking from illegally imported bottles. It reminded me of the staff cloakroom at Wasbrook's, only there was less powder and more swearing.

Out in the club again, we found somewhere to sit. It wasn't a desirable spot, a bench against the wall tucked away almost behind one of the little bars, not on the mezzanine where the older, wealthier, more confident clubbers leaned and preened and sipped their cocktails, but on the bottom floor, where the music was so loud we could only communicate by speaking right into the other's ear, with one hand cupped around our mouths to protect the words.

We didn't have to wait long before two young men came over and offered to buy us drinks, which we accepted of course. We couldn't hear a word they said. The DJ was playing disco hit after disco hit. My young man, a square-shouldered, shaven-headed soldier with bitten-down finger-nails and metallic breath, kept trying to kiss me, which I didn't much like, so when we finished our drinks Anneli and I slipped away on to the dance-floor. We hadn't been there five minutes when somebody stepped on Anneli's foot, and that somebody was Luca. He was there with Marc and a small group of Portiston boys and the younger members of the town's Sunday League football team. I looked all round, but there was nobody else. There was no Nathalie.

We couldn't hear one another. Luca's face was green and then blue and then red and then covered in silver raindrops in the disco lights. But we laughed and embraced and he shouted in my ear that this was his informal stag night.

'Not the proper one with Pop and my uncles and cousins. We're going to bloody Naples to meet up with the rest of the Felicone mafia. This is my getting-hammered-and-falling-over stag night,' he shouted.

'No stripper?' I shouted back.

'Not yet,' he replied, 'but I live in hope.'

It was natural that we would dance together. Why wouldn't we? I felt on fire, it must have been the vodka hitting my bloodstream, I was mad for dancing. I shimmied and I shivered and I flicked my hips and I glowered out from under my hair (a look that I'd practised for hours in front of the mirror and that I thought was alluring), and then some stupid song would come on – 'Thriller' or something – and we were together, doing the actions, laughing so much I thought my mouth would split at the corners and I knew Luca was looking at my chest and that my small breasts were pretty in the lacy confines of a tight, low-cut little top and I was so, so happy.

When Luca's hair was stuck to his face and his shirt was dark with sweat stains, he indicated that we should leave the dance-floor to cool off for a moment. We went out of the double doors to the lobby, where the draught from the entrance was chimneyed up the staircase. It was blissfully cool. I leaned up against the flock wall, easing my feet out of my tight shoes. There was a blister on the side of my little toe. Luca knelt to examine it and told me it wasn't terminal. He blew on my foot to cool it down. There were lots of other people milling around, people snogging, people crying, people shouting at one another. To our right, a girl was being sick into an overgrown plant pot which contained a plastic tree done up with red fairy lights. Her friend was holding her hair back away from her face and rubbing her back sympathetically. The sick girl had lost a shoe and her tights were horribly laddered. I turned away.

Luca stood up and lit a cigarette and took a drag and then somehow the cigarette was gone and he was kissing me, his hands in my hair, his mouth sour with tobacco all over mine and I could feel him pressed hard against me. For the first time in my whole life, I felt I was exactly where I was supposed to be, doing exactly what I was supposed to do. I heard the doors into the club open and expel a burst of noise and heat, and then shut somewhere to my right, and glanced over Luca's shoulder to make sure nobody we knew was in the lobby, and nobody was.

'Oh God, Liv,' Luca gasped into my ear, leaning against

me. 'Let's get out of here . . .'

'No, no, shush,' I whispered, touching his damp face with my fingertips and then dropping my hand down to the zip of his jeans strained tight. Nobody could see, Luca was covering me with his body and the wall was behind me. My right leg was bent at the knee, my bare foot on the wall. 'It's your stag night, you can't disappear.'

Luca groaned. 'Don't do that, please don't do that.'

'Shhhh,' I said, undoing the zip and working my fingers into the tropical heat of his pants.

Every atom of my body was zinging. I felt like a universe of nerve endings, all of them sparking and twitching. Luca nuzzled his face into my neck, his mouth was on my ear, he was breathing deeply and quickly like somebody who is afraid.

'If you keep your hand there one more second I will come,' he whispered.

'Onc . . .' I whispered back.

A little later, we returned to the dance-floor. Luca looped his arms around me and breathed thanks and wonderment into my hair.

It was terribly crowded in the club now, there wasn't room to dance and Luca looked dazed and fawn-like. Marc kept trying to dance with me, which was getting on my nerves. I wanted him to go away. In fact I wanted all of them to go away, and to leave me and my darling on our own. It didn't happen, though. The millionth time Marc's face bobbed up grinning in front of mine, I picked up Anneli's handbag with what was left of the vodka in it and headed for the ladies'.

'What is it?' she asked, trotting after me on her high heels. 'Did Luca say something? Did something happen?'

'No, nothing,' I said. There was a queue outside the ladies', sick-looking girls panda-eyed with mascara. The music was beginning to thrum in my head. I did a quick check to make sure no staff or bouncers were watching, and had a good swig of the vodka. Then another. The bottle was almost empty. The floor was sticky with spilled drink.

'Something's going on,' said Anneli. 'You're not telling me something.'

I wiped my lips with the back of my adulterous hand. Oh, the smell of him. I shook my head.

'Something's different. You're different.'

'No, no, nothing's changed.'

Anneli bit her lip. I stepped towards her but she stepped back, away from me.

'You kissed him, didn't you?'

'Or he kissed me. Oh, it was nothing. He's drunk.'

Anneli frowned.

'Don't look like that. It didn't mean anything.'

'You're not going to do anything silly, are you?'

I gave a high little laugh. Even to me it sounded artificial.

'No, of course not,' I said.

'He's engaged, Liv. He's getting married in eight weeks. You get in the way of that now and it'll be a million times worse than what happened with Mr Parker.'

I took her hands in mine. My pornographic hands on her pure ones.

'Anneli, I promise I won't do anything wrong.'

Later, Luca and I slow-danced to 'If You're Looking for a Way Out'. His lips were in my hair, tasting my shampoo, his big, bony hands holding me close to him. Marc was dancing with Anneli. She kept her face determinedly turned away from us; Marc kept watching, watching.

At the end of the song, most of the other couples on the dance-floor started to kiss, those deep, wet, tongue kisses of drunk people who don't know each other well. Luca and I, however, stepped decorously back away from one another. Anneli was pointing at her watch and to the door: our taxi would be outside.

I picked up my bag and waved my fingers at Luca.

'Can I see you tomorrow?' he mouthed. 'Can you come to Marinella's?'

I nodded. 'I'll come for coffee when I wake up.'

And I did. And that's where it really started.

forty-three

The plane journey back to Watersford felt like a long, extended goodbye and the thought of what might happen once we got back filled me with unspeakable dread. I'd been horribly twitchy at Shannon Airport in case Mrs McGuire was returning on the same plane. She'd told Marc she was on holiday with her daughter for the whole of the following week, but that didn't convince me that we were safe. She might, out of some dog-like sense of loyalty to Angela, come to the airport to spy on us.

'And what if we bump into any of your friends from the stag night?'

'We won't! Most of them went back this morning and the rest have gone on to Dublin.'

'But they might have missed their plane.'

'Liv, stop it. You're wearing me out.'

'You're not taking this seriously enough.'

'Why are you suddenly going all paranoid on me now?'

'Mrs McGuire saw us.'

'She doesn't know you. She doesn't know there was anything untoward going on. And even if she suspected, what's the worst that could happen?'

'Oh, nothing much. Just the end of your world.'

Marc shrugged and scowled and turned away. He walked off towards the duty-free shop and I sank back on to a chair and covered my eyes with my hand.

Once on the plane, reassured that nobody we knew was on board, I tried to enjoy the view from the window, the ice crystals on the glass and the magical lightscape of the top surface of the clouds, but the wine felt like acid in my stomach and every little jolt and creak of the plane made my heart race and prickled my fingertips. Marc, I think, was feeling the same. He held my hand on the armrest that separated us and asked me far too many times if I was all right. I was dreading the parting at the airport, dreading having to linger at the baggage carousel while he walked out into the arms of Nathalie, or Maurizio.

'We can't do this any more,' I whispered.

Marc squeezed my fingers.

'I never meant to have an affair with you,' I said.

'Don't say that.'

'Well that's what it is.'

'No it's not. Affairs are tacky and dirty.'

'That's what other people would say about us.'

'Liv, please, there is no point worrying about things that haven't happened yet. Forget Mrs McGuire. She only saw you for a moment. She didn't recognize you. And even if she did, it would still be a big leap of imagination for her to work out that we were together.'

'It wouldn't be a big leap,' I said. 'It would be the only logical conclusion.'

Marc sighed, let go of my hand and put his head back on the headrest. My ears popped. In our safe, private, high-altitude dusk, we were starting the descent into Watersford.

'Is that what you want, Liv? Do you really want us to stop seeing one another?'

'No. I don't know. I don't want to be without you but . . .'

'What?'

'Stopping is the only possible ending to you and me.'

'We don't have to stop until we're ready.'

'We have to stop before anybody gets hurt. Nathalie, I mean.'

Marc shrugged. 'I don't know why you worry about her. She doesn't care much for you.'

'She has no reason to.'

As we came down through the cloud, the plane banked to the left and, through the window, we could see the lights of the traffic circling the roundabout to come into the airport. Nathalie was probably in one of those cars. She'd have timed the journey perfectly. She'd be listening to some classical music. Her hair would be shiny, her breath fresh, her clothes pressed. She'd be tapping her short fingernails on the steering wheel. She'd have left the children at home, in the flat above Marinella's, being looked after by their grandparents. Baby Ben would be in his cot, in his blue bunny pyjamas, lying on his back, his arms thrown out at either side of his head, breathing milkily through rosebud lips. And the other two, probably, would be watching TV in the living room. Kirsty would be curled up on the sofa, her feet tucked beneath her, twirling a strand of dark hair round her perfect little fingers. Billy would be on his stomach, on the carpet, his chin in his hands, grubby socks falling off his fat little feet behind him, transfixed by the screen.

My mind was made up.

'I want to stop, Marc. I want to end this here.'

'Whatever you want,' he said, but he didn't sound convinced.

forty-four

Luca and Nathalie were due to be married on Christmas Eve. Luca and I started seeing one another at the end of October. By the beginning of November, we were lovers. By the end of November, Luca told me that what we had wasn't just the final wild-oat-sowing of a soon-to-be-married man.

A painfully cold autumn was gearing up for a record-breakingly icy winter. Privacy in Portiston was all but impossible for me and Luca. Despite Angela and Nathalie's double-act of coldness and unfriendliness, I frequented Marinella's with increasing regularity, simply to enjoy the reassuring feeling of being near Luca. At work, I day-dreamed and idled. After a disastrous hour in the glassware department one Saturday morning, the supervisor said I was neither use nor ornament and sent me home, assuming I was sickening with the flu. In truth, I'd smuggled Luca into my bedroom the night before and we hadn't slept for a moment, our delight at being naked together totally spoiled by the fear of discovery. Every creak of that prudish old house sounded like my mother's footstep on the stair, every whisper of wind outside startled us.

Sooner or later, we knew we would be found out. Our desire was spurring us on to acts of increasing recklessness. One Sunday, we fucked standing up in the tiny courtyard at the back of Marinella's, and then Luca went back inside to serve roast dinners to a coach party from Lytham St Anne's. Another time, when Angela and Nathalie had gone to Watersford to sort out exactly what was required of the wedding photographer, Luca summoned me to the ferry ramp and we had ten minutes of extremely cold bliss in my old haunt. Luca was still wearing his Marinella's uniform and when he left his trousers were streaked with oil and the green of seaweed. Occasionally he managed to come to Watersford on some errand or other, and would meet me at Wasbrook's and then we could enjoy the privacy of his old car for half an hour. We never once discussed the future.

We never talked. We never had time. We had no mobile phones, we had no opportunity, we had no privacy, but nothing deterred us from being together as often as we could.

Afterwards, everyone assumed we had been plotting and planning, but that simply wasn't true. I never considered the future. I was just greedy for the present because I thought that was all I was ever going to have.

December, of course, was Wasbrook's busiest month. My supervisor kept asking me to stay on and work overtime and I always agreed because I needed the money for my escape fund and it took my mind off Luca's wedding. Also, working meant I didn't have to go home. Working was fun at Christmas, although the shoppers left the store in a dreadful state and the shoplifting that went on was unbelievable. Racks of merchandise disappeared into the shopping bags of the predominantly middle-class women who frequented the store. I grew sick of the piped Christmas music, the pa-rum-pum-pum-pum and the have-yourself-a-merry, but I enjoyed the bustle and the busyness as red-nosed shoppers, stressed and short of time and money, struggled to find the perfect presents. I liked coming out of the shop into the winter dark, the city garlanded with lights every way you looked. Sometimes the Salvation Army band would be playing carols on the podium in the centre of the shopping area, and once I saw Father Christmas on a motorized sleigh throwing sweets to the shoppers and waving a mittened hand like he was the Queen. His pixie told me they were collecting for the Firefighters' Benevolent Fund.

I was on a permanent adrenalin high. I saw Luca's face everywhere. I saw the slope of his shoulders, or the swing of his hair, or the way he stood with his feet apart and his thumbs in the pocket of his jeans, and I would cross the department floor time and time again to find it wasn't Luca but somebody who bore a tiny physical resemblance.

This permanent state of sexual anxiety made my eyes bright and my cheeks pink and never in the whole of my life did I receive so much attention. Young men would come up to me in the store. Some of them were polite and courtly. They asked if they could take me for a coffee in my break. Others – the ones I preferred – were full of smiles and bravado. They flattered and teased and worked round to what they were trying to say which was usually did I fancy a drink after work. Older men tried to give me presents. The boys at work showered me with small acts of kindness. I told them all thank you but I had a boyfriend. Then, when it came to the staff Christmas party, I was stuck, because of course I didn't. Not one who belonged to me, anyway.

The party was due to take place on 17 December, which was the Friday before Christmas Eve and Luca and Nathalie's wedding day. It occurred to me that Luca might be prepared to drop me off at the party and then make an excuse for not staying. That would keep everyone happy and my position as spoken-for would not be compromised. I could see no harm in this plan. There was no risk to Luca.

When I stepped out of the dark winter evening and into the bright, welcoming warmth of Marinella's to make the necessary arrangements, it was clear that the wedding preparations were well under way. Cardboard boxes of glasses and champagne were piled up behind the counter. A little stage had been erected at one end of the restaurant, perhaps for a band, and somebody had installed small spotlights on a runner on the ceiling. Big, high-standing vases were lined up at the other end of the room and the Christmas decorations, which were, as always, beautiful, were all green and purple and twined with the tiniest, prettiest fairy lights I'd ever seen. At the counter, Fabio was laboriously making tiny mauve roses out of icing paste. There was a smell of celebration in the air.

Angela, as usual, didn't have a hair out of place, but she was so fraught that she forgot to even pretend to be polite to me as I stood at the counter.

'What is it, Olivia?' she asked without any preamble.

'I'd like a coffee, please,' I said.

'You can't just have coffee,' said Angela. 'We're too busy. You have to have a meal too.'

Four American tourists were sitting at the table right beside me, drinking coffee. My eyes flickered to them, and then back to Angela, but she wasn't even looking at me any more; she had turned to speak to one of the staff who was standing behind her drying her hands on a dishcloth.

Normally I would have turned and left at this point, but this was important.

I coughed. Angela turned her head. 'Yes?'

'Could I just have a quick word with Luca, please?'

'No. He's at the church having a dress rehearsal with Nathalie.'

'Can I help?'

Marc had come into the restaurant behind his mother, his arms full of Christmas linen. He had a friendly smile on his face, and I had an idea.

'Yes, sure.'

'Do you want a coffee?'

Angela shot me a look of pure spite, but didn't intervene, so I nodded and Marc fetched us both an espresso and we sat down at a table by the window. It was wet with condensation. There was no snow yet, but the feel of snow was in the air, like the promise of Christmas.

'So how are you?' asked Marc, sipping his coffee from a teaspoon.

'I'm OK,' I said. 'Actually I was wondering if you were doing anything tomorrow evening?'

'At a guess I would say I'll be talking weddings.' He grinned up at me, blowing steam off his spoon. 'God, it's boring, Liv.'

'Well, would you like to come to a party with me instead?'

Marc sat back and opened and closed his mouth.

'Oh look, don't worry,' I said, busying myself with a twist of sugar. 'I'm sure you've got far too much to do and . . .'

'No, it's not that, I'd love to.' Marc smiled widely. 'I just never thought you'd, you know . . .'

'What?'

'Ask me on a date. God, you know how I feel about you, Liv. I've been dreaming of this for years.'

I could think of no way to ameliorate the situation. Any use of the words 'just' or 'friends' would have been too wounding. So instead I ignored him and said breezily, 'OK! Will you come and call for me about six?'

'I'll be there, don't worry.'

'There'll be lots of free drink and food and stuff and they've got a comedian for the cabaret. Probably be really boring but . . .'

'No, no, it sounds great. Better than being stuck here listening to Mama trying to get Luca to show a bit of interest in the colour of the napkins. By the way, what was it you wanted him for?'

I shrugged. 'Oh, it was nothing. Just a message from Mum about something to do with the ushers at the church.'

'Shall I get him to call you?'

'Yes,' I said. 'Yes, please.'

forty-five

Watersford in the summer was beautiful, a city of trees and gardens. The May blossom lasted well into June, scenting the warm evening air with the fragrance of honey. The late-evening light turned the buildings apricot and pink and people sat outside pubs with their jumpers round their waists and their shirtsleeves rolled up and drank cold beer and smiled.

After the trip to Ireland, I was glad to be back in my flat, on my own. I was sleeping better because I was getting up earlier and my appetite had returned. I felt healthier. I realized there were parts of my daily ritual that I actually quite enjoyed. I didn't call Marc and he didn't call me, and I dared to hope that we had survived both the bereavement and the affair without anybody being hurt. I missed him, but it was nothing compared to the missing of Luca and even that wasn't so bad now, not so weighty.

I'd taken to stopping in the café every morning for coffee and toast. The bodybuilder chef and I were friends now. He was called Chris. I looked forward to our conversations. Chris was always very well informed due to starting work so early. He listened to Radio Four while he fried up the first eggs for the early commuters and the council workers coming off night shift. Because I was always in the café at the same time of day, I began to recognize the regular clientele, and they recognized me. We enquired after each other's health and well-being. I learned the names of wives, husbands and children. I knew whose nephew played bass in a rock band called Mumm-Ra, whose mother had won £100 on a scratchcard, who was studying Spanish at evening class and whose four-year-old had been diagnosed with autism. Accidentally, I had become part of a close-knit and diverse little community.

After the café, I would walk to work. Jenny always got there before me, even on her hangover days and sore-feet days after a long shift at the noodle bar. Sometimes the professor came, sometimes he didn't. Either way I would switch on my computer, organize my notes while it buzzed into life and then type in more carefully researched information about Marian Rutherford. It was a story unfolding in no particular order in front of my eyes, and I had begun to look forward to the next piece of information.

I would tuck my feet under my chair, and put my mug of coffee on one side of the keyboard and the sheaf of notes on the other, together with a huge old dictionary, its pages soft and yellow, and a coloured pencil for marking any part of the manuscript that was illegible, undecipherable and unguessable.

Meanwhile the professor was his usual quiet, shadowy self. He paid me small kindnesses and compliments, but always in a manner that suggested he was going through the motions. He didn't try to persuade me to talk about myself and he didn't mention his own experience again, for which I was grateful. I had never met anybody before who moved so effortlessly amongst people, but who gave away so little of himself. It was as if he shed no skin, exhaled no carbon dioxide and left no fingerprints. One day, I thought, maybe there would be a time when it would be right to talk. In the meantime, he didn't pry beneath any of my rocks. At work there was no anxiety. The big, light, untidy office was a haven to me and to the professor too.

Then, three weeks after our return from Ireland, I heard from Marc. I switched on my phone after a particularly pleasant day at work and there were several missed calls from Marc, and a message saying not to call him under any circumstances.

My knees went weak.

'Is everything all right, Olivia?' asked the professor, who had come out of the history department behind me in order to lock the door.

'Yes, fine,' I said.

He didn't look convinced.

'You've gone a very funny colour.'

'Just a bit of bad news.'

'Is there anything I can do?'

'No, no, thank you, it's nothing serious.'

I said, 'Goodbye, have a nice weekend,' and set off at a fast walk in the direction of Fore Street.

*

Mrs McGuire was back and had said something to Angela. She must have done. I was oblivious to the beauty of the city as I tried to compose an alibi to explain my presence at one of southern Ireland's most famous beauty spots at the same time as Marc. Just because we were together didn't necessarily mean anything, as Marc had pointed out. Incredible coincidences take place all the time. People bump into one another in the strangest places, I thought, and then I thought, Yes, in books and films they do.

Back at the flat, I drank two glasses of wine one after the other and then changed into my jeans and one of Luca's old, unwashed T-shirts, and went out again.

I hadn't meant to become involved in an affair, I really hadn't, and I was sure Marc hadn't either. It had been an unconscious thing, our coming together, a reaction to the pain of losing Luca and a way of alleviating the grief. It had been selfish and dangerous, but sort of inevitable, and now we had come to our senses we had done the right thing. We had decided to stop seeing one another in any way except as brother and sister-in-law. We had agreed that the death that had brought us together was the reason we now had to part. Hadn't we?

The thought of Luca was enough to turn my feet in the direction of the cemetery, but although it was still light the gates were already locked.

Some of the old loneliness and the frustration at being separated from Luca returned. I couldn't bear the thought of wandering around Watersford on a Friday evening on my own, so I turned back the way I had come and was just going into the off-licence when Marc called.

He was trying to sound calm, but it was clear from the furtive tone of voice that this was a panic call.

'Where are you?'

'At home. In the flat.'

'But that noise . . . ?'

'I'm in the bathroom. I've put the shower on so Nathalie can't hear. She's watching me.'

I stepped back out of the shop and walked a little way down the street, moving back against the wall to make way for a gang of cheerful teenagers.

'What's happened? Does she know?'

'She thinks I'm seeing you.'

My heart gave a little jump. I could feel the muscle squeezing itself in fright.

'Oh God.'

'Don't worry, she doesn't know anything for sure, but . . .'

'Mrs McGuire! She told Angela?'

'No, no, it's nothing to do with Mrs McGuire.'

I bent over in relief, rubbing my forehead with my hand and feeling nauseous.

'Oh, thank goodness. It's just a suspicion then. And it's OK because we aren't seeing each other any more. Apart from Mrs McGuire there's nothing to ever put us together.'

I heard Marc sigh. Over the storm of the shower water I heard him sigh like a man who fears all is lost.

'What? Marc, what is it?'

'It's not just a suspicion. She found the photo.'

'What photo?'

'The photo of you on my phone.'

I was genuinely confused.

'You've got a photo of me on your phone?'

'You know, the one I took of you on the beach.'

'But you said you'd deleted it . . .'

'I couldn't. It was all I had of you.'

This time I sank right down on my heels. My breath was coming in short little gasps. My fingertips were tingling, my mouth was dry.

'I'm so sorry . . .'

'Oh Marc, oh God! I was practically naked. What are we going to do?'

'Are you all right, love?' A powder-faced old lady was leaning down over me.

I looked up and nodded, but I wasn't all right.

'Has somebody attacked you?'

'No, really, I'm all right, thank you.'

The old lady probably thought I was a drug addict. She looked at me suspiciously, but she wandered away. She had a tiny little dirty-white dog on the end of a lead. The dog looked on its last legs.

'Marc? Are you still there?'

'Yes.'

'What did you tell her?'

'I told her Luca sent me the picture last summer.'

'But why would he do that?'

'Well, he might have done. You looked so sexy. I told her I'd just forgotten it was there.'

'Did she believe you?'

'I don't know, Liv. You know how she feels about you. Even if she does believe me, she's pretty upset.'

'Poor Nathalie,' I whispered.

I stood up again, breathing coming a little easier, and shook my head.

'I can't believe you kept the picture. I can't believe it.'

'Well, it's gone now.'

'And she has nothing to fear because what we had is over.'

'You believe that?'

'We agreed it was over on the plane.'

'I'm finding it hard without you,' said Marc. 'I can't just switch off grief or love or whatever this is. That picture, it felt like it was all I had left of you.'

'Enough, Marc.'

'If she calls you . . .'

'I know what the story is now.'

'I'm sorry, Liv, I . . .'

But I had had enough. I was tired of Marc, tired of feeling anxious, tired of the whole business.

'I've got to go,' I said. 'Have your shower. Leave me alone.'

forty-six

Luca came round to my house. It was late-ish. I'd had a bath and was sitting cross-legged on my bed, in my pyjamas, listening to Bob Marley. My hair was wet and I was twisting it into tiny plaits so that when I combed it out in the morning it would all be wavy and would look nice for the party. I heard a gentle knocking at the door and knew it was for me. It was past ten and Mum was already in bed.

I ran down the stairs and opened the door to find Luca there. The first snow was falling; it was stuck to his fringe and his eyelashes, and his nose and cheeks were red.

'What's the matter?' I asked in an urgent whisper, but Mum was already on the landing, leaning over.

'What's going on, Olivia?'

'Nothing,' I called back over my shoulder. I beckoned Luca inside so that I could shut the door and stop the rest of the heat escaping.

'Who is it?'

'Just a friend.'

'Tell them to go away.'

'I'm just lending a book.'

I did a little pantomime of opening and closing the door again and shouting, 'Bye, see you soon!'

Then, stifling the urge to giggle, I put my finger to my lips and Luca tiptoed after me into the kitchen. It was directly below Mum's room. If she came out, we would hear her and Luca could escape through the back door.

I didn't put on the kitchen light, but the room wasn't dark thanks to the luminescence of the snow, which had covered the garden and was mirroring light from the sky and from the windows of the houses in the street and the street-lamps beyond. My feet were cold on the lino. Luca, huge in his coat, pulled me to him and held me tight. I tried to pull away so that I could look into his face, but he wouldn't let go.

'What's the matter?' I whispered.

'Don't go to the party with Marc.'

'Oh Luca, it's nothing. I wanted to ask you to take me but you weren't there and . . .'

Luca, forgetting for a moment the importance of silence, pulled out a chair from under the kitchen table. It screeched. Immediately my mother's feet swung out of the bed and landed on the other side of the ceiling above us.

Before she could make it to the stairs, I took my coat off the hook and stepped into my wellingtons and we were out, through the back door. We had to climb over two fences and traipse through the back gardens of two neighbours before we reached the alley. Once there we ran, or at least Luca ran and I, hanging on to his gloved hand, struggled to keep up as I scuffed along in the boots which were too big and which didn't keep out the cold at all.

'We'll go to the pub,' said Luca.

'I'm in my pyjamas.'

'Shit, fuck. Well, where can we go?'

I shrugged. I was shivering. 'Nowhere.'

'You're freezing.'

'That's what happens when you don't have a fucking plan,' I giggled, quoting Sandra at work. 'Things go tits-up.'

Luca grinned and pulled me close.

'That's what I like about you, Liv.'

'What?'

'That you're standing here on Portiston High Street in your pyjamas in the middle of the night in the snow and you still have a mouth like a philosophical sewer.'

'It's the only thing keeping me warm.'

'What about the chip shop?'

'It would take about two nanoseconds for the news that you and I were there together to get back to Marinella's.'

I was cold, really cold. The rat's tails at the ends of my damp hair had actually frozen.

'Come on,' said Luca.

He led me back towards Marinella's and told me to wait a moment around the side, hidden from view by the bins. He ran inside and returned a few minutes later with the key to the van, an armful of blankets, and supplies. The van was parked up a side road, far enough away from the restaurant for nobody to hear it starting up. I climbed up on to the passenger seat and Luca took the wheel, passing his bundle of supplies to me. I kicked off the boots, tucked my icy, bare feet under me and wrapped myself in the blankets. We drove, carefully, to the far end of the seafront and Luca parked the van so that we were looking out to sea. The lights of Seal Island were only just visible through the snow, which landed in black splatches on the windscreen of the van. Luca kept the engine running for warmth, and every few seconds the wipers cleared the screen and visibility was resumed for a moment.

'It won't take them long to work out where we are,' I said. Ours were the only tyre tracks in the snow. From the passenger window, I could look over my shoulder and trace our journey back to the end of the road.

'Let's hope they don't come looking,' said Luca. He switched on the radio and fiddled with the dial until he found music. Then he fished under his seat and produced a bottle of wine.

'It's for the wedding,' he said by way of explanation.

'Won't Angela notice it's missing?'

'Nope. Pop's been at it for weeks.'

He tore off the plastic top with his teeth. 'Shit, we haven't got a corkscrew.'

It took some time, but eventually, with the help of a screwdriver we found under the seat, the cork went into the bottle and we took it in turns to drink. I spilled wine all down my chin and the front of my pyjamas. We giggled like infants.

'We're like an old married couple,' said Luca.

'What? Drinking wine in a stolen van in a snowstorm?'

'No, coming to the seafront and sitting in our car looking out to sea. It's what they all do.'

There was a packet of Marlboro on the dashboard. Inside was one cigarette. Luca shook it out of the box and lit it from the van's lighter. The cabin filled with smoke. He passed it to me, and in between we kissed. Tracy Chapman sang on the radio. I melted.

'I don't think you should marry Nathalie,' I whispered. 'It's not your destiny.'

'I know.'

'How are you going to get out of it?'

Luca blew out a stream of smoke. 'We need to get out of here.'

'Out of Portiston?'

'Yep.'

'We?'

'You and me. They'll blame you, Liv, when I don't marry Nathalie. I've thought about it a lot. We can't stay here.'

'We could just keep on seeing each other in secret.'

'No.' Luca took a deep drag on the cigarette. 'Why should we have to act like criminals? We'll go somewhere where we belong, together.'

'So what do you mean exactly? That we elope?'

The word had a magical, spell-like quality. It was a *Romeo and Juliet* word. I don't think I'd ever used it before. It didn't sound like the sort of word I'd ever need.

'We can elope if you want. Or we could just run away.'

The snow was coming down more heavily now. Already the car-park wall was covered, and the beach itself was starting to disappear. The wipers were being blocked from doing their job by a build-up of snow on the screen, which was making the inside of the cab feel even darker and more private.

'I can't marry Nathalie,' said Luca. 'I can't. She's a lovely girl and all that, and she's brilliant at Marinella's and she's one of the family and Mama and Pop love her but . . .'

'What?'

'We just don't have any fun. Not like I have with you.'

Luca's profile was dark and handsome beside me. His eyelashes rested on his cheeks as he flicked ash into the footwell. I drank in the curve of his chin and the line of his nose, the outline of his lips backlit by the dashboard lights. I didn't want to be without him, I knew it then.

'When are we going to run away, Luca?'

'Tomorrow?'

'OK.'

'OK?'

'I don't have anything else planned.'

I'd forgotten about the party. I'd forgotten my date with Marc.

forty-seven

The professor had spent the morning trying to catch my eye. It was getting on my nerves. I was completely immersed in the story of Marian Rutherford. I didn't want any distractions when I was working. I had moved through the looking glass into the professor's world. During office hours, I now existed in his modus operandi. I never, ever bothered him while he was at his desk so it was irritating that he was distracting me.

I was finding it difficult to concentrate with the professor hovering continually on the outskirts of my vision. In the end I leaned back from the keyboard and folded my arms across my chest and asked, perhaps a little rudely, 'What?'

The professor, who was standing by the bookshelves, wiped his palms on the legs of his trousers.

'I want to ask you something,' he said. 'But please don't feel under the slightest obligation to say yes. I won't be the least offended if you decline and either way my intention is for us to carry on exactly as we have been doing.'

'OK . . .'

The professor took off his glasses and wiped the lenses

with a corner of his shirt which he'd pulled out of his waist-band.

'It's the faculty dinner next week. I usually go on my own. I wondered if you'd like to come with me.'

'Oh, I . . .'

'It'll be a nice evening. Up at the Grove House Hotel. Three-course meal, wine, dancing, you name it . . .'

'It sounds lovely,' I said.

'So you'll come?'

'It would be my pleasure.'

'Good,' said the professor. 'Very good.'

He went back to his desk and sat down behind it. Normal service had been resumed.

forty-eight

I looked at my bedroom like I'd never looked at it before. This was the last night I'd ever spend there; I knew in my bones I'd never come back. The bulb in the lamp wasn't strong enough to illuminate the corners of the room. It was narrow and high-ceilinged with mustard-coloured Anaglypta hiding the deformities in the plaster. I tried to muster up some nostalgia, or even affection, for the room but couldn't find any. Hardly anything good had happened to me there. There were spiders under the bed and the carpet was hard and threadbare. I'd done my best to counter Mum's penchant for plainness by covering the heavy-wood dressing table with cosmetics and scent bottles and pretty little knick-knacks, and my collection of china ponies stood on the window-ledge, some of them grazing, some of them gazing out of the window, one of them rearing with his ears flat against his mane. Pictures of pop stars and photographs were Blu-tacked to the Anaglypta, but they only reached two-thirds of the way up those ugly walls.

I was terribly cold, but there was nothing warm or inviting about my bed with its old-fashioned, slippery eiderdown and its scratchy blankets. Instead, I crept across the landing to Lynnette's room.

Last time she'd been back, she had slept in her little single bed, Sean had slept in my bed, and I'd been in a sleeping bag on the floor in Lynnette's room (Mum's way of ensuring no funny business took place). I had offered to swap with Sean when Mum was asleep but Lynnette said it wasn't worth the hassle and anyway it was nice for the two of us to share a room. It *was* nice. We whispered into the early hours. Lynnette reached down from her bed and touched my cheek with her fingers and we held hands for a while. We talked about our father and how we had both, separately, decided not to seek him out. Not yet, anyway. Lynnette told me that she and Sean were going to get married and that I could come and live with them in London if I liked. I remembered all this as I parted the sheets and climbed into her bed.

It was cold, but it was comforting to smell my sister's shampoo on the pillowcase. I hugged the old bear that lay on top of the bed, and felt a shiver of excitement at the prospect of tomorrow. There were things we'd need to do: letters, goodbyes, packing and suchlike. I started to make a list in my head, but before I'd finished it was morning and Mum was calling me to get up and go to work.

I got dressed as normal in my Wasbrook's uniform, the navy skirt and white blouse and dark tights and sensible, flat shoes.

In the kitchen, Mum was eating All Bran. I could tell from the line of her shoulders that she was angry. She knew

I had gone out the previous night. I didn't know how to apologize for that, or for what I was about to do.

Through the window I could see the garden, everything hidden by the most beautiful white snow. It sparkled in the sunshine. I felt so moved by the significance of the new beauty of the world that my eyes grew hot. I supported myself on the back of a chair and watched as a robin hopped across the back of the bench.

'You need to remember to put some food out for the birds,' I said.

'They'll survive,' said Mum. 'God will provide.'

She looked up at me. 'You look pale. Don't expect any sympathy from me if you've caught a chill.'

'I won't. I don't.'

I felt the kettle with the heel of my hand. It was still warm. I made myself a cup of tea. Mum said she didn't want one, in a tone of voice that implied she wouldn't accept anything from me.

'Why did you tell us Dad was dead?' I asked.

'Not now, Olivia.'

'Please, Mum.'

'It was better that way.'

'Better for who?'

'Whom. All of us. There's nothing worse, Olivia, than public humiliation. And that's what would have happened if people knew what your father had done to us.'

I sipped my tea. I was feeling slightly shivery, but I couldn't tell if there was a virus in my bloodstream or if I was just frightened.

273

'I'm sorry, Mum,' I said.

'So you should be.'

'No, I mean I'm sorry for any humiliation that's my fault.'

'I think people know that what happened with Mr Parker was down to you and nothing to do with me. But it reflected on me, on the way I'd brought you up.'

I nodded. 'But you didn't have to tell Mrs Parker about the diary. You could have kept it quiet. Nobody needed to know at all.'

'That wouldn't have been right.'

'It would have saved a lot of bother.'

'No. The truth will always out. Sooner or later it would have come to light. It was best to get it out in the open straight away.'

'Oh,' I said.

'You'd better get a move on,' said Mum. 'You'll miss your bus.'

I fetched my coat from its hook in the hallway and put it on.

'Are you going up to the church?'

'It's Friday. It's Women's Institute. Of course I'm going.'

'Good,' I said. I buttoned my coat and pulled a woollen hat down over my ears. I checked my face in the hall mirror. My eyes were pink and watery and there were two red spots in the middle of my cheeks.

'I think I've got a cold,' I said.

'That's what you get for sneaking out in the night like a common thief,' said Mum.

I crossed over to her, put my hands on her shoulders and kissed her temple. She smelled of dust and bacon. She pushed my hands away from her.

'What have you done?'

'Nothing.'

'Why did you do that then?'

'I just felt like kissing you.'

Mum snorted and stood up, making dismissive gestures with her hand. 'Get out of here,' she said. 'I've never heard anything so stupid.'

Which was a shame because those were the last words she ever said to me.

forty-nine

I stopped off at the café on the way home. It was a balmy evening, and this leafy part of the city was noisy with traffic and birdsong. Music and voices spilled out of the open windows of cars and taxis and vans, and in the flats above the shops people opened their sash windows wide and leaned out to water the plants in their windowboxes and watch the commuters below.

Chris had set a couple of tables and chairs out on the pavement. I went inside to order a glass of sparkling water, but the smell of tomato and basil was so evocative that I ordered the pasta as well. I went to sit outside with my drink and a copy of the *Watersford Evening Echo*. Shortly, Chris brought my pasta to the table, along with a bowl of freshly shaved Parmesan and a huge wooden pepper pot.

'Mind if I sit down for a quick smoke while I watch you eat?'

'Excuse me, are you flirting with me?'

'I have been for ages, you just haven't noticed before.'

'Sorry. I've had a lot on my mind.'

'I know.'

'This is delicious.'

'Good.'

'It tastes just like Luca used to make it.'

'Who's Luca?'

'My husband. The one who died.'

'Oh, sorry. I've done it again.'

'No, don't be sorry! I never thought I'd taste pasta like this again. It's lovely.'

Chris smiled and looked down at his big red hands. The cigarette smoke wisped up from between his fingers. He was, I realized, nice-looking in a shaven-haired, big-muscled sort of way.

'Maybe,' he said, 'one day I could cook a meal just for you. Just the two of us.'

I licked the sauce from my lips and looked up at his face.

'I ought to warn you that I'm a bit of a mess,' I said.

'I'm good at tidying up.'

We beamed at one another.

Chris dropped the end of his cigarette on to the paving stones and crushed it with the heel of his boot.

'One day soon then, eh?' he said, standing up.

'Yes,' I said. 'Definitely.'

fifty

I didn't get the bus to work. I walked to the bus stop, my footprints merging in the snow with those of all the commuters who'd already made the journey, and when I got there I made a little pantomime of pretending to have forgotten my purse, for the benefit of the other people waiting for the bus, and turned round and headed back home again. I lurked in the newsagent's shop at the end of the road until Mum went past, wrapped in her long brown coat and headscarf, her feet in flat brown boots with fake sheepskin at the rim. I watched her as she walked away from me towards the church, treading carefully, afraid of slipping on the compacted snow on the pavement. I felt a pang of sadness, but only for a second. When she turned the corner and disappeared from view I skated along the snow back to the house. Inside I put the kettle on, for by now I had a terrible sore throat, and ran upstairs to pack my suitcase.

I couldn't decide what to take. I packed the obvious things – underwear, jumpers, jeans, toiletries – and by then the suitcase was near enough full with the bulky winter items, but I thought I ought to take some summer clothes too. I had an idea that it was much warmer in London and I'd need some nice stuff for when we went out. And then there were my other belongings: my records and books and painting things, my posters, my school photographs, my vast collection of cheap jewellery.

After what felt like a long time taking things out and putting other things into the case, I suddenly felt very hot and shivery and had to sit down on the bed. At that point, the enormity of what we were about to do came crashing down on me like a wave and I thought it was a stupid idea, that we were mad for even considering it. I realized that Luca was probably thinking exactly the same thing. Or maybe he never had any intention of leaving at all? Maybe it was just his idea of a joke? Running away was the sort of desperate plan anyone would come up with a week before they were due to promise complete and unending fidelity to somebody who wasn't much fun. Talking about it was one thing. Doing it was another.

I lay down on the bed. When Mum came back I'd tell her I was too ill to go to work. No, I'd say I'd gone in and they'd sent me home so it wasn't my fault. I closed my eyes and snowflakes danced in front of me and then I was aware of the pleasant sensation of drifting into dark oblivion. I was disturbed by somebody shaking my arm. I opened my eyes and there was Luca, looking pale and urgent.

'Come on, Liv, we need to be quick,' he said.

I sat up. Luca was buckling the straps on my suitcase. I swung my legs off the bed.

'I haven't done a letter.'

'Well do one, quick.'

I had my pad and a pen ready.

Dear Mum, I wrote. 'What did *you* say?'

'Huh?'

'In your letter.'

'Fuck's sake, Liv. We haven't time for this.'

I exhaled. He relented and sat on the bed beside me and put his arm round me.

'I did three letters. I wrote them last night when I got back.'

'Three?'

'One for Nat, one for Mama and Pop and one for Marc. I told Nat I would only make her unhappy and that she deserved better, and to the parents I told the truth, that I was going away with you and that I was sorry for everything but it was what I had to do.'

'And Marc?'

'That was the hardest. I just said I hoped he'd forgive me and that one day he would understand. I said I'd call as soon as we found somewhere to live and that he could come and join us if he wanted.'

'That's a good idea.'

'He's going to bear the brunt of the fall-out, poor sod.'

Luca was chewing the side of his thumbnail.

'He'll be OK,' I said.

'I hope so,' said Luca. 'Please hurry up, Liv, we need to get out of here.'

I wrote a few more words to Mum, I don't remember what exactly. I didn't bother trying to explain, I just apologized and reiterated that no harm or hurt had ever been intended. I put the note in an envelope and licked the seal.

'OK.'

'OK.'

Luca carried my suitcase out of the room. I glanced round quickly, scooped up the china ponies from the windowsill and put them in my pockets. They would get broken, I knew, but I couldn't bear to leave them.

That was it. Leaving my whole life behind was as easy as that.

I propped the envelope between the salt and pepper pots in the middle of the kitchen table where Mum couldn't fail to see it. I hoped that she'd come home with Mr Hensley after she'd finished her business at the church. I didn't like the thought of her finding it on her own. Luca was going through the cupboards, looking for provisions.

'I couldn't take anything from Marinella's, I'm supposed to be going to the wholesaler,' he said.

'Does that mean that as well as losing you they're going to be short of supplies tonight?'

'They won't open the restaurant tonight,' said Luca. 'They'll be too busy looking for us. That's why we need to go now.'

One last sweep of the kitchen where I'd eaten my meals for eighteen years, and then we left. I shut the door behind me and heard it click on the latch. Luca had my suitcase in one hand, and took my gloved hand in his other.

'It's going to be OK,' he said, squeezing my fingers. 'We

are going to be happy. Really, really happy. We are going to be the happiest runaways on the planet.'

He was right.

fifty-one

The week before the birthday he used to share with Luca, Marc came to see me. I hadn't seen him for a few weeks, and was stupidly happy when he called. I ran down the stairs of the flat to open the door, and embraced him. He held me very close and stroked my back and breathed into my hair. The stud of his earring dug into my scalp.

'Liv,' he whispered, 'Liv.' As if he were saying a spell or a prayer.

He asked if I'd like to go to the café, but I said I'd rather we had a drink in the pub. So we went to the Horse and Plume, which had its doors and windows open and contained the usual mix of regulars and tourists. We took our beers out into the yard at the back. It was walled on all four sides, a complete suntrap with thirsty-looking roses struggling to grow up a wooden trellis tacked to the yellow rendering.

All the tables and seats were taken, so we sat down on the browning, stub-littered grass in the far corner and leaned against the wall, our shoulders touching.

'I don't want to be with Nathalie,' Marc said, without

preamble. 'I want to be with you. I won't ever ask again, but if you give me the word, I will leave her.'

I balanced my bottle between my knees and pulled at a daisy. I let my hair hang over my face.

'I can't make your decisions for you,' I said. 'But I don't want you to leave Nathalie. Please don't do that. You and me, what we had, was about Luca. It wasn't about you and me.'

Marc took a swallow of beer. I made a slot in the daisy stalk with my thumbnail.

'That's where we're different,' he said. 'From my perspective, what we had wasn't just about Luca. It was about you. You mean the world to me.'

I glanced up at him through my hair. He was staring into the middle distance, not looking at me.

'I am not your world,' I said quietly. 'There will always be Nathalie and the children. And Marinella's. And this thing between us, it was never straightforward. It's all mixed up with Luca, no matter what you say. It would never have happened if Luca hadn't . . .'

He nodded, his face expressionless. I watched his throat swell as he swallowed.

'I've always wanted to be with you, Liv.'

'No you haven't.'

'I have. Think about it. I was the one who held a torch for you always.'

I swallowed some beer and tipped my head back and closed my eyes.

'Don't tell me your secrets, Marc, I don't want to know.'

'Luca knew.'

'What did he know?'

'How I felt about you.'

I sat upright. 'Oh, Marc, surely not . . .'

'He did. That's why it took so long for us to get back to normal, him and me, after you left together.'

'Why didn't you ever ask me out then, or say anything?'

'You engineered it so that I was going out with Anneli, remember, and you were seeing that skinny lad who worked the ferry. And then when I finally thought I had my chance, the very night that we were supposed to have a date, you ran away with my brother.'

'Oh, Marc! I'm so sorry. I never meant to . . .'

'I know you didn't.'

'We only decided we were leaving the night before. It wasn't something we'd been planning for ages.'

'Luca had been planning it.'

'He hadn't. Why do you say that?'

'Things he'd done. Preparations. He filched some money out of Pop's account.'

I shook my head. 'He can't have.'

'He did. And he had the car fixed. He told the garage to send the bill to Marinella's. That was a good few days before you two buggered off.'

Marc sighed. He took out his tobacco tin and laid a paper on his knee.

'Don't tell me any more,' I said. 'I don't want to know.'

We were silent for a few moments. Marc made his cigarette and went through the ritual of flicking it repeatedly with a blue disposable lighter before it caught. Meanwhile

I trawled through my memories for signs that Luca had been planning to leave, and couldn't find any. He'd never spoken to me of making preparations; certainly I had no idea he'd stolen any money. They would have blamed me for that, Angela and Nathalie. They'd have thought it was me putting ideas into his head. I threaded the stalk of a daisy through the slot in its sister's stalk, and repeated the process.

'Why did you marry Nathalie, Marc?'

Marc shrugged. He waved a fly away from the rim of his glass.

'We were both in the same boat. Both pretty devastated. Pretty pissed off.'

'I'm so sorry.'

'I guess we both understood how the other was feeling.'

'Bit like you and me, after Luca,' I said.

'A bit,' said Marc. 'She loved Luca, you know. Never me, not really.'

'I'm sure that's not true.'

'And after Luca went, when we realized he wasn't going to come back, it just seemed natural for me to step into his shoes and take over the restaurant with Nat. I think I was Mama's Plan B.'

I couldn't help smiling. 'You make Angela sound like a complete control freak.'

'No,' said Marc, shaking his head. 'She's just a mother who loves her family, who would do anything to protect them, and who wants the best for them. And she loves Nathalie as much as any of her sons.'

'Fair enough.'

'But Nathalie and me, we were just going through the motions. We still are.'

We drank some more beer in the pub garden, we talked some more. It was pretty sad but it was good. I thought it was a dignified and adult end to the affair. We both knew it was over, we tied up some emotional loose ends, we were considerate of the other's emotions.

Later, we walked back to the flat. The daisy chain was strung around my neck. We stood outside the door. I didn't invite him in.

'Will you be all right?' He smoothed my cheek with his knuckle.

I nodded. 'Will you?'

'I've survived worse.'

'It's not like we'll never see each other.'

Marc kissed my forehead.

'I'll never forget anything, Liv. None of it. You got me through this last six months, nobody else, and I'll always be grateful for that.'

'Me too.'

'God, I hate goodbyes,' said Marc.

'Just go then.'

'OK, but Liv . . .'

'What?'

'Thank you.'

I thought that was the end of it, we both did. Still no real harm had been done.

fifty-two

So Luca and I ran away together. We ran away to London, but *en route* I became really ill so we stopped at Leeds and found a cheap hotel and holed up for what was supposed to be a couple of nights. Our room was cold and damp and dirty and my cold turned into bronchitis but we were afraid of going to a doctor because we knew that would mean retrieving my medical records from old Dr Clayton at Portiston and he would be bound to reveal our whereabouts to Mum and Angela. He had never believed in the sanctity of the patient–GP relationship and had outed many an embarrassing condition disclosed in assumed confidentiality.

In the end, it became so difficult for me to breathe that Luca took me to Casualty and I was admitted into Leeds General Infirmary with what turned out to be pneumonia. On the day he was supposed to be marrying Nathalie, Luca phoned my mother to tell her that I hadn't been in touch because I was in hospital. Mum told him she didn't care if I died; in fact, she said, it would be a blessing. Luca only told me about this conversation many years later when I'd tried, and failed for the thousandth time, to build bridges back to Mum. He said she was a cold, hard, unloving woman. Lynnette said Mum had just had an unhappy life.

After he'd phoned Mum, Luca called Marinella's. Angela answered the phone so quickly that Luca suspected she had been sleeping beside it. She had let loose a stream of invective in Italian, much of it directed against me. Luca didn't tell me about this either, but Angela, naturally, blamed me for leading her beloved son astray. Angela thought I'd used my sexuality to lure Luca away from the virginal and almost holy Nathalie. She called me a sexual terrorist. She told him my speciality was blowing apart decent relationships with no regard for the wounds that would be inflicted on innocent victims. Nathalie, poor girl, had been destroyed, she told Luca. She then tried to persuade him to return. He would, she said, be completely exonerated if he were to return home immediately. Nobody blamed him. They knew it was all my fault. They were even prepared to compromise on the wedding. They could talk about it if he didn't feel ready to commit, if that was what the problem was. Nobody would force him to marry Nathalie if he didn't feel ready for it. All he had to do was come back to Marinella's and this whole episode would be forgotten and never mentioned again. No harm done. No bottles broken.

The money in the phone ran out before the discussion could go any further. Luca had been calling from a booth in the waiting area of the hospital. It was full of people who had slipped over in the ice and had suspected fractures. The phone was normally used to communicate very happy or very sad news. Births and deaths. Luca, in his exhausted, hungry, scared and lonely condition, thought his situation consisted of a bit of both. He bought a newspaper and ate a hot lunch in the hospital cafeteria. The room was strung with tinsel and faded paper chains which had clearly been recycled from the year before. A few large, collapsible silver- and gold-foil snowflakes spun in a melancholy fashion from the ceiling. The windows were steamed up. The serving ladies were wearing cracker crowns and a couple had mistletoe pinned behind their ears. Mournful cathedral carols were being piped into the room. Some of the tables were occupied by loud, laughing nurses and auxiliaries. Stooped, anxious people sat around others, picking at their food and stirring their drinks endlessly. Children whined and fretted in pushchairs.

There was a special turkey dinner available. It was cheap. So on the day when Luca should have been feasting on pasta Alfredo and marinated beef in Marinella's, when he should have been guest of honour at the party to end all parties, when his ears should have been ringing to the sound of members of an extended Italian family standing up and shouting, '*Evviva gli sposi*,' instead Luca, my beloved, sat alone in the cafeteria in the Leeds General Infirmary and ate processed turkey and rock-hard roast potatoes in reconstituted gravy.

Later, when he came up to see me on the ward, gasping for breath, propped up on pillows with oxygen being fed into my nostrils, he told me it was the best meal of his life.

'There's nowhere in the world I'd rather be,' he said.
'You do talk a load of rubbish,' I gasped out.

He was right though. It was an inauspicious beginning to a truly beautiful relationship.

fifty-three

I took a bus to Watersford city centre to buy a dress for the faculty dinner. It wasn't difficult at all; I couldn't imagine why I'd found public transport so frightening just months earlier.

I browsed in Top Shop and River Island and Zara, but I knew where I wanted to go, and when I'd failed to find anything that was both decorous and sexy along the High Street, I went into Wasbrook's.

It was laid out exactly as it had been when I used to work there. The point-of-sale displays were much more sophisticated than they used to be, and the carpet had been replaced by wood-effect flooring, but the assistants still wore the same uniform, and all the departments were in their traditional places.

I took the escalator up two floors to the wedding department. Two mannequins, which I swear were the originals from fifteen years earlier, posed on the podium, one in a shepherdess-type dress of the kind favoured by Nathalie, the other in a slim, ivory sheath. There was a young girl in a blue skirt and a white blouse standing behind the desk, sorting the jewellery. I smiled at her.

'I used to work here when I was about your age,' I said.

'That's amazing!' she said. I gave her a £5 tip out of nostalgia. She thanked me nicely.

I travelled down a floor to womenswear, and wandered round looking at all the clothes. It had been such a long time since I'd bought anything that I didn't know what suited me any longer. In the end I bought a demure, long-sleeved, navy-blue dress, and a pair of strappy, heeled shoes which weren't so demure to go with it. I didn't think the professor would like me to stand out from the crowd, so I took the 'less is more' approach.

That evening, I bathed and washed my hair, and listened to the Sugababes while I dressed. I'd bought some new make-up: foundation and mascara and a pinky-brown eye-shadow. For the first time since Luca's death, I plucked my eyebrows and waxed my legs. I glued on some false nails. I stood on the bed to look at myself in the mirror. I looked OK.

The professor had sent a taxi to pick me up and take me to the hotel. In the lobby, I panicked. There were hundreds of people milling about and I didn't know any of them. Most of the men were of an age where their hair was either receding or had totally disappeared. The women wore sleeveless dresses and shawls, and the flesh on their arms wobbled. I scanned the crowd for a face I recognized. Then Jenny appeared from nowhere, gorgeous in Karen Millen, with Yusuf on her arm, and they led me to the professor who was in a crowded lounge, deep in discussion with a Polish man with a long beard and a bald head.

'Olivia, how lovely to see you,' said the professor with polite enthusiasm. He didn't kiss me, but placed a gentle, proprietorial hand on my hip and introduced me the Polish historian.

During the meal, I didn't say much. We were sitting at a round table, and the conversation was predominantly about literature and history and everyone seemed to be showing off, in the nicest possible way, so I ate my fish in parsley sauce very slowly and cut my new potatoes up small so as not to finish before everyone else, and made sure I drank more water than wine, so as not to embarrass myself or the professor, and I successfully deflected intellectual questions. All in all, I think the evening was a success.

There were a lot of tedious, self-congratulatory speeches after the meal, when the temptation to drink did get the better of me, and I finished off a bottle of red all on my own. I was still sober enough to know that as long as I kept my mouth shut and didn't fall over, I would be OK.

When the speeches were finally over, the professor invited me into the hotel garden for a nightcap before the taxi came to take us home.

At the back of the hotel was a long, stone terrace. Night-scented plants exuded the most delicious fragrances over the terrace, where some of the younger couples were canoodling in an intellectual kind of way. The women had kicked off their shoes and the men were smoking cigars.

The professor led me down some steps in the centre of the terrace into a sunken garden, where an illuminated fountain played on a fishpond and moths had gathered in search of the moon.

'You've nearly finished the Rutherford manuscript,' said the professor. 'You're the first person who's managed to stay the course.'

'I've enjoyed it,' I said. 'It's so interesting. It's going to be a great book.'

'You haven't reached the best bit yet.'

'Oh?' I sipped my Cointreau, silently thanking God for summer nights and moonlight and orange liqueur.

'You'll see.'

I was more than a little drunk. 'Excuse me for asking,' I said, 'but how long did it take you to stop missing your wife? After she'd left?'

The professor cupped his glass. 'Grief is an illness. Different people respond to it in different ways. And they find different ways of treating the symptoms.'

I picked a sprig of lavender and crushed it beneath my fingers. It scented the warm air.

'It's like a virus,' he said, warming to his theme. 'Once it's in your blood you can't fight it and there is no cure. You just have to travel with it and see where it takes you.'

'So how long have you been on your own?'

'Ten years.'

'Ten years? And you're still not cured?'

The professor sat down on a curved stone bench and held his glass between his knees and watched the beads of water from the fountain tumble and dance as they fell. A smile turned up the edges of his lips.

'I sound a bit self-indulgent, don't I?'

'Just a bit.'

'I should get over myself, shouldn't I?'

'Yes.'

'I appreciate your honesty, Olivia.'

'Any time, professor, any time.'

It was all OK, it was a nice evening and on Monday, when I went to work, everything was exactly as it always was, as it should be.

fifty-four

Eventually Luca and I made it to London and we started off our life together in a bedsit on the second floor of an old terrace in Woolwich. It was filthy-romantic, with damp blooms of mould on the ceiling, peeling wallpaper and an infested mattress on the floor. The window-glass vibrated to the tune of the trains that passed below our window. There was a schizophrenic poet and an old lady with a little Jack Russell dog called Minette in the rooms on the ground floor and some shy refugees on the floor below us. There was a shared bathroom. Luca used to pee in the sink. I loved him so much that I liked the fruity, farmyard smell of the drain when I brushed my teeth in the morning. We had sex all the time, everywhere. We smoked a lot of dope. We were on a permanent high. We were thin and good-looking. We went to a lot of parties. We loved London.

Mum had disowned me; Lynnette was quietly sympathetic. She and Sean took us out for meals and watched with the pleasure of parents as we ate like gannets, finishing off their leftovers, eating the sugar out of the bowl. Lynnette and I grew very close. We made plans to track down our missing father. Lynnette brought round food in Tupperware containers. She told us to heat it up but we were always so hungry that we ate it with our fingers straight out of the tub as soon as she was gone. Pasta bake, risotto, curry.

It was more difficult for Luca. Stefano, not yet with Bridget but living in London, came to see us. He was supposed to be angry but his heart softened the moment he saw Luca's sorry, dark-lashed eyes. He hugged his brother and they both wept. I stood in the corner, my sleeves pulled down over my hands, and fidgeted. Luca missed his whole family terribly. He particularly missed Marc. Sometimes he would creep away to the phone box on the corner. He would return with sore eyes and lie down on the mattress, his face to the wall, one arm curled protectively over his head. I left him alone at those times. He wrote letters to Marc and gave them to Stefano. Stefano told us that Marc, left to clear up the mess that we had left behind us, tried to hate his selfish brother, but couldn't. Still, it took months before the first bridge was built between them.

On sunny days and rainy evenings, we would walk the streets of London, hand in hand and starry-eyed, too broke for even a McDonald's but generally too happy to care. We stole quite a lot. Just the essentials – food, toiletries, condoms, cigarettes, records, make-up. It can't have been easy, but we managed.

Luca soon found a job in a restaurant and Lynnette called in a favour from a friend and found me work as a receptionist in a fairly swanky PR agency.

A year after we had left, Luca and I went back to Portiston for the first time. By then, unable to cope with yet another scandal, my mother had sold the house and left Portiston. I knew from Lynnette that Mr Hensley had arranged for her to stay with an associate of his who was chair of the governors at a church school in Hull. Angela, Maurizio, Fabio and Marc and Nathalie were still running Marinella's. Angela and Maurizio had, however, bought a house in Watersford and had given the flat over the restaurant to Marc. Marc was already engaged to Nathalie.

I wasn't allowed into Marinella's.

Angela had told Luca over the phone that I wouldn't be welcome, but he thought that when we got there she would change her mind. She didn't. I stayed in my overheated but comfortable room in the bed-and-breakfast that had, at one time, been Andrew Bird's house, while Luca visited his family. I lay on the bed and read a battered old paperback copy of *Valley of the Dolls* for hours and ate Minstrels. When that became too tedious, and there was still no word from Luca, I walked along the beach, picking up pebbles and throwing them into the sea, which was spraying and tossing playful little waves. The wind whipped my hair across my cheeks and my scalp was itchy beneath my woollen hat. At the ferry ramp I stopped, for old times' sake, and wrapped my arms around myself and kicked the shingle around with the toe of my boot and smiled at the memory of Georgie. Then I turned round and wandered back up into town.

I didn't look at Marinella's, but I had to walk past its façade. The day was bright and blustery, a silvery-grey

December day, yet the light behind the glass in the restaurant was golden and warm. I didn't look, but I was aware of people moving behind the glass, the shadows of the family I had loved and who I'd wanted to love me.

It wasn't as cold as it had been the year before, but it was still just a few days before Christmas and my breath veiled my face as I walked. I went along the High Street, past the windows of the little shops with their festive decorations and blinking lights. Thankfully the chip shop was open, its windows steamed from top to bottom, and a billow of fishy warmth cushioned me as I opened the door and stepped inside.

I recognized the girl behind the counter; she'd been in the year above me at school. She was pregnant beneath her white apron, her cheeks were rosy and her forearms were spattered with little burn marks.

'Yes?' she smiled at me, a stub of a pencil between her fingers to write my order on the wrapping paper.

'Just a bag of chips, please.'

She grabbed the scoop and plunged it into the cooker, piling golden chips on to the paper. I was so hungry my stomach gave a lurch of pleasure.

'It's Olivia, isn't it?' asked the girl, salting the chips.

I nodded.

'You and that Felicone lad caused a bit of a fuss last Christmas.'

'Sorry.'

'Oh, you're all right.' The girl smiled and folded the

paper. 'I thought it was very romantic myself. His family didn't take it too well, though, did they?'

I handed her some money. 'Luca's over there now trying to sort things out.'

'It'll be all right soon enough,' said the girl, giving me my change. 'These things blow over. It'll all be forgotten.'

I thanked her, and took my lunch back out into the chill air. I ate it in the shelter near the ferry terminal. It smelled of pee and motor oil. An empty beer can rolled mournfully in the gap beneath my feet. The chips were delicious, fat and salty and so hot they burned my tongue and then sat heavy and comforting in my stomach.

Afterwards, I went back to the bed-and-breakfast and fell asleep on the bed. Luca came back red-eyed and dejected. He said Angela had invited him to stay for Christmas, but not me. He said Nathalie had refused to meet his eye and Maurizio looked old and disappointed. Only Marc had asked after me. He had sent me some cake, wrapped in tin foil. I ate it in the passenger seat of Luca's car as we headed out of Portiston back to the lonely route south, picking off the lemon icing and letting it melt on my tongue.

fifty-five

September 1 was the date of Luca and Marc's birthday. I did not know how I was going to get through the day. Yet it was a beautiful morning and when I looked in the mirror as I looped my hair into a ponytail, I saw my own face, and I knew it was a face which Luca had loved, and that made me feel almost happy.

It was going to be a long day. First, there was the professor's landmark lecture about the life and loves of Marian Rutherford in the Watersford City Museum. After that, I had promised myself an hour or two alone with Luca. Then I didn't know what I would do. I decided to go where the day took me.

In the café, Chris had put a posy of sweet william in a vase in the centre of my table. The intense, peppery scent mingled with the smell of espresso. He had the tiny coffee cup on the table for me almost before I had sat down, and with it was a glass of iced water.

'Nothing but the best for you, madam,' said Chris, shaking out a napkin for me.

He brought me frittata – a new recipe, he said, eggs soft

and yellow and mixed with sweet vegetables. I hadn't been hungry, but I cleared the plate he set before me and then bit into a vanilla pastry sprinkled with almonds and sugar, and swallowed a second espresso. By now the blood was dancing in my veins and my eyes were wide open. The day no longer felt like an ordeal to be endured, but just a day, like any other only with more memories.

'You must stop feeding me like this, Chris,' I said. 'I'll end up the size of a house.'

I licked my fingertip and picked up the pastry crumbs from my plate.

He sat down opposite me, as was his custom, to smoke a cigarette.

'No real man likes a skinny woman.'

'That's what Luca used to say.'

'He sounds like a top man, your husband.'

'He was,' I said.

'What was he like?'

He was lovely. He was perfect. He was my world. I couldn't find the words.

'Don't you want to talk about him?'

'It's just . . . It would have been his birthday today.'

Chris slapped his forehead with his hand. 'Why don't you stop me before I keep saying inappropriate things?'

'Actually,' I said, 'it's really nice to talk about Luca with somebody who doesn't go all tragically sympathetic on me.'

Chris smiled. 'Actually I am quite sympathetic, you know.'

'I know.'

'I just find it hard to show it.'

I shook my head. For some stupid reason my eyes were growing dangerously hot.

'It's the testosterone. Us alpha males are hormonally incapable of . . . Oh Christ, are you crying? Oh God, I'm sorry!'

I wiped my eyes with my wrist and shook my head but I couldn't trust myself to speak. Chris pulled his chair closer and put his arms around me and although at first I stiffened in his embrace, I soon relaxed and let him be my friend.

fifty-six

Eighteen months after we left Portiston Marc married
Nathalie. Luca was invited to the wedding, but I wasn't.
I told him to go, I begged him to go. We argued about it. I
said he owed it to Marc to be there – not to prove anything,
or to show that he wasn't ashamed or anything, just for
Marc's sake.

'Not unless you're there beside me,' said Luca.

'I don't mind not being there,' I said for the millionth
time.

'Well I do mind, very much,' said Luca. And he kissed
me full on the mouth and I think even though I was still so
young I realized how wonderful it was to be loved by a man
who minded about me so very, very much.

In the end, neither of us went to the wedding, but Luca
wrote Marc a long letter full of love and Marc sent one back.
There were snapshots in the envelope. Luca pored over the
family groupings, picking out uncles and aunts who had
travelled from Italy, and identifying grown children.

I noticed that Nathalie was wearing a different dress, not
the one she'd picked out for marrying Luca. It wasn't quite

such a pretty dress, it was a little more adult. She looked better in it, less like a pantomime dame and more like a woman trying to make the most of herself. Nathalie was smiling in the posed pictures, but in her off-guard moments I thought she looked a little pinched. Marc was handsome as ever, gorgeous in his dark suit and purple cravat.

'He looks like a waiter,' said Luca.

I glanced at him covertly to see if he was jealous, but he had already turned away. He should have been there, I thought. I was angry with Angela. She was trying to drive a wedge between Luca and me by making him choose between me and his family. All she was succeeding in doing was hurting her son.

'Bitch,' I muttered to her heart-shaped face in the photograph. Beneath her charming little blue hat, Angela smiled out at me as if her heart was muscle and blood and not stone.

Luca was working hard; he was a good cook, and the punters loved him. He had inherited Maurizio's showing-off genes and knew how to put on a performance in a restaurant.

If he was in a good mood, he would sing in the kitchen, and the diners would say that there was music in his food. It was good, honest, Italian food. His reputation went before him and Luca was never out of work. Soon, given the plethora of good Italian restaurants in London, he was able to pick and choose.

The people at the PR agency seemed to like me, and I

was good at being a receptionist. I liked meeting people and chatting to them and putting them at their ease. There was talk of training and promotion. I went into Miss Selfridge and bought myself some new clothes. I had my hair cut at a salon in Chelsea. I met Lynnette for lunch and we sipped minestrone piled high with Parmesan and she told me I looked lovely. I swear there was a tear in her eye. We still talked about finding our father, but we both knew we wouldn't. By this time, Mum was completely immersed in her good works and was living a life of almost monastic austerity in Hull, complete with the big-eared Mr Hensley. I'm certain their relationship was entirely platonic. I didn't miss her much. For family, I had Lynnette and Luca, and they were the ones I loved. They were all the family I needed.

Marc and Nathalie's first baby came along in due course. Luca was invited to the christening. I wasn't. Marc telephoned to find out why Luca hadn't come. I answered.

'Liv,' he said, his voice so hesitant that I knew he had toyed with the idea of putting the phone down rather than speaking to me. 'How are you?'

'I'm fine,' I said, and then, anxious to let Marc know that it wasn't me keeping Luca from him, 'I keep telling Luca to go and see you, I tell him, Marc, it doesn't matter about me but he . . .'

Marc sighed. 'Marry Luca, Liv. Get married and then she won't have any reason to stop you coming. You'll be part of the family then.'

I didn't know if by 'she' Marc meant Angela or Nathalie. Either way, I waited up for Luca that evening and when he came home from work I was ready with a beer that had cooled in the freezer and a proposal.

'Fuck a duck,' said Luca, kissing me full on the mouth. His lips were wet and cold. 'That's not a bad idea.'

So Luca and I were married at Croydon Register Office. It was a low-key affair. Luca wore washed-out jeans, a baggy T-shirt and a pair of sunglasses, and I wore a white summer dress from Top Shop, bangles and espadrilles. Representing our respective families were Stefano and Bridget and Lynnette and Sean. In the photographs that Lynnette took with her little Kodak camera, Luca and I look like brother and sister. Our hair is long, dark and wavy. We are both smiling widely, showing a lot of teeth. In the picture where Lynnette posed us beside a fountain to make us look romantic, Luca is making rabbit ears above my head with two fingers. After the ceremony we went to Dino's, just near the Tate Gallery, which was where Luca was working at the time, and ate pasta and drank Chianti. Luca's colleagues had made an amazing cake which they presented to us in a flurry of sparklers and petals. It was the best wedding ever.

And Marc was right. Now that we were married, I was invited to Felicone family gatherings as Luca's wife. Angela and Nathalie never made me feel welcome, but at least Luca was back with his family and that made him happy, and really that was all that mattered to me.

fifty-seven

The professor was giving his lecture and I was assisting. I was responsible for the slideshow that illustrated his talk. He stood on the stage in the lecture hall, looking like the handsome academic he was, with his sleeves rolled up past his elbows and the top button on his shirt undone. It was awfully hot in the room. An impressive number of students had turned up to listen to him talk about the life and loves of Marian Rutherford. There was also a small group of professors at the back of the theatre, and even a couple of arts-magazine journalists, friends of his whom he'd invited.

It was no secret that the professor was going to drop a literary bombshell during the course of this lecture. I felt deliciously proud to be the only person in the room, beside the professor, who knew the nature of this revelation. I had transcribed it myself just a few days earlier.

For one so quiet, the professor was a surprisingly good presenter. I was sitting on the steps in the middle of two blocks of seats, and the audience was enthralled. The professor and I had practised what he called 'the show' several times and our timing was down to a fine art. I stretched my legs out in front of me; they were going brown now, and my feet were bare inside a pair of sandals. I'd painted my toe-nails bronze to match the straps of the sandals. I clicked on the mouse and a picture of Marian Rutherford standing outside her little house appeared on the screen.

She was buttoned into a high-necked jacket and only the toes of her boots protruded from beneath her heavy skirt. Her hair was pulled rather severely back from her face, but she had a tilt to her chin which implied good humour. As was the fashion in late-Victorian photographs, she was not smiling, yet there was a definite glint in her eye and in the neat little arches of her eyebrows. Her eyes were very dark and there was a slightly foppish curve in the wrist of her left hand which was balanced on an ivory umbrella handle, carved in the shape of a swan's head.

'Marian was a favourite of the great and the good of Watersford,' said the professor as I clicked again, and there was a picture of the writer posing beside one of the city's former mayors – a huge ball of a man complete with whiskers, medals and ermine.

'She became a society darling, and a mainstay of the literary and social circuit. In her time, she was a huge celebrity, the equivalent, perhaps, of David Beckham today. However, she always professed to be happiest strolling along the seafront, or on the cliffs at Portiston, and enjoying the simpler pleasures of the seaside town.'

Cue a picturesque shot of the town taken during our earlier visit. On the large screen it was possible to make out

the love of my life

the frontage of Marinella's in the centre of the picture. My heart gave a little lurch.

There was no time for nostalgia.

'Marian never married,' said the professor, 'and it certainly wasn't for lack of opportunity or admirers.'

Cue several slides of Marian's beaux, all of them literary, and extremely hairy men with a predilection for felt fedoras and pipes.

'There were rumours,' said the professor, 'that she was romantically involved with a much younger man, the son of the vicar, no less. It was rumoured that one of the sexiest fictional characters in nineteenth-century literature, Dan du Bruin, was based on the man in question, yet the fictional hero bears little physical resemblance to any of these real-life possibilities.'

I curled my toes with anticipation. I knew what was coming. I glanced to my right, where the journalists were sitting. One of them, a very tall, bony man, was leaning forwards, balancing one elbow on the knee of his crossed legs, his chin in his hands, his spine making a perfect C. He was wearing Jesus sandals and I could see the curly hairs on his toes and their big yellow nails. The other was older, suited, with grey hair combed over a large, pink head. Neither of them was making notes. The professor made a little nod towards them, as if to tip them off that what came next was the important part.

I returned to the job in hand. There was a flurry of slides as the professor described how Miss Rutherford never returned to America and never left her pretty little rented house. She lived to the grand old age of eighty-six, eventually dying in her sleep in her bedroom.

'It was,' said the professor, 'according to Marian's long-time friend and companion Daniella Urbin, a most peaceful and serene death.'

He cleared his throat, and his eyes darted around the lecture hall. Nobody had made the connection yet.

'Not much is known about Daniella. I came across a picture of her in the course of my research, and the letter from which I just quoted was actually framed on the wall of a bed-and-breakfast establishment in Portiston, so it's quite incredible that nobody picked up on it before. Anyway, this is Daniella . . .'

I clicked and on the screen appeared a young woman. She was attractive in a rather rakish and decidedly unconventional way but the first thing anybody would notice about this young woman was the fact that she was wearing an eye patch.

The audience weren't stupid. They'd read their Rutherford. They all knew that Daniel du Bruin had lost his left eye in a duel and ever after had to wear a patch. It didn't take anyone long to solve the obvious wordplay.

There was uproar in the lecture hall. There was applause and cheers and the professors, many of them women with an interest in lesbian influences on Victorian literature, crowded around my professor. There was talk of changing the nature of the Portiston Literary Festival next year. The professor was going to be a hero. He didn't know it then, but within the month he would have been interviewed by the national newspapers. He would be invited to appear on TV arts discussion programmes and his face and voice would become well known and respected internationally. That was the professor's future, but for now I, his assistant, had a promise to keep in the cemetery.

The professor knew I had to go. I caught his eye and he held up his hand to wave goodbye. He smiled and mouthed, 'Thanks,' and I mouthed back, 'My pleasure.' I put the slide of Daniella Urbin in the zip-up pocket of my handbag, where it would be safe, and left the rest to be tidied up by Jenny. Then I trotted out of the room, blinking, into the summer sunlight.

fifty-eight

I was almost looking forward to visiting the cemetery on Luca's birthday. I wanted it to be a special occasion. So after the lecture I went back to the flat and blew a kiss in Luca's direction through the window, and then had a bath and washed my hair. It was so warm, I didn't bother with the drier, but combed it out over my shoulders and walked round the flat in my towel tidying up bits and pieces. I poured myself a small glass of cold orange juice and fingered a couple of black olives out of a jar in the fridge. I played Irene Grandi, being in the mood for Italian love songs.

There weren't many summer clothes in my wardrobe. I hadn't brought much from London, and I hadn't had occasion to buy clothes except for work, but I wanted to dress up for Luca. Humming to myself, I went through the wardrobe, dropping unsatisfactory and rejected items on the floor. I ended up in a very old pair of Luca's jeans which I held up with his leather belt pulled tight so that the waist bunched, and a white *broderie anglaise* top. I remembered Luca standing behind me and kissing the balls of my shoulders one day last summer when I was wearing that top. Possibly there were still some of Luca's cells in the fabric. I liked the thought of his DNA being so close to my skin.

I made myself up. The whole works: foundation, eyeliner, eyeshadow, mascara, lip-gloss, blusher. I highlighted my cheek- and browbones. I sprayed perfume on my wrists and throat. I smiled at myself in the mirror. I looked as good as it was possible for me to look. Luca would have been proud.

In my handbag were my car keys, my mobile phone and my purse. On the shelf by the door was a card for Marc and a bottle of wine in a shiny red gift bag. I had originally bought him a pale blue cotton shirt for his birthday, but had decided it was too personal. I didn't want to give him anything he could remember me by. I thought I could leave the card and present on the doorstep of Marinella's later. The family would probably be having a party for Marc and I didn't want to interrupt that, but I also wanted him to know I hadn't forgotten. Also on the shelf was a poem and present for Luca. I had bought him a silver eternity ring from a stall outside Watersford Cathedral. My intention was to bury it for him. Then when I wasn't there, he would at least have something of me close by, for ever.

I drove up to the cemetery. I was feeling light and insubstantial, as if my feet were floating fractionally above the ground.

I parked the car at the bottom end of the ceremonial garden, nodded to a woman who was changing the flowers on a grave, took out the poem and held it with the ring tight in my hand as I began the long walk up the hill.

It was one of those balmy, late-summer evenings when the air is hazy with midges and the day's leftover heat. Flowers were wilting, dropping their heads over the edges of their vases as if disappointed, and overhead balletic swallows swooped and rushed while lazy pigeons gave their comforting calls from the trees.

I walked up the path, which was fringed with buttercups and daisies. The grass had grown to seedheads and was dotted with meadow-flowers, and moths and butterflies were busy around my ankles. The sun was low and gentle now, as if it too were tired. I passed an old man with a watering can who said, 'Good-evening,' and a young man holding the hand of a small girl who looked at his feet and wouldn't catch my eye.

Up I went to Luca's grave, my heart beating a little faster as he drew closer, my breath coming a little quicker through a combination of exertion and anticipation.

But when I turned left at the ash tree that marked the point directly opposite where Luca had been buried, the grave was not as I had expected. When I saw what they had done, my hands flew to my mouth and the poem fluttered to the ground some way below me and the ring dropped into the long grass and was immediately lost.

There was a black marble headstone on Luca's grave, which was piled high with flowers.

Of course the family would have been to visit today, but there were so many flowers I was shocked, and I hadn't

known about the headstone. Nobody had consulted me.
Nobody had even told me about it.

My heart was pounding as I stepped forward to read it.
It said:

IN MEMORY OF LUCA FELICONE
Dearly Beloved Son and Brother
For ever in our Hearts
And Always Loved
Angela, Maurizio, Carlo, Stefano,
Marc, Fabio and Nathalie

That was all it said.

There was no mention of the fact that Luca had also
been a husband.

There was no mention of me.

'You're a bit late for the party, love,' said a kindly voice
at my shoulder. It was the cemetery superintendent.

'Yes,' I said. I felt shaky.

'Is it a birthday or something?'

'Yes,' I said. 'Yes, today would have been his thirty-fifth
birthday.'

'I thought so. I'm sorry.'

I gave him a little widow's smile to disguise whatever
emotion it was that was hammering in my chest. 'Did they
all come together? The family?'

'Oh aye. It's a shame you missed it. It was a lovely ceremony. There must have been about twenty people here.'

The flowers, heaped on Luca's grave and deprived of

water, were already beginning to smell oversweet and slightly rotten. It didn't feel like Luca's grave any more. I didn't know where Luca was. I had never felt so far away from my husband.

The superintendent wandered off and I stood there in the heat, staring at a headstone which, for all eternity, had erased me out of Luca's life. At my feet were the remains of a ceremony and commemoration to which I hadn't been invited.

I felt a great pool of sadness inside me. It was heavy and lapped against me, black and deep and cold. There was a rumble of thunder in the distance, a long way off, like the possibility of trouble to come.

Then something happened.

The water in the pool of grief began to bubble and boil. Instead of sadness I felt anger. Not just a little anger but a great, steaming fury.

I turned and took off my sandals and ran down the hill, pushing past the superintendent with his wheelbarrow and the young man and child. I jumped into my car and screeched out of the cemetery. I don't remember the journey to Portiston, but I do remember that I had a huge energy and a huge anger and it was great, it was magnificent.

I skidded the car to a halt outside Marinella's, slammed the door with a strength I didn't know I had and climbed the steps. I pushed open the door so hard that it swung all the way back and the inside handle banged on the wall behind it. This small act of violence had the desired effect.

The family and friends who were milling around inside the restaurant helping Marc celebrate his birthday stopped in the middle of their small-talk and their memories and their condolences and turned to look at me.

The restaurant had been decked out for a party, but in a more subdued way than normal. There were no balloons or HAPPY BIRTHDAY banners, just coloured tablecloths, flowers and wine on the tables. The children were wearing their Sunday clothes, fresh from the church and the cemetery.

The last time I had seen many of the assembled faces had been at Luca's funeral. I recognized a couple of his old schoolfriends amongst Angela and Maurizio's neighbours and friends. Carlo was there, and Sheila with her slapped-arse face; Fabio, oblivious of the tension, wiped glasses behind the bar; Maurizio was probably in the kitchen but Angela was standing closest to me, a stack of plates in her hands, and Nathalie was looking right at me, one hand on her belly, and beside her was Marc. My dear Marc. My comforter, my lover, my confessor, the only person in the world who understood the depth of my grief, was standing with his arm around Nathalie's shoulder. My anger erupted spectacularly just as the thunder boomed over Portiston, flickering the lights and frightening the little children.

'Olivia,' said Angela calmly, putting the plates on a table and stepping forward towards me, one arm extended in greeting. 'We knew this would be a difficult day. Why don't you sit down and have a glass of wine and . . .'

'Don't touch me!' I said in a voice that didn't belong

to me, and I pushed her so hard that she stumbled into the table, which rocked, sending the plates crashing to the floor. There was a communal intake of breath. I felt furious. I felt strong. I felt marvellous. I was seeing them for what they were now. For the first time ever I was seeing the truth about this family.

'Liv . . .'

This time Marc stepped forward. His face was pale and pinched. 'Liv, sweetheart . . .'

'You knew!' I cried, staring right into his eyes. 'You must have known about the headstone but you didn't tell me! You didn't make them talk to me! You bastard!'

'There's no need for language,' said one of the neighbours.

Marc gave a helpless shrug. 'I didn't want to upset you. Please, Liv . . .'

'Please what?'

A flash of lightning lit up the restaurant and I saw Nathalie's face and I swear she looked happy. She was happy that I had come to this crisis. I wondered if the whole thing had been planned by her and Angela to make me look like a madwoman in front of everyone.

If that was the case, then they had made a mistake. They didn't know that they were actually the vulnerable ones. Not me. I had the power to bring their world crashing down about them. It would take just a few words.

'Please don't . . .' whispered Marc.

'What you said a few days ago . . .' I said, but quietly. 'What a load of lies that was.'

He shook his head. He was wringing his hands.

'Please . . .' he mouthed.

Nathalie stepped forward. 'I think it's best if you leave, Olivia,' she said. 'This is our home and you're not welcome here behaving like this.'

'Hear, hear,' murmured some of the guests.

Marc stepped forward. 'Liv . . .'

'Don't you touch me!' I hissed. 'Don't you ever touch me again.'

Angela was looking shaken and worried. She was moving almost imperceptibly towards me, as was Carlo. I wished I had a knife or something, some kind of weapon to keep them all at bay, but I didn't. All I had was my anger. Outside rain began to crack against the window like gunshot.

Nathalie was looking from Marc to me. I knew she was thinking about the photograph she'd found on his phone. I knew she had doubts. Her hand was still on her belly and I recognized the top she was wearing, printed with sprigs of roses. It was her preferred maternity top.

One of the children was crying. He was frightened of the thunder. Or maybe he was frightened of me. Outside, the sky had turned almost black. Inside it wasn't much better.

Marc tried again.

'Liv, I'm begging you . . .'

'Begging me not to tell the truth, Marc? God, you've changed your tune.'

'What does she mean, Marc?' asked Nathalie, tugging at the back of his sleeve. 'What is she talking about?'

Marc was pale as a ghost. He was panicked. I despised him. He wasn't half the man Luca was.

'Tell her, Marc,' I said. 'Go on, tell her.'

Marc turned to Nathalie and took both her hands in his. 'Nat, I . . .'

'Olivia.' It was Maurizio. His hand was gentle on my arm. 'Don't do this. Think of Luca.'

I thought of Luca.

Marc was watching me. Nathalie's poor, plain face was vulnerable as a baby's. Maurizio put one hand on my shoulder, and squeezed.

I gave up.

What was the point of destroying her again? I had done enough damage the first time.

'There's nothing to know, Nathalie,' I said, quieter now. 'You have nothing to fear from me. I don't want anything to do with any of you any more.'

My voice had to compete with the rain which was banging on the window like a million tiny fists desperate to come in. I took a step sideways, away from Maurizio. I didn't want his kindness now. It was too late. I looked at their faces, half of them linked by blood and genes, and I thought I understood. They didn't hate me, they were jealous of me. They were jealous because Luca had chosen me over them. The epitaph on the gravestone was just another symptom of that jealousy.

'You're hypocrites,' I said. 'All of you. You said you loved Luca and that you wanted what was best for him. But you didn't, none of you. Because what was best for Luca was me.'

the love of my life

It had all gone very quiet inside Marinella's. Outside, the evening had plunged itself into dark grey and still the rain lashed against the window and I felt very tired. Marc, his face collapsed in gratitude, passed me a glass. It was some kind of clear spirit. I drank it in one. I felt as if my knees might buckle and steadied myself on the back of a chair.

Once I heard an astronomer talking on the radio. She explained that nothing is ever really lost or over. She said it would take eight years for light from Earth to reach the closest habitable planet in the universe. This meant that an extra-terrestrial being looking at Marinella's through a telescope on that planet at that precise moment in time would see Luca, standing right here beside me at his and Marc's birthday party eight years ago. How I envied that alien and his telescope.

fifty-nine

I walked out of the restaurant. They were all watching me. I walked out and I didn't look at them and I knew I would never go back.

The door swung shut behind me. I stood beside the giant plastic ice-cream cone on the terrace and looked out across the sea. The rain was still falling hard, and it softened the outlines of the railings and the seafront shelters and the ferry ramp. In the distance, Seal Island was a pale grey shape like something sleeping, something forgotten. The whole world was different shades of grey and it smelled of wet pavement and regret.

The rain came down and I had to keep blinking to get it out of my eyes and soon it was trickling down my neck and my bare arms and my clothes were stuck to me and I stood there and felt my history wash away. All of it. It puddled at my feet and then ran away down the terrace steps and into the stream that was coursing down the road towards the drain that would take it directly into the sea.

I felt the door open behind me. I felt the warmer air. Maurizio came quietly to stand beside me still in his shirtsleeves and apron. He had brought an umbrella. He opened it and held it above me and we stood side by side, watching the rain pricking millions of holes in the green-grey sea.

After a while he said, 'Olivia, will you forgive us?'

I could not speak. What could I say to him?

'We all knew the truth,' he continued. 'We all knew how Luca felt, long before he took you to London. We should have stood behind you both instead of always getting in the way.'

I shook my head. It was too late. It was all too late.

'We let Luca down,' said Maurizio. 'He did what he had to do and instead of blaming ourselves for forcing him into that situation, we blamed you. All this time we blamed you. I'm sorry, Olivia, so sorry.'

I closed my eyes.

Maurizio sighed.

'It was easier that way,' he said. 'Especially for Angela. But it was wrong.'

The little white waves broke on the pebbles. The sea sucked the water back down through the stones and then the waves broke again. The rain fell and went back into the sea. Everything went round and round and back to where it started.

I went back to London.

sixty

Lynnette insisted I stay with her and Sean. She made up the bed in the spare room and put a vase of flowers on the dressing table, bought me magazines and Lucozade and seedless grapes as if I were an invalid. She gave me Sean's old laptop and told me to write it all down. She said it would be cathartic, and she was right.

Over the last few months, she and Sean have been gentle and kind and patient as saints. They make me drinks and sandwiches and ask me to help them with pleasant little chores: dead-heading the roses in the garden, painting the window-frames, sewing new cushion covers, that kind of thing. Lynnette tries to engage me in conversations about television programmes. She is addicted to documentaries about people buying old barns and disused shops and converting them into beautiful homes. Sean tries to make me laugh. He supplies me with strong drink and the sweet, familiar smell of roll-ups. While they are at work I write my confession and lie on my bed. Sometimes I walk on the common. The black dog of depression is with me at all times. I understand that it will stay until I am ready to be on my own.

I miss Chris and the café. I called him to explain why I had disappeared and he said he was just glad it wasn't something he'd said. He made me laugh. He told me he missed me too and that one day he would come to London so I could show him the sights. Every so often he sends me a postcard with a recipe on the back. Lynnette and I follow the recipes but we have come to realize that neither of us will ever be any good at cooking.

I am trying to find a café where I will feel comfortably anonymous. In the park there is a lake, and in the middle of the lake is an island with a café that can only be reached via a little wooden footbridge. Swans, ducks and geese float underfoot, hoping for bread. I have noticed, lately, that there are tadpoles in the water too and the air has a thrill of spring about it, especially in the mornings.

The lake café looks promising. The chef is a woman with fleshy arms and dewlaps on her chin. She laughs a good deal and calls everyone 'ducks' and her huge breasts wobble when she puts my coffee down on the table. The café is a good place to read a library book and to look at flyers about art exhibitions and concerts and protests.

Stefano and Bridget and the children come round for Sunday lunch or else we are invited to their house. We talk about Luca a good deal, but we don't mention Marc, only in passing. Stefano said that the family might have taken Luca's grave from me and claimed it as their own, but that's nothing because Luca's heart will always belong to me. The time we had together, he and I, is sacred and safe. It sounds like another cliché, but I treasure it. We all drink too much, even Lynnette, and we get emotional and affectionate and put on rose-coloured spectacles in order to look back at our childhoods and our crossing paths.

The best news is that I have found a job. I start work this week. My previous experience as research assistant to the Professor of History at Watersford University stood me in good stead. It was accidental, of course, but I had been working on what was probably the highest-profile literary-history project of the decade. Outing Marian Rutherford as a lesbian has spawned a whole new genre of research. All her books are being reprinted, re-read and reinterpreted. Syllabuses are being adjusted to incorporate this latest slant on Miss Rutherford's work.

The professor has left Watersford. It made sense for him to come to London, given the fact that he has been asked to research, produce and star in a television documentary on this very subject. He has asked me to be his research assistant because he knows how well we work together in our separate ways. I have accepted his offer.

And Luca?

Luca has died but he has not left me. He is in the blood that goes through my veins, he is in every thought that crosses my mind, he is in every footstep I take, every flower I pick, every bird, every leaf, every raindrop, every word, every colour, every fingerprint, every star, every dawn and every sunset.

He is in every breath and heartbeat.

Luca.

The love of my life.